THE WINTER VERDICT

DAN BUZZETTA

Severn River Publishing
www.SevernRiverBooks.com

ISBN: 978-1-64875-757-0 (Paperback)

ALSO BY DAN BUZZETTA

The Tom Berte Legal Thrillers

The Manipulator

The Winter Verdict

System of Justice

Join the reader list at

severnriverbooks.com

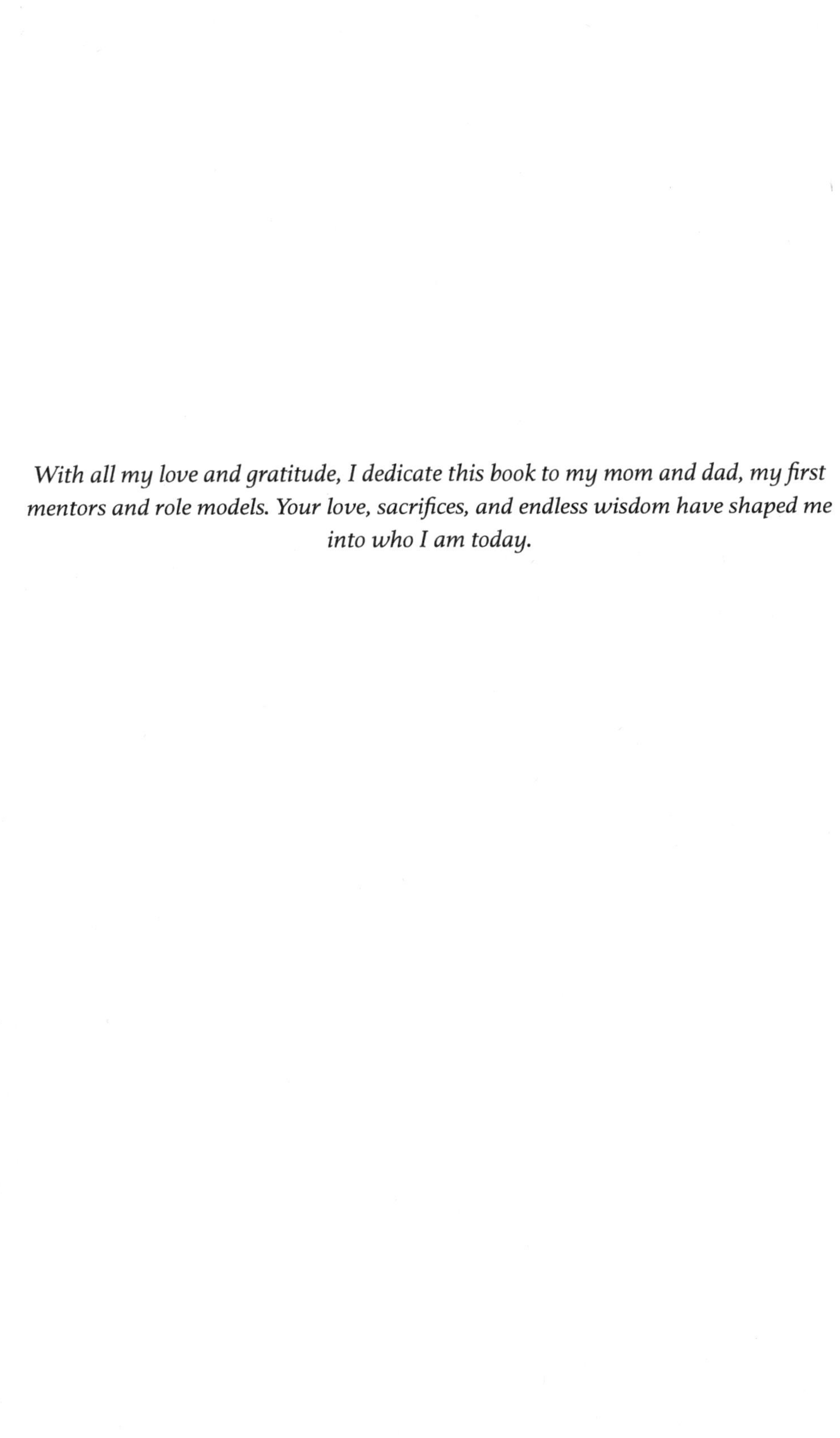

With all my love and gratitude, I dedicate this book to my mom and dad, my first mentors and role models. Your love, sacrifices, and endless wisdom have shaped me into who I am today.

PART I

1

Like he did most mornings from Thanksgiving until—if mother nature cooperated—the first week of April, Tom dug his feet into his ski boots and clasped the buckles tight. He flung his twin-tip skis over his shoulder and trekked through fluffy white powder for exactly thirty-two and a half yards from the rear door of his cedar-shingled cabin to the edge of Knight's Run, a winding green trail with shallow drops and gentle curves. It was a crisp, cold, cloudless morning and snowcat operators had been out all night carving and sculpting trails on terrain that was firm but soft. Six inches of newly fallen snow on top of a snowpack that was already a hundred inches deep will do that. Not bad for early January. Treetops along the peak of Castle Ridge Mountain, or the Castle as locals called it, glistened as if dusted with confectioners' sugar, while clumps of fresh snow clung to lower branches shimmering in the dawning sunlight. From the steepest peaks to the widest glades, miles of groomed corduroy awaited Tom on his favorite morning commute.

With a bright blue jacket insulating him from the morning chill, and a neck and ski hood combo under his helmet, he slipped into the bindings. Without any poles—Tom didn't use poles for leisurely skiing—he glided effortlessly down the wide expansive run, marveling at the multi-million-dollar chalets along both sides of the trail. Cruising the smooth, sugary slope and across and sometimes under snow-covered bridges, Tom grinned as he allowed himself to pretend for a few minutes that he, too, was a millionaire living among the rich and famous in Castle Ridge—at least those sunbirds who spent a few months each winter "on the mountain."

There was a time when Tom wanted nothing more than to be a first-chair trial lawyer. Now his goal was riding the first chair up the Castle in the morning while stamping fresh tracks on first runs down. The best was when Brooke and Aneilia, his three-year-old baby girl, were with him. But not today. Brooke was readying Aneilia for her big day at Regal Preschool where an indoor petting corral had been set up with small animals from local farms dotting the valley along the foothills of the Castle Ridge Mountains.

When Tom reached The Turret, Castle Ridge Ski Resort's high-speed chairlift that would whisk him more than forty-six hundred feet to the summit, he found he had again achieved his goal. It was 7:55 a.m. and he was the first and only person in the lift line. The air was quiet and the base area empty with no skiers in sight—and thankfully no snowboarders—just how Tom liked it. The only sound came from the whirring hum of the lift wheel providing a soothing melody accompanying him on his morning ritual.

At two minutes to eight, Chet gave Tom a nod signaling the next chair was his. Riding the chairlift alone in the tranquil early morning gave Tom time to clear his mind and think. Life had been good to him these past five years, ever since he and Brooke moved to Castle Ridge, and he was enjoying his fifteen minutes of glory. He'd accomplished what most former big firm lawyers only dream of. He opened his own general practice law firm in a small town and even hung a wooden shingle on a light post outside his second-floor walk-up office on Main Street above an art gallery. The shingle, made of pure milled walnut, was inscribed with the words "Thomas Berte, Counselor at Law." Tom had long ago stopped using his first initial C. Too many bad memories and not enough good ones.

He wasn't the only lawyer in town, but the one who was there first, Millard Jensen, who had been a judge earlier in his career, was now in his late eighties and had achieved perfection so many times for his clients, that he didn't need to practice anymore. Tom was only too happy to take his spot when Millard retired, and he even hired his secretary, Janet, as full-time help around the office.

His practice was flourishing, and he was considering hiring an associate to deal with the increasing caseload, a mixed bag of bread-and-butter real estate deals, personal injury and business litigations, an occasional bankruptcy or two, corporate and partnership transactions, and preparing wills and trusts for his more well-heeled clients. He also spent several hours every month working on *pro bono* matters, primarily helping veterans get disability benefits and representing single mothers seeking to recover child support payments from dead-beat dads.

But the matter that monopolized most of his time, and the one he was thinking about as he rode the chairlift that early morning, was a case he filed a few months earlier against Phoenix Holdings Group. He represented Faith McReynolds, the CEO and President of Castle Ridge Ski Resort, and the Castle Ridge Town Council, whose mayor also happened to be Faith. She desperately wanted to prevent Phoenix Holdings from developing a few acres of dense forest it owned between the edge of the resort and the banks of Bensonville Reservoir. In the past several months, there had been a lot of activity on that land, with construction crews working day and night cutting a pathway from the main road down to the reservoir. The townspeople were up in arms about the incessant noise and truck traffic, and they petitioned Faith to do something about it. She, in turn, retained Tom. He quickly found a number of state statutes and local ordinances, some dating back to the 1800s, that Phoenix was violating since much of its land sat in a conservation easement given its proximity to Bensonville Reservoir, the largest in central New York state. It provided drinking water to over eight and a half million residents of New York City some two hundred and fifty miles to the south. Last month, Tom obtained a preliminary injunction preventing Phoenix from carving up its property, or doing much else with it for that matter, pending a trial that was set for April, and the two sides had been battling it out ever since.

Although he wasn't practicing law anymore for the money, the fees from that case alone were going to make it a banner year for the little firm of Thomas Berte, Counselor at law, which had just celebrated its fourth anniversary. It wasn't Balatoni, Cartel & Colin by a long mile, but Tom loved his new life as a small-time country lawyer. His little firm was growing, paid its bills on time, and even turned a modest profit. And with Brooke opening her own family counseling center just down the road from Tom's office last year, Tom, Brooke, Aneilia, and Bentley, their rescue beagle-labrador-shepherd mix, were living comfortably in a tidy three-bedroom slopeside cabin in the woods in one of the most affluent towns in the Northeast.

Eight minutes after boarding The Turret, Tom reached the summit. Wide open vistas ran for miles in every direction, with undulating snow-capped peaks, escarpments, and hills as far as the eye could see. At the base of the mountain sat the hamlet of Castle Ridge, and in the distance the ice-covered Bensonville Reservoir was clearly visible. Tom never tired of the view, and he still managed to spot something new every time he gazed at the serene landscape. From the summit, he had his choice of six trails including two greens, two blues, one nasty black diamond, and an extreme double black diamond called Dungeon Alley which initially dropped at a near vertical pitch before "leveling off" to an insane sixty-five-degree angle with jagged outcroppings and knee-jarring moguls.

He had skied them all and was comfortable most days on any trail, even though he felt like he cheated death every time he made it down Dungeon Alley. But he wasn't looking for any thrills today. He had an important meeting at 2:00 p.m. with the attorney for Phoenix Holdings Group and he needed all his wits, and limbs, intact for what he expected to be some contentious negotiations.

He dropped the visor on his helmet to help with the sun glare off the crystal-white snow and to keep the cold out of his eyes. With a few kicks of his legs digging into the base, he headed for Majesty Mile, an easy blue that meandered its way down Castle Ridge Mountain like a garland around a Christmas tree. The only reason it even qualified as blue was because of a thicket of trees lining both sides of the tapered trail. Shifting his weight from side to side, and with the edges of his skis barely skimming the snow, Tom crouched lower and leaned forward to reduce drag and gain speed. He raced over smooth grooves and chiseled tight turns into the snowpack as he carved arcs down the belly of the Castle.

As he approached the shed, an unused, worn-down lean-to open on two sides in the woods about seventy-five feet off the right side of Majesty

Mile marking the halfway point down the trail, Tom thought he glimpsed movement in the woods over his right shoulder. He slowed his momentum, came to a stop, and raised his visor. He didn't realize it at first, but his thighs burned and his heart was pounding. Time to hit the gym harder, he thought. He waited for his eyes to adjust to the whiteness around him as he surveyed the woods, forcing himself to listen. Silence. Moving closer to the edge of the trail, he squinted through the leafless trees and glanced at the snow-covered ground. He saw nothing. Newly fallen snow leading off the trail was untouched and pristine, like a blanket of puffy white powder. Satisfied he was alone, Tom smirked and mentally kicked himself for thinking someone was lurking in the woods at that early hour. Wiping morning grit from his eyes with his gloved hand, he lowered his visor again, pivoted left, dug into the snow, and headed for the lodge.

Seconds later Tom heard a shrill shriek coming from the right side of the trail. He banked hard and forced a quick stop. He looked uphill and saw only his tracks. He peered into the woods again but saw nothing except a mantle of whiteness, just like before. He lifted his visor and craned his head from side to side.

"Is anyone there? Is someone hurt?"

Tom wondered if a hiker or snowshoer was lost in the woods, just waiting to be rescued.

Shifting his weight to keep from sliding downhill, he scanned the terrain again. He removed his helmet and adjusted his ski hood over his head.

"Hello? Is someone injured?"

Just then he saw something move to his left deep in the woods. It was a person.

"Hold on. I'm coming to help you. I'll be right there."

He stepped on the heel release of his left ski to unlock the binding and then used his left boot to unlock his right ski. Stepping off the skis quickly, Tom kept his eyes trained on the trees at his ten o'clock. He scrambled gingerly down the icy embankment and steadied himself while training his sights on the spot where he had seen movement.

The thunderous blow to the right side of his face and head hit him with herculean force. Tom stumbled forward, crashing headfirst into a maze of trees. His eyesight narrowed as piercing pain shot down his spine. Frothy blood quickly filled his mouth and nostrils. He was choking and losing consciousness. Sight and sound became distant. Time stood still.

Through dimming, blurred vision he saw the faint outline of a shotgun aimed at his eyes. He saw the bright flash at the end of the long barrel just as he heard the muffled blast of the single round.

2

Terrie was shredding powder on Windsor Gate trail when she heard the thunderclap of a shotgun blast over the chorus of Journey's *Don't Stop Believin'* playing in her earbuds. She instantly crouched low and leaned back on her skis, hitting the frozen ground on her left side as if sliding into second base. If it were November, it could have been a hunter shooting wildly at his prey, she thought, but this wasn't hunting season and that wasn't a hunters' rifle shot. She quickly reached for her iPhone in the outside breast pocket of her red parka with a huge white plus insignia on the back and pressed stop. The echo from the blast was still reverberating through the valley, funneled by the mountains' high peaks. She scrambled onto her stomach while making sure her skis didn't get crossed under her. Out of the corner of her eye she saw a figure clad in white, from snow pants to ski jacket to helmet and gloves, moving through the woods separating Windsor Gate from Majesty Mile. The person was moving away from her, putting more and more distance between them. For a second, she thought the figure was hovering down the mountain without ever touching the snow.

The crackle of static over the walkie-talkie mic fastened to the lapel loop on her parka broke her stare.

"Caution, all ski patrol and all emergency personnel, a loud boom, possibly from a large caliber shotgun, was heard moments ago from the area between Majesty Mile and Windsor Gate, near the lean-to hut. Proceed with caution." After a long pause, the walkie-talkie came to life again: "All available personnel get there ASAP."

Terrie lowered her head toward the mic and collected her thoughts. She cleared her throat and pressed the talk button: "Sentinel Base from ski patrol Terrie. I'm on Windsor Gate, on the other side of the lean-to from Majesty Mile. Figure in white, possibly the shooter, is making his way down the mountain, in the woods between Windsor and Majesty. Looks like he may be riding a snowboard. No other victims or persons are in my visual. Will be investigating. Over."

Releasing the talk button, Terrie took in a deep breath and noticed her hands were shaking.

Using her poles to unlock the bindings, she kicked the skis off to the side. Looking uphill and down, she surveyed the trail and scanned the woods. There were no tracks in the snow other than her own. Her heart raced and she was panting heavily. She felt small beads of sweat form on her upper lip despite the morning chill. Slowly, she got to her knees and then rose to her feet. She steadied herself, regained her balance, and made her way to a huge snow-covered boulder, probably created millennia ago when tectonic plates pushed these gorges and mountains up from the sea floor. She trudged through the knee-high snow toward the area where she first saw the figure in white. The tangle of trees and dense underbrush made it difficult to walk in a straight line. Rounding the trunk of an enormous evergreen, she spotted droplets of fresh blood on the snow. Falling to her knees and crawling on all fours, Terrie followed the blood trail down a narrow ravine. She slid to her left, around a mass of rocks, and noticed a small patch of bright blue fabric poking up from a ditch. She cleared snow and underbrush with her hands, and quickly realized a person was buried under the snow. Blood and dirt were smeared across the person's face, and a hood covered the person's head which dangled to one side in a muddy pool of reddish water, surrounded by blood-stained twigs and branches.

Ripping off her ski gloves, Terrie frantically grabbed sterile gloves from her fanny pack, and slid her cold, trembling hands into them. She scrambled to check for a pulse but felt none. Seeing no rise in the chest, she lowered her head to listen for a heartbeat, but the bulky clothing made it difficult to detect one. She pulled out scissors and began cutting layers of clothing, first the neck cover and hood, then a sweater and turtleneck, and finally a thermal undershirt. She soon confirmed what she thought when she first knelt next to the skier: the victim was male. She half expected his garments to be soaked in blood, but they weren't. The bare chest revealed no visible wounds, from a gunshot or otherwise, but given the vast amount of blood puddling around the victim's head, she thought a bullet might have penetrated his skull. Terrie was a trained EMT and comfortable with basic life support, but this patient needed more intervention than she could render. Craning her head toward her mic, Terrie pressed the talk button with her right hand while still trying to feel for a pulse with her left.

"Sentinel Base from ski patrol Terrie. I've located an adult male. Likely in his late thirties or early forties. Approximately fifty yards downhill of the lean-to hut, between Majesty Mile and Windsor Gate." Her voice was trembling her stomach churned. Trying hard to control her breathing, she swallowed hard and focused on the victim bleeding profusely before her. She lowered her mouth again to the mic and pressed the talk button.

"Subject is non-responsive and not breathing with significant head trauma. Massive bleeding. Negative for pulse. Commencing CPR. Request immediate medical assistance from medics with AED and a rescue sled. Over."

Terrie tilted the man's head and slowly lifted it out of the bloody crevice to clear his airway. As she laid her hands on the man's chest to begin compressions, she noticed his lips quiver and his eyes twitch. He was conscious. Grabbing a fistful of snow, she quickly wiped away dirt and blood that had caked on the man's face in a sticky mess.

Terrie gasped, taking in a quick gulp of cold air.

"Sentinel Base from ski patrol Terrie. Where the hell is everyone?" Terrie shouted. "Request medevac helicopter stat. Injured skier is alive—but barely! It's Tom Berte!"

3

Stark white lights pierce the darkness, even though my eyes are closed. Sounds, distant at first, become louder. Faint murmurs and hushed wails turn into a cacophony of thumping drumbeats and clanging cymbals making it difficult to rest. Words are becoming more distinct too. Soft and comforting at first, they're more intense now. I'm beginning to recognize the voices. They're familiar and soothing but betray a sense of urgency. Time is ticking down. It's approaching zero. The wait is coming to an end. It's now or never.

Mustering all my strength, I turn my back to the dark tunnel in the distance and fight to escape through the narrow opening. The pain is severe, and my legs weigh me down, but I will myself to slog forward, straining to run away from the intense beam of light. I see their faces. I need to reach them. I can't go back. There is no going back. I extend my arms as far as they reach and lunge for them but I only brush their cold, moist cheeks for an instant with the tips of my red-tinged fingers. But even my fleeting touch is enough to wipe away their tears.

The sound of her voice overwhelms me. "Tom, can you hear me? I love you. Please come back to us! I need you. Aneilia needs you! We love you. Please don't leave us. We need you, Tom. We need you!"

Tom forced his eyes open and jolted himself awake. He was breathing rapidly and covered in sweat but felt cold and clammy. His mouth was dry. He tried pulling the blanket over him but didn't have the strength. He lay still for a moment. It was the same dream. The one that tormented him every time he managed to doze off. The same one he'd been having ever since he found himself on a hospital gurney with doctors and nurses prodding and poking him with needles and blades. But at least the pain was less intense now. The throbbing in his head was fading, and he could open his eyes and focus his vision. His thoughts made sense and his hearing had returned.

"Babe! Are you ok?" Brooke wiped his face with a soft warm cloth. "You must have been dreaming. You nearly fell out of bed."

Brooke had been by Tom's bedside for the last three days, ever since he arrived at Mercy Hospital in Larange, the closest hospital to Castle Ridge with a level one trauma center. Castle Ridge Constable Stuart Ozzie had waited to contact her until he knew Tom was going to make it. Soon after Tom was medevac'd to Mercy Hospital and was stable, Constable Ozzie directed his deputies to get to the Berte's residence and escort Brooke to the hospital. At first, he had a hard time convincing the state police to join in the convoy, but after placing a few calls to people in high places, Brooke was part of a four-car motorcade with lights and sirens blaring that cleared the left lane of the New York Thruway, allowing her to make the sixty-mile trip in under forty minutes.

Tom sat up in bed and asked for water. He was tired, but breathing on his own, and fewer tubes and cords tethered him to machines today than yesterday. He was making progress.

"I'm feeling better," Tom said softly in hopes of comforting Brooke. She looked wan and bleary-eyed, and the dark circles under her eyes told him she hadn't slept much.

"Your attack's been big news. It was on the front page of all the upstate newspapers and led the local TV news coverage for the last few days. People are cancelling reservations at the ski resort and all the nearby hotels because they're worried a crazed ax-wielding gunman is on the loose in upstate New York. Folks are really freaked out about this."

"Constable Ozzie said it was a blunt object that made contact with my skull, sweetie. He didn't say anything about an ax." A sly smile crossed his sweat-covered face, but he quickly realized Brooke wasn't amused.

"Come on, Tom, I'm serious. Until the madman who did this to you is caught, no one is going to feel safe around here. The governor even held a news conference today to provide an update on the search for your attacker to try to calm fears. But I don't think it worked. Janet called and said state troopers are posted all over town, and folks have formed a neighborhood watch group, working in twelve-hour shifts standing in front of businesses with long guns. Janet says Main Street looks like a war zone. Peoples' nerves are frayed."

"Oh, that'll be great for tourism. 'Come to Castle Ridge, where you can ski, dine and get shot on Main Street if you step out of line.'" Tom cut himself off. "Where's Aneilia?" he asked.

"She's with my parents. They took her back to New Jersey for a few days. Bentley too. Aneilia was here yesterday to say goodbye before she left but you were asleep, and the doctors said it was best not to wake you. She asked if you were tired because you had played too long with your friends. Thank goodness she's too young to understand what's going on." Brooke let out a nervous laugh, but her eyes quickly filled with tears.

"Tom, I'm scared. What if this wasn't a random attack? What if they're coming for you?"

"Come on, sweetie, aren't you being a little paranoid?"

Tom knew she was doing what she always did, trying to solve the crime and find out *who done it*. But this time Tom wanted to know it, too. Was his attack planned, and was he specifically targeted? Despite his curiosity, he wanted to show Brooke he was calm and carefree. "Why would anyone want to attack me, on a ski mountain no less? I have no enemies in this town." A quick glance at Brooke told him he wasn't convincing.

"You come on!" Tears streamed down her face and she wiped them with the back of her hand. "State troopers are guarding our house and your office, and this entire wing of the hospital has been cleared of patients. There's practically an armed encampment in town!" She took a deep breath and wiped her nose. "It's happening again, isn't it? Someone's after you. And this time you almost died! You almost died, Tom! Next time they may actually succeed!" Her voice cracked and her hands were trembling as she tried to catch her breath. "I haven't been this scared since ..." Her voice trailed off. She began to sob and buried her face in her hands.

"Please don't cry." Tom wanted to hug her, but the IV and cuff on each of his arms limited his reach. "Everything's going to be ok, I promise. I'm getting stronger every day. The doctors said there was no permanent damage from the blow to my head, and thankfully I wasn't shot. In a couple of days I'll be released and will be back home."

Although life had been going well for him these last five years, there were times Tom still wondered if someone was lurking in the shadows. He was constantly looking over his shoulder, and he shuddered every time he heard loud noises. To this day, the fluttering sound of helicopters overhead sent his heart racing. He tried not to let fear consume him, but some days were harder than others. Today was especially difficult, but he needed to put on a brave face for Brooke's sake.

"Sweetie, Monte Carlo was a long time ago," Tom said as softly as he could. "All those people are long gone or are in prison and will remain there for a long time. There's nothing to suggest that what happened to me on the mountain has anything to do with the events that occurred five years ago."

Brooke lowered her eyes, let out a deep sigh, and looked away. Tom sensed she was going to say something he didn't want to hear.

"Douglas Aronson is here. He arrived this morning and wants to speak with you."

Tom's eyes narrowed and he furrowed his brow. He hadn't heard that name in years. "Aronson from the FBI? He's here? In the hospital? And he wants to speak with me?"

"Yes, Tom, and I'm sure he didn't come all this way to reminisce about old times. He must be here because your attack is connected to your past." Her voice was intense and rose an octave. "The police said the shotgun blast right after the blow to your head was a warning shot. A warning, Tom. The shooter intentionally missed you, but wanted to send you a message. Next time it may not be a warning. Anyone around here who doesn't know who you are will soon find out who the real Tom Berte is. Babe, I have a sinking feeling our past is finally catching up with us. We should leave now, while we can. Go somewhere. Anywhere. Someplace they can't find us."

Tom let his head fall against the pillow. He'd worked so hard to start a new life, a simpler life, with a clean slate. Gone were the trappings of success and glory that once surrounded him, before discovering he'd been manipulated in a game of deception which ended with his own manipulation of his father. He tried desperately to put that life behind him. When he left Washington, he resolved not to dwell on what the past took from him, but instead to live in the present and for what the future had to offer: a life with Brooke and Aneilia by his side, where they could be happy. He promised himself he'd do everything in his power to keep them safe and protect them from the forces that almost destroyed him years earlier.

He pinched his eyes shut, hoping the nightmare of the last few days was only a dream. But he knew full well it was real, as real as the gash on the side of head that had been sutured closed. As he lay in that hospital bed listening to Brooke sobbing in the corner, Tom questioned whether he could still protect those he loved.

He silently prayed that his future wouldn't be haunted by his past.

4

"Good afternoon, Counselor."

Tom dreaded the thought of speaking with Aronson, but Brooke insisted they meet. She said that if their family was in danger because of Tom's past, she wanted to know it and wanted to know it now. He couldn't disagree. She told him Aronson had been stingy with information and she hadn't gotten much out of him. He kept saying it was best if he spoke with Tom first. She made him promise to fill her in as soon as they were alone.

"Can't say I'm happy to see you," Tom said, stone-faced.

"Nice to see you, too, Tom. Glad to hear you're doing better. Doctors say you're expected to make a full recovery. That's good news."

"You've spoken with my doctors about my medical condition? When was that added to the FBI handbook?"

Aronson smirked, which made Tom dislike him even more.

"No, Tom. Your wife told me when she and I chatted outside. Come on. I came here because I'm concerned about your well-being. I'm glad you weren't injured more seriously."

"Sorry, but since you didn't walk in with flowers, I assumed this wasn't a social visit." Tom's scowl put his contempt on full display.

"I see you're still holding a grudge."

"Yeah, I tend to do that with people who barge into my home, knock my wife to the ground, scare my family nearly to death, and accuse my wife and me of selling government secrets for money. The statute of limitations hasn't expired on that yet."

"Counselor, you know as well as I do, I was just doing my job back then. We had probable cause to execute the search warrant and I was following orders."

Tom knew he was being a hard ass, but he was still haunted by the story Brooke told him about Aronson and his armed FBI buddies storming into his apartment, and how frightened Brooke and his mother Mary were during the whole shit-show. It pained him to hear how they'd been treated, and he was still angry about it, even after all these years. There was a time when Tom would let things go and turn the other cheek, willing to explain away a slight or ignore an insult. But that was the old Tom.

After a long pause, Aronson spoke up again. "How's your mother? She didn't deserve what she went through."

Tom looked away and let out a deep sigh. He wasn't about to bring his mother into this conversation. She made her choices and had to face the consequences. Although Brooke visited Mary with Aneilia a couple of times, he hadn't spoken to her since she told him the truth about his life and his family. He still couldn't accept, or forgive, what she'd done. He needed more time to heal and more distance to deal with it all. His mother hadn't yet found her way back into his heart. But that was a story for another time, and it was his business to sort out, not a topic to be discussed with Aronson.

"So what brings the Deputy Director of the Federal Bureau of Investigations to Larange?"

"You've kept tabs on me, I see. You're aware of my promotion and all. I guess I should be grateful you never accepted the position the President offered you five years ago, which would have indirectly made you my boss, I guess. If you had, and since you're still holding a grudge, I might be walking a beat through a corn field in Nebraska."

Tom maintained his glare as he considered a distant memory. Whenever he thought about it, which wasn't often, he came to the same conclusion: he was glad he turned down the job of Attorney General of the United States. It would have meant continuing to live in the spotlight, with a target emblazoned on his back, and under intense scrutiny amid daily reminders of the life he once had. He had no regrets and wouldn't take a mulligan if he could. Then again, at a time like this, sitting in a hospital bed with a huge bandage on his head after having been savagely beaten by an unknown assailant, Tom wouldn't mind a security detail like the one protecting the AG wherever she goes.

In the end, though, he knew accepting the AG position would have meant his family's past being dredged up every time his name was mentioned in the press. He never would have escaped the circumstances that landed him that job, and he never would have enjoyed the anonymity that came with being a small-time country lawyer.

"If I congratulate you on your promotion, will you cut to the chase and tell me why the second highest official in the FBI is interested in a simple assault and battery?"

"If you consider being nearly killed by blunt force trauma to the head a simple assault and battery, I guess you recovered better than I would have from the events in Monaco."

Tom looked away and refused to take the bait.

"Come on Tom. It shouldn't surprise you the FBI is interested in your well-being and has been for the last five years. You performed a tremendous service for your country, and you sacrificed more than anyone should. President Ferguson meant it when she said our nation and our government owe you a tremendous debt of gratitude, and so does the FBI. Me included."

"And you've come here to pay off that debt?

"Yes and no. We check in regularly with the Constable's office to make sure you and your family are living peacefully and aren't facing any threats we need to be aware of."

"So, you've been keeping tabs on me too, I see."

"We're not pulling any strings, Tom," Aronson snapped back. "You've had enough of those pulled for you in your life."

The words stung. Tom clenched his jaw, and considered telling Aronson to go fuck himself, but after a few seconds he conceded ground. He realized he was acting like a spoiled prick instead of being grateful the FBI hadn't cast him aside after being done with him.

"Look, Tom, there was a time not that long ago when you were an important asset for our government. The dangers and risks you faced haven't entirely gone away and so, from time to time, we like to make sure you and your family are safe. If we had reason to intervene we would, but so far we haven't needed to."

"Until now?" Tom asked hesitantly, a pained look on his face.

"Well, that's what I'm here to tell you."

Tom held his breath.

"We've been in touch with all the major players who are still around from five years ago, listening to chatter, and trying to decipher clues and uncover any plots. We've kept a close eye on everyone. Including Cosimo Benedetto."

Tom stiffened at hearing his father's name.

"We've done it quietly and out of sight, but methodically, and we've been thorough to ensure we're prepared to take action if necessary to thwart any threat before it happens."

"So, have you uncovered evidence connecting my past work on the Syndicate to my assault?"

"No, we haven't. And that's the biggest news I'm delivering today. We've done a complete assessment and investigation. We've spoken with all of our sources in the days since your attack in an attempt to learn who was behind it and why. But we've come up empty. The state police shared with us the results of their investigation as well as ballistics analysis of the shell casing at the scene. Based on the trajectory of the casing fragments embedded in trees, their best guess is that whoever pulled the trigger missed you intentionally and didn't intend to kill you. Their working theory is that it was a warning shot. Likely to scare the Jesus out of you."

"It worked," Tom said, only half joking.

"There's more."

Tom inhaled deeply and eyed Aronson.

"Since your attack, the FBI, with the help of state police, have reviewed a compilation of hours of security camera footage taken over the past several months from various locations all over town. Near your office. The road in front of your home. On and around the mountain. The coffee shop you stop in every morning. The station where you're a volunteer firefighter.

And, of course, the courthouse. You'd be surprised how many folks in these parts have cameras rolling."

"And?" Tom said, eager for more details.

"For several weeks you've been under surveillance, and you've been closely watched. One, two, sometimes three persons or more have been trailing you. Monitoring your routine. Places you go, who you meet with, times you do things. They go to great lengths to cover their tracks, change their appearance, and hide their faces so we can't match them using facial recognition software. We can't conclusively say the surveillance is related to your attack, but we believe there's a connection."

Tom was stunned.

"You're a pretty regimented guy, Tom, and you follow a clear pattern without much variation. It's clear you like to ski early, and alone, almost every morning just as the mountain is waking up. I hate to say you were an easy target, but you were an easy target. Perhaps you should vary your routine from now on."

"Brooke was right. This wasn't a random attack," Tom said absently.

"She's a smart woman. No, it wasn't random. You were targeted."

Tom felt dizzy and a wave of nausea hit him hard.

"Listen, we don't know who attacked you within an inch of your life, or why. We don't believe whoever it was wanted to kill you because it would have been too easy to knock you off if that was their goal. What I can tell you, though, with almost complete certainty, is that your attack is unrelated to the Benedetto Syndicate or your work for the DOJ."

Aronson paused for a moment. Then he looked squarely at Tom.

"But there's someone else out there who wants to harm you."

Tom sank deep into the bed. The lines on the video monitor spiked as his heart pounded. His mind raced with possibilities. If his attack was unrelated to his past, then his future and the safety of his family were even more uncertain now than ever.

5

After a week or so, Tom's doctors gave him a clean bill of health and cleared him to return to his normal activities. He'd already been back to the office for a few days and even made a couple of court appearances. The only visible sign of his attack was some residual swelling and bruising across his right temple and cheek. Even the hair on the right side of his head, which had been shaved so doctors could suture the deep gash, revealing a five-year-old scar above his right ear, was starting to grow back, although it looked grayer than it did just a few weeks ago. But Tom didn't care, and he looked forward to the day when all the physical scars of his past would be hidden again.

He was in his office putting the finishing touches on a brief due later in the week in a case involving a novice skier who'd had been seriously injured at the resort by an out-of-control snowboarder, when Janet's voice came through the intercom. She announced his visitor, Anastasia Maine, had arrived for her appointment. He glanced at his watch and smiled. It was ten minutes to three. Tom appreciated his guests arriving early. It showed they valued his time as much as he did. This was going to be an important meeting, or so Tom thought about a month earlier when he had received a call from Phoenix Holdings Group's attorney saying she wanted to discuss a potential settlement deal. The meeting had originally been scheduled for that fateful day when Tom's world had turned upside down.

So far there had been no arrests stemming from his assault, and the police recently admitted they had no leads and no suspects. Brooke was relieved knowing the attack wasn't related to his family's past or his work at the DOJ, but she still spent almost every night trying to figure out who wanted to hurt him so badly—and why. But every suspicion turned into a dead end. Since they moved to Castle Ridge, Tom and Brooke had more friends than they'd ever had and never got crosswise with anyone. Their enemies list simply had no enemies. Tom even asked Janet to review all his old files to see if there was a disgruntled client along the way, or perhaps an adversary who was unhappy with the way a case ended. Although he was certain he'd remember something like that—in four years of running his own practice, he'd only had about fifty clients and couldn't recall any of them being upset to the point they'd want to harm him—he still asked Janet to take a fresh look at the files.

The hysteria in town had begun to die down, too. Gone were the army of police officers and the neighborhood watch group that had patrolled Main Street and stationed themselves outside every restaurant and bar in town. Even the Castle was busy again. While crowds had been lighter than normal the first weekend following the assault, they were back with a vengeance by MLK weekend. A couple of mass shootings out west, a threatened transit strike in New York City, and the hijacking of a commercial freighter in the Red Sea by rebels from Yemen were enough to divert attention away from a figure in white who had attacked a local lawyer. Life in town was slowly getting back to normal—except for the police car Constable Ozzie insisted be parked in front of Tom and Brooke's cabin and his office. Truth is, Tom and Brooke were relieved the police were guarding their home. Aneilia liked it, too, and she begged Brooke every afternoon to bake cookies for the "police *mens*."

Knowing his attacker was still out there, and being unable to figure out a motive for it, made it impossible for Tom to feel safe. Although each passing day put more distance between him and his brutal attack, he knew life would never be the same until whoever was responsible for it was apprehended and brought to justice. Until then, his fifteen minutes of gloom persisted in a time warp. Instead of a fading memory, the moments leading to his assault were seared in his brain's hard drive, a constant reminder to remain vigilant against faceless forces who wanted to harm him.

Tom reached for the folder Janet prepared for the meeting and re-read the notes he'd made when he first spoke with Anastasia Maine, Phoenix Holdings' attorney, a few weeks earlier. She said then she wanted to discuss a proposal to resolve the litigation between their clients, and felt an in-person meeting was best. Flipping to the second page, Tom saw the deed to the property Phoenix Holdings owned on the banks of the Bensonville Reservoir and was reminded of the five-million-dollar price tag the company paid for it a little over a year ago. That was a king's ransom for seven acres, Tom thought. Even though land values had risen considerably in and around Castle Ridge in the last several years, he was certain Phoenix Holdings seriously overpaid for land that sat almost entirely within a conservation buffer zone, and whose only access from the main road at the time was a narrow dirt path that ran through a forest. But rich dumb people making bad decisions never ceased to amaze him. Fortunately, it also meant lawyers like him continued to be in high demand.

He glanced at the last sheet of paper in the folder. It was his retainer agreement with his electronic signature in place. He smiled when he saw his hourly rate was up to $375. What a bargain, he thought, compared to the inflated fees BCC was charging years earlier for junior associates with hardly any experience. Closing the folder, he grabbed his suit jacket from the back of his high-back leather chair and slipped it on as he made his way to the conference room down the hall. Old habits were hard to break.

Anastasia Maine was seated in an armchair at the head of the oval table when Tom walked into the room.

"Ms. Maine, it's a pleasure to meet you."

Anastasia rose gracefully, without resting her hands on the table or the arms of the chair, and walked toward Tom, offering her outstretched hand. Although her name was on the brief submitted to the court as Phoenix Holdings' lead lawyer, she wasn't in court for the hearing that resulted in the preliminary injunction, so this was the first time Tom was meeting her. It was Anastasia's young associate who had attended the hearing, and while he did an admirable job, he still lost. Now, for this settlement meeting, Phoenix Holdings was sending in its big guns—Anastasia Maine herself, several years removed from Yale Law School.

Anastasia looked young, with long dark hair, dark eyes, and tanned skin suggesting she didn't spend her winters in Castle Ridge. She stood a bit taller than Tom, but only because her high-heeled boots added several inches to her height, making her appear more statuesque. She wore a red dress with a black scarf hanging loosely around her neck that framed a thick diamond pendant hanging in the center of her plunging V-neck. The pendant matched her diamond hoop earrings, and Tom noticed a gold and diamond encrusted bracelet encircling her left forearm, preventing her dress sleeve from covering it. A large oval diamond mounted on a gold setting nearly straddled several fingers of her right hand, which Tom saw when he reached out to accept her handshake which she extended gracefully, giving her an aura of power and sophistication. He also noticed her fur coat casually draped over a chair to the right of the one she'd been sitting in, slightly covering her Louis Vuitton satchel. Even in a town as affluent as Castle Ridge, no one looked and dressed the way Anastasia Maine did.

"The pleasure is mine, Mr. Berte. Thank you for seeing me so soon after your..." She paused as if searching for the right words. "Your unfortunate incident."

Tom thought Anastasia's choice of words was curious, but he'd run into a lot of folks since he was released from the hospital who seemed uncomfortable talking about his assault. He decided to ignore it and turned to the sideboard across from the conference table to offer Anastasia a selection of coffees and teas.

She accepted a cup of tea and then looked around the room as if she was afraid to touch anything. "You have a charming office."

Tom detected a slight British accent, something he hadn't picked up on when they spoke on the phone weeks earlier. He also sensed an air of formality about her that was both off-putting and intriguing, and it made it difficult for him to determine if she was sincere—or being a critic.

"Thank you, Ms. Maine. I'm not much for decorating, but I wanted to create an inviting and comfortable space, inspired by the mountain landscape and country setting." Tom liked how his office looked and felt. It wasn't stuffy or pretentious, and you wouldn't find any gold leaf, marble or crystal anywhere in the place.

She smiled and nodded. "Yes, well, it's," pausing again as if at a loss for words, Anastasia glanced at the ceiling and finally said, "Shall we say cozy and quaint."

Tom stood up from reaching for a *Yoo-hoo* in the small refrigerator custom built into the bottom portion of the sideboard and looked around the room. It was adorned with mahogany shelves lined with law books and his growing collection of antique, leather-bound classics. On one end of the room, in front of a fireplace where flames flickered keeping the room warm, were two wingback armchairs grouped in front of a coffee table and matching side tables topped with brass lamps. On the other end sat a cream-colored sofa under a pair of paintings depicting fox-hunting dogs and riders on horseback gathering in a country field. Patterned coordinating drapes framed three large windows overlooking Main Street, as well as those in the semicircular apse. And taking pride of place in the center of the apse was a sturdy plinth holding the bronze bust of President Lincoln, a gift he received when he stepped down from the DOJ five years earlier, an almost daily reminder of the best job he'd had in his still-young career. Surveying his conference room, Tom felt satisfied and content. "Cozy and quaint sound good to me."

Tom invited Anastasia to take her seat. Normally he would have taken the chair at the head of the table and invited Anastasia to sit to his left facing the windows, but since she had already claimed the head seat for herself, Tom moved down several chairs, taking a seat at the middle of the table. He placed his folder, pen, a new unused legal pad, and his bottle of *Yoo-hoo* in front of him.

"I hope you had a nice drive up to Castle Ridge, Ms. Maine."

"Please, call me Anastasia. I insist. And I trust I can call you Thomas?"

Tom took a sip of his *Yoo-hoo*. He assumed she was trying to soften him up for the negotiations to come and decided to play along, for a while at least.

"Tom will do," he said. "And because you insist, I'll call you Anastasia."

Tom noticed a Mona Lisa smile cross her face.

"The drive was pleasant enough. Some of the vistas on the way were absolutely spectacular. And I was fortunate the weather was pleasant. I can't imagine driving up the mountain when it is snowing. Some of the hills and curves I traversed were treacherous. Fortunately, I'm driving a Range Rover and that made the drive even more pleasant."

Let the pretentious name-dropping begin, Tom thought. "Yes, well, welcome to upstate New York in the winter. Our road crews are excellent, though, and they do a terrific job of clearing snow and salting the roads. Even for those who don't drive Range Rovers," a wry smile crossing his face this time.

"That's good to know. I was surprised, however, to see some of the abandoned and worn properties along the way after leaving the Thruway. There was more blight than I expected on the approach road, considering the immense beauty of Castle Ridge."

What a blowhard. Tom could have scooped the condescension in her voice with a snow shovel. It was clear Anastasia Maine was out of her element and uncomfortable with the rural beauty of the area. He quickly decided he and Anastasia weren't going to become fast friends and it was better to get down to business. Time for small talk was over.

"So, you said you had a proposal in mind to resolve the dispute between our clients. I'm all ears."

"I appreciate your wanting to get right to the point. As I mentioned when we first spoke, Phoenix Holdings is not in the business of litigating. My client is relatively new to town, as you know, and it wants to be a good neighbor and steward of the land it acquired. Phoenix Holdings prefers to live and let live as it were, without creating unnecessary strife. We want peace, not conflict."

Tom sat back in his chair. He was pleased to hear Anastasia willing to tone down her rhetoric. It was the exact opposite tact she took in her court filings where she used strident language to accuse Tom's clients of bullying. Numerous times she wrote that Faith McReynolds had an incurable conflict of interest because she was using her position as mayor to benefit her company at the expense of a tax paying property owner. Anastasia adamantly argued the town and ski resort were depriving her client of the right to use their land however they saw fit and were violating state and federal laws, and even the United States Constitution itself.

"It's interesting you say that, Anastasia, because my clients and I know almost nothing about Phoenix Holdings other than it is owned by a group of wealthy foreign investors. What are their intentions? What do they plan to do with the land? Most of it can't be developed because of its zoning designation, and yet there was quite a bit of activity on the land before we obtained the preliminary injunction stopping any further construction."

Tom noticed Anastasia didn't flinch at his questions. She was ice cold and showed no emotion, making her impossible to read.

"My client thought it rather unfortunate that you filed the lawsuit. It would have much preferred if you had contacted us first."

"My clients felt they needed to move quickly. The truck traffic was unbearable as was the round-the-clock noise. And the judge obviously agreed, which is why she issued the injunction. What was your client doing there with so many trucks entering and leaving anyway?"

Anastasia smiled as she uncrossed and recrossed her legs.

"We view the judge's ruling as only a minor setback and we expect to prevail at trial. But that's not really the point of this meeting. My client is interested in finding a mutually agreeable resolution. As for your question about my client's intentions, even though I don't believe it is any of your business, it is really quite simple. My client believes investing in Castle Ridge is a wise decision, and certainly the increase in land values over the last few years confirms that strategy. Phoenix Holdings is not interested in large-scale development, but in doing something that is in keeping with the rural charm of the area. Perhaps a nature preserve or animal sanctuary. Or an endeavor devoted to scientific study. They are even considering establishing an equine-assisted therapy center for children."

Tom perked up. He'd long heard Brooke talk about the benefits of animal therapy for young children with physical, emotional, and developmental disabilities, like the kids she worked with. She'd be excited to have such a facility in Castle Ridge. But he needed to play it cool. This was business after all, and he had a job to do. Plus, he wasn't convinced Anastasia was being completely forthcoming. Spending five million dollars on land to build a therapy center didn't make much business sense. He suspected there was more to the story, but he also wasn't sure he cared enough to press for the truth. Faith had retained him specifically to prevent development on what was environmentally sensitive land and, so far, he'd succeeded. Analyzing Phoenix Holdings' business plan wasn't within the scope of his job.

"Do you live in the area with your family, Tom?"

Tom shifted in his chair. Anastasia's comment caught him off guard. He reached for his *Yoo-hoo* and took a small sip. He almost never spoke about his family, especially with people he didn't know, and Anastasia certainly fit that bill. He didn't want to appear rude, but he also had no intention of discussing his family with her.

"Yes, I do. Now, let's please turn to what you came here to discuss. The matter between our clients."

"You are a talented lawyer, Tom. I see why you've had much success in your career."

She was at it again, trying to flatter him, but he wasn't buying it. Besides, what successes was she referring to? The real ones or the contrived ones? He decided to stay silent and let Anastasia keep talking.

"You're a highly credentialed attorney. Your pedigree is very impressive, from the schools you attended, to the law firm you were associated with, to the high-level position you held with the Justice Department. My client respects high-achievers, and based on your resume, it is clear you are."

This was the first time since he started his own practice that anyone mentioned his pedigree or his past work. His resume looked impressive, but it bore no resemblance to his reality or to what he would have achieved without the assistance he received along the way. He understood that now, and had come to terms with it. No one in Castle Ridge cared what law school he attended, or where he worked previously, and he preferred it that way. But Anastasia and the people she worked for seemed to care and apparently believed his background mattered. Tom debated what to say. He was determined to succeed on the basis of his talents now, not the padded resume he once had, and the only way to prove it was to brush aside what Anastasia and her clients thought of him and do the job he was retained to do.

"That's very kind of you, Anastasia, but it has nothing to do with the issues we're litigating. You said you had a proposal to share. Let's have it."

"You seem anxious, Tom. I'm sorry if I said something to make you uncomfortable."

Tom noticed the Mona Lisa smile again.

"You should know that I've spoken with Bradley Mitchelson about you and he thinks the world of you. He has nothing but the highest praise for your legal talents."

Tom's eyes widened as he leaned forward.

"You know the former Attorney General? Why didn't you mention that earlier?"

"Would it have mattered? Attorney General Mitchelson has advised my client on several deals over the past few years and they've kept in touch. When my client's representative mentioned to Bradley the issues we're having in Castle Ridge, your name came up. Bradley said he knew you well. He's quite fond of you."

Tom hadn't spoken with his former boss in over a year, although he'd received flowers from Mitchelson while recovering in the hospital. He assumed Mitchelson had learned of his attack from news reports. After leaving his post, the AG took some time off to write his memoir, and then landed a swanky job as a senior advisor in a small but highly regarded international consulting firm based in London with offices in Washington, D.C. and Abu Dhabi. In the first few years after Tom left Washington, Mitchelson would often tell him he'd try to recommend him to his clients and contacts, but Tom just assumed he was being friendly and saying what most lawyers say when networking—they'd love to refer business if the right opportunity came up. Although he thought it odd that Mitchelson hadn't called him after speaking with Anastasia, he was also grateful his old boss hadn't seen fit to intervene on behalf of a client.

"Bradley Mitchelson is a wonderful man and an excellent attorney. I'm fond of him too."

That was about as much as Tom was willing to say on the subject. Mitchelson was someone from Tom's past, and although he felt great affection for the man who helped salvage his career, and maybe save his life, he wasn't about to let it affect his judgment or take his eye off the ball.

"Now, for the third time, will you tell me your settlement proposal?"

6

"Phoenix Holdings wants to acquire Castle Ridge Ski Resort."

Tom grabbed his pen and was staring at his pad intending to jot down the settlement proposal when Anastasia spoke. But he wasn't sure he heard her. He lifted his head and looked at her with a quizzical look on his face.

"Repeat that."

"My clients want to purchase Castle Ridge Ski Resort."

A million thoughts swept through Tom's mind. The resort wasn't for sale. If it was, he'd know. He and Brooke were good friends with Faith McReynolds, the ski resort's third-generation owner. Faith's family had owned the land the resort sits on since the late 1940's when Earl McReynolds, Faith's grandfather, bought 750 acres of steep wooded terrain on the north side of Castle Ridge Mountain with a vision of turning it into a premier skiing destination just a few hours' drive from at least three post-war booming cities. As the ski resort grew, it was consistently rated among the best in the United States, providing a first-rate winter playground for families and celebrities alike. In more recent times, calling it a ski resort was a misnomer of sorts because just as many snowboarders flocked to the Castle as skiers, much to Tom's chagrin. But Faith was a traditionalist, and although she welcomed snowboarders to ride her mountain, she drew the line at changing the name to Castle Ridge Ski and Ride Resort.

Tom realized he had remained quiet for too long.

"I wasn't aware the resort is for sale," he said. "I know Faith McReynolds and she's never mentioned selling her business."

"It may not be. And I'm well aware of your acquaintance with Ms. McReynolds," Anastasia said with a shrug of her padded shoulders. "It is of no importance to my client, really, whether the resort is currently for sale or not. Everyone has a price, and the people behind Phoenix Holdings are prepared to make a very generous offer. They're willing to spend whatever it takes, and they wish to move quickly."

Not a smart negotiating ploy, Tom thought. Anastasia and her client were violating a cardinal rule of negotiating 101: never let an unmotivated seller know you're more interested in buying than they are in selling.

"Anastasia, I'm not sure I'm following what you're proposing. Your client wants to buy a company that's not for sale and it's willing to pay top-dollar to acquire it? Without doing any due diligence or looking at the resort's books? And your client wants to make that happen as part of a deal to settle litigation between our clients?"

Anastasia flashed a confident smile and sat up straight as an arrow.

"As I said, my client is not interested in litigation. Phoenix Holdings is run by savvy businesspeople and their primary goal is to make money for their investors. They view litigation as an unnecessary expense and a distraction from more fruitful endeavors. And as for the resort's value, my clients have done their homework. They know what the resort is worth—to them."

"What are your client's intentions? Would it continue to operate it as a resort?"

"Yes, of course. As you likely know, Phoenix Holdings possesses vast holdings in oil and gas, real estate, and manufacturing in the UK and throughout Europe. Its board of directors wishes to enter the US leisure and hospitality sector, and they want to make Castle Ridge Ski Resort their first investment. They have thoroughly researched the company, and they view it as a very desirable investment. They intend to maintain it as a first-class winter resort and install experienced professionals to operate the venture, perhaps eventually transforming it into a four-season recreation and entertainment destination. They have very ambitious aspirations."

Anastasia paused and took a sip of her tea, "And I'm sure they'll want to spruce up the surrounding area."

Tom raised his eyebrows and pursed his lips.

"Anastasia, Castle Ridge is a small town and many of the folks have lived here for generations. The McReynolds family itself has owned the mountain along with half the town for decades. Change doesn't come easy in these parts. People around here tend to like things just the way they are. I'm not sure your proposal to transform the town or resort will play particularly well with the townsfolk or the McReynolds family."

"Ah, yes, well that's where your services come into play. My client is well aware of your solid reputation in the community. You're held in high regard by the locals. You're viewed as a successful businessman and a respected family man with strong values. Your judgment and opinions carry a lot of weight. We're hoping you'll view our proposal as a win-win for everyone involved and you'll use your good office to convince Ms. McReynolds and everyone else on the Castle Ridge town council that needs convincing that our offer makes a great deal of sense."

Tom sat back in his chair. Offering to settle litigation over development rights to a spit of land by combining it with an unsolicited offer to purchase the entire ski resort made no sense. And he was certain it would make no sense to Faith.

"Tom, the people behind Phoenix Holdings are sophisticated, smart investors. They do their homework before they leap. They didn't obtain their wealth and *power* overnight."

Tom heard Anastasia's emphasis on the word *power*. He thought of countering her, but quickly remembered a lesson he learned long ago from a smart lawyer who was like a father figure to him: *in negotiations it is often better to listen than to speak. That's why God gave us two ears but only one mouth. You learn twice as much by listening rather than speaking.*

Tom decided to remain silent.

"My client has sufficient resources to litigate forever, if it chooses to. Phoenix Holdings can bankrupt the town of Castle Ridge and the resort by forcing it to pay legal fees for the next decade. Is that really what the Mayor wants? We realize you're a worthy opponent, as is Ms. McReynolds, with vast resources of her own, but I assure you those resources pale in comparison to those of my client. We are proposing a business solution that makes sense for everyone. The McReynolds family walks away with a sizeable return on their investment, the town of Castle Ridge gets a new business owner that will continue to fill its tax coffers for years to come, and Phoenix Holdings gets to manage its property and business on its terms while being a gracious neighbor to the good people of Castle Ridge."

Hearing Anastasia put it that way made it difficult to argue with her logic. Sure, it was like using a chain saw to cut a hang nail, but both Faith and the town would profit handsomely and everyone would get to live in peace and harmony. There was only one problem. Tom wasn't at all convinced Faith would agree to sell her most prized possession.

"And how much are you offering?"

"My client is prepared to offer five hundred million dollars in cash to purchase the resort, and it will assume the company's debt," Anastasia said without hesitation, looking relaxed and cool. "It's a significant multiple of the company's expected earnings over the next decade."

Tom inched closer to the edge of his chair. For the second time he thought he'd misheard Anastasia.

"Five hundred million dollars?" Tom forgot his game face for a moment and got caught up in the mental math he was doing in his head. After a few seconds, he collected his thoughts, regained his composure, and sat back.

"It's a generous offer, isn't it, Tom?"

"Generous indeed. But I'm not sure your client's largesse will entice my client to part with her business. Ms. McReynolds loves the resort and the town of Castle Ridge. This is her home. She considers her employees her family. I don't think there's enough treasure in all the world's bodies of water that would convince Faith McReynolds to sell her company."

For the first time Tom sensed Anastasia become uneasy. She shifted in her chair, sighed deeply, and clasped her hands, pausing for a long while before speaking.

"That would be unfortunate. Continuing the litigation you started would be a colossal waste of time and resources. And a huge mistake. There will be no winners in the end. And many losers. Faith McReynolds is your good friend, and my client is confident you'll be able to persuade her and her family that offers like these come along once in a lifetime, if they come along at all. It would be a shame for the McReynolds family to miss out on this opportunity." Anastaisa looked around the conference room again. "The same is true for you and everyone involved."

Tom understood a veiled threat when he heard one. He could push back, or he could use his time to figure out how to present the offer to his client. He opted for the latter for now. He was certain Faith would turn it down, even for the incredible sum of half a billion dollars.

Anastasia was approaching the entrance to the Thruway when her cell phone rang. She took a long drag from her vape pen before pressing the talk button.

"Was the offer conveyed?"

"Yes," Anastasia said while exhaling. "The lawyer appeared intrigued, as I suspected he would, but he was skeptical his client would accept. He will convey it to Faith McReynolds and I expect to hear from him in a few days. We will know shortly whether she will accept. If not, we will need to change course and execute our alternate strategy. I recommend we maintain our surveillance of the lawyer, but at a distance."

Anastasia took another deep pull from her vape pen before speaking up again.

"It is our divine right to triumph in the vindication of our cause. The sacrifice of our people must never be forgotten. Praise be to you, and glory to our collective destiny which shall be vindicated through the Grand Plan on the Fourth of July. May Your Eminence continue to reign supreme."

7

Tom watched Anastasia from his conference room window as she gingerly strode to her Range Rover while balancing herself on her stiletto boots. "What a piece of work," he muttered to himself.

Glancing up and down Main Street, he noticed traffic was light and storefronts quiet. The police car that had been a constant presence outside his office ever since his attack was still there with the sheriff's deputy sitting in the driver's seat probably playing solitaire on his phone. It was a typical calm mid-week afternoon in Castle Ridge, a welcomed respite to the snarled roadways and choked sidewalks that usually began as early as Thursdays at noon in the winter months. Slate gray clouds hung low, casting an ashen pallor over the town, and a biting wind from the west meant another storm was brewing. Forecasters were calling for up to a foot of fresh snow to fall the following day, and Tom was eager to get home and restock the firewood rack in case the power went out.

He slumped into one of the wingback chairs next to the fireplace and stared intently at the random whisps of flames dancing in the fireplace. Just as they reached their peak, their intensity gave way, becoming less potent as they flickered closer to the logs, until a burst of oxygen fueled their ferocity again, repeating the pattern. Tom's mind was racing just like the flames in the hearth.

He was unsure what to make of Anastasia's proposal and had more questions than answers. The search he'd done on Phoenix Holdings when Faith first retained him was consistent with Anastasia's description of the company and its business interests, but he still found it odd that a group of wealthy foreign investors would choose to make a huge investment in the tiny hamlet of Castle Ridge. And although Castle Ridge Ski Resort was wildly popular and profitable, he found it curious that businesspeople with no experience in the leisure and hospitality sector, to say nothing of the ski and snowboarding business, were interested in investing hundreds of millions of dollars to acquire a resort in upstate New York. If it was the Swiss Alps, or even the Rockies, maybe it'd make sense, he thought. But perhaps starting small was a smart move after all. Phoenix Holdings could cut its teeth with a smaller venture in a smaller market, before extending its reach out west or to Europe. As the song goes, if it could make it in New York, it could make it anywhere.

What he found even more interesting was the connection Phoenix Holdings had with his old boss. Sure former Attorney General Bradley Mitchelson was well-credentialed and highly regarded, especially after his stint running the Justice Department, so perhaps it made sense for an international conglomerate like Phoenix Holdings to find its way to him. He decided to reach out to Mitchelson and do some more reconnaissance on Anastasia and her client. It might shed some light on Phoenix's intentions.

Unfortunately, when Tom called Mitchelson, he was told the former Attorney General was travelling in Asia and would be for the next several weeks. Mitchelson's executive assistant, Hope, who had worked for the Attorney General at the Justice Department and knew Tom from his days as Mitchelson's number two, thanked Tom for the note he sent after receiving Mitchelson's flowers. She assured Tom she would pass along his message.

It was almost three-thirty, and Tom wanted to get home. He called Faith to schedule a meeting with her to present Anastasia's offer, but when he did, she too was out of the office. With everyone he needed to speak to unavailable, and no other appointments on his schedule, Tom decided to call it quits for the day and head home.

Brooke and Aneilia were in the kitchen when Tom walked in and dropped his briefcase in the tiny mudroom off the garage. The smell of chocolate chip cookies baking in the oven wafted throughout the small cabin as Aneilia came running toward him with her chocolate-covered hands held high in the air, followed by Brooke.

"Hi, daddy. We're making cookies for the police *mens* outside. Want to help?"

Tom scooped her up in his arms and nuzzled her neck. She giggled as Tom licked her fingers and tickled her belly.

"Daddy, is your boo-boo better?" Anelia craned her head up, puckered her lips and mashed her face into the right side of his head. Tom's heart was full as he hugged his sweet baby girl tightly.

"Yes, sweetie, and your kisses make it feel even better."

Brooke rushed over to join the hug fest and Tom gave her a gentle kiss.

"Tell daddy how many cookies we're making."

"We made a whole lots," Anelia said, holding her sticky, chocolatey hands up. "Mommy said we can take them to the police station too."

The three of them walked over to the counter and Tom poured milk into a mug so he and Aneilia could enjoy their favorite snack together.

"What's the rule about milk and cookies?" he asked.

"Don't put your fingers in the milk," Aneilia said, giggling through a mouth full of soggy cookies, which made Brooke and Tom both laugh.

He wanted so much to share news of the offer to buy the resort with Brooke, but he resisted the urge. He never shared details of his work with anyone, not even his wife who was his best friend. But he decided to tell her that he had reached out to Mitchelson. Brooke had grown close to Mitchelson and his wife, Beverly, in the days and weeks after the events in Monaco five years ago. The Mitchelsons even arranged for dinner to be delivered to Tom and Brooke's apartment every day for an entire month while they adjusted to their new reality before moving to Castle Ridge.

"Bradley Mitchelson's name came up today in connection with one of my matters," he said while Aneilia kept dipping cookies and the tips of her fingers into the milk. "I called him but was told he's out of the country travelling on business. When's the last time you spoke with Beverly?" Tom asked, trying to sound indifferent.

"Around Thanksgiving, I guess. She told me she and Bradley were planning to be abroad during winter and spring, including a cruise around the Greek Isles. I thought I mentioned it to you."

"Maybe you did, I can't remember." Tom shuddered when he heard Brooke mention a cruise. He hadn't been near water in five years. If she had mentioned it, he likely tuned it out of his mind.

"So what's the connection? Did he refer a new client to you?"

"See, this is why I hesitate to tell you anything about my work," Tom said grinning. "You know I never share details about my clients or my work."

"Oh, please. You're a small-town lawyer now, babe, not a high-powered Wall Street litigator making the world safe for millionaires and billionaires so they can keep lining their pockets with gold."

The two laughed again and shared a knowing look. The pace of Tom's practice had certainly slowed since his days at BCC. No more all-nighters or answering emails and texts at all hours of the day and night. In fact, Tom rarely looked at his phone when he was home, almost never brought work home with him, and never worked on weekends. When he decided to open his own law office, a year after they moved to Castle Ridge, he vowed he'd never practice law again for the money. Years of billing three thousand hours so he could earn a high six figure salary, plus a hefty bonus, were behind him. His time at the DOJ, working with dedicated public servants who devoted their careers to promoting the rule of law for a fraction of what partners at Wall Street firms earned, confirmed for him that the greatest reward for practicing law was knowing justice was done, not collecting a fat paycheck. He still took his work seriously, though, and he was still committed to maintaining his clients' secrets.

"OK. You can continue to keep me in the dark, for now. Just please tell Bradley that I miss him and Beverly and would love to visit with them this summer."

He smiled and nodded as Brooke moved to the stove to stir the simmering pot of stew she was preparing for dinner. Glancing at Aneilia sitting on the floor with Bentley who was licking cookie crumbs and milk from her fingers, he felt happier than he had in a long time and was looking forward to enjoying a quiet dinner at home with his beautiful wife and baby girl.

Little could he imagine at that moment the grave danger he would soon face—danger from a sinister plot no one ever thought possible.

8

The technician made his way deliberately to the two-story-tall glass cistern filled with water. Encased from head to toe in a self-contained silver acrylic mobility jumpsuit, with lead gloves and steel-toed boots, he looked like he belonged on a launchpad waiting to blast off into outer space instead of in a subterranean desert laboratory thousands of miles from Castle Ridge. The protective cover-all prevented exposed skin from coming into contact with the viral agent he carefully poured into the black payload capsule. The umbilical tube tethered to the back of his jumpsuit pumped oxygen-rich air into his helmet allowing for prolonged breathing, longer than would be possible with just a backpack-style breathing apparatus. The longer work shifts were necessary to achieve the July Fourth deadline.

After pouring the last batch of agent into the payload capsule, he flipped a switch which slowly lowered the capsule to the bottom of the cistern. Closing and locking the cistern's hatch, the technician turned to his assistant and nodded. The assistant picked up the handheld device strapped to the side of the cistern's outer wall and typed the code that had been given to him. Almost immediately the payload capsule sitting on the floor of the cistern detonated with a small burst, releasing thousands of tiny bubbles that instantly dissolved, infusing the water in the cistern with the viral agent encased in the capsule.

After a few seconds, the technician opened a small door to a glass-domed cage adjacent to the cistern. Dozens of tiny, furry white creatures scampered into the cage in search of water to quench their thirst. They eventually made their way to a row of bottles lining the side of the cage that had quickly filled with the liquid mixture from the cistern. The tiny creatures began sucking at nipples attached to the bottom of the bottles, drinking in the liquid mixture. The result was as expected. Within seconds of their first sip, their tiny bodies stiffened. Some began seizing and foaming at their mouths, eyes bulging wide. Others immediately suffocated and collapsed. One by one the tiny creatures succumbed to the poison. Death came quickly. Survival was impossible.

Monitoring the results on a large video screen from her Manhattan luxury penthouse halfway around the world, Anastasia looked away, unable to watch the tiny creatures' suffering after ingesting the crippling liquid. Before she averted her eyes, she saw His Eminence seated in the viewing room perched high above the laboratory.

"The same result occurs each time," the technician said in a steely voice. It was crystal clear even from thousands of miles away. "Upon detonation of the payload capsule, the viral agent Zincar is released. Based on our studies, we will require 150 tons of Zincar to achieve the objective of the Grand Plan."

The technician paused, and Anastasia could hear the rustling of papers before he continued.

"Immersion of multiple payload capsules containing Zincar on July 1 will allow the viral agent to reach its destination by the morning of July 4. Results of our efforts will be noticed immediately."

Anastasia took in a deep breath and stared intently at His Eminence. Within seconds she saw the look of approval on his scarred, craggy face.

9

"You look great. I hope you're fully recovered from that awful incident," Faith said as she took a seat across from Tom at Peak's Perk Coffee Chalet, his favorite coffee spot on Main Street. He often retreated there when he needed peace and quiet and an out-of-the-way place to work. Not in the front of the house, which was always packed and noisy, but in a back room that, according to legend, had been a speakeasy in the roaring twenties. Now it was used only by a select few friends of the coffee shop's owners for discreet meetings. Most customers didn't even know it existed. It had shag carpet, a plush sofa, and a few mis-matched chairs around a small table. Tom would ask to use the room from time to time when his office and home were too chaotic to finish an important brief or prepare a critical witness for deposition. This morning, it served as an ideal place for him to brief Faith on Phoenix Holdings' offer for the ski resort. He arranged the meeting late last night via an exchange of text messages with Faith.

"I'm almost at a hundred percent and feeling better every day."

"You had us all scared nearly to death. When I heard the blast on the mountain, I was prepared for the worst. And then I heard Terrie yelling on the two-way radio that you were injured, and I couldn't believe it. I got on a snowmobile and raced up the mountain as fast as I could. The entire ski patrol team arrived within minutes, and thank goodness the medevac helicopter was in the staging area. I couldn't imagine having to wait for it to arrive from Larange. I mean, there was so much blood, and ..." Faith's voice trailed off as she shook her head.

It was just as well. Tom didn't want to relive the details of the assault. Going through the harrowing experience once was enough.

"Luck was on my side that day in a lot of ways. Especially because of Terrie's quick response. I've told her a million times she saved my life. Without her, I probably wouldn't be here today. But you know Terrie, she's so humble she doesn't want to hear it."

"We're lucky she's part of our team. I've nominated her to receive a special commendation from the Castle Ridge Town Council. The announcement will be coming out this week. It would be great if you and Brooke could attend the next Council meeting and join us for the ceremony."

"I wouldn't miss it for the world."

"I spoke with Constable Ozzie again this morning. Darryl, who leads the resort's security team, has been working closely with him and his deputies and the state police. The Constable tells me they have no leads on who did this to you. The trail's run cold."

"So I hear," Tom said, desperately trying to change the subject from the only thing everyone in town seemed to want to talk about over the past few weeks.

"I'm sure Constable Ozzie and his deputies are doing everything they can, and hopefully they'll catch a break soon," Faith said. "In the meantime, I'm going to help them by announcing a one-hundred-thousand-dollar reward for information leading to an arrest of the madman who did this to you."

"I don't know what to say, Faith. Thank you very much. That's incredibly generous of you."

Tom didn't want to prolong the discussion by sharing details of what he'd learned from FBI Deputy Director Aronson, including that he was a marked man and not the victim of a random attack, but he assumed Faith already knew all that. She was in her third term as mayor and controlled the Castle Ridge Town Council and its five-member board. She was also the largest landowner and biggest employer in town and contributed the most to the town's tax coffers. Few people were as plugged in as she was. Whatever happened in Castle Ridge, Faith was either responsible for it or knew who was long before anyone else.

"On the bright side, this season seems to be going really well for the resort," Tom said, segueing to a different topic. "The snow's been great so far, and the mountain's as packed as I've ever seen it. Did you notice the crowd out front? Skiers and riders are three deep at the counter waiting for their cup of joe before heading to the slopes."

"It has been a great season so far. We've sold out every weekend except for one."

Tom knew exactly which weekend. Castle Ridge was a virtual ghost town that first weekend after his attack. Thanks to the governor's press conference, everyone on the East Coast thought a crazed sasquatch was on the loose. Fortunately, the hysteria had died down, with deep-pocketed families looking for winter fun on the slopes flocking back to the Castle in droves.

"The good Lord has blessed my family with this resort, and mother nature keeps blessing us with abundant snow. I owe it all to Grandpa Earle. He was a real visionary when he arrived here after World War II and started building this place. When I think about the courage it took for him to embark on this journey, I am just in awe." Faith looked down and stared at her cup. "Sometimes I feel like an imposter. I mean, I question whether I deserve to be carrying on his vision, and whether I've earned the right to be here." Faith paused and took a sip of coffee. "This was his dream. It was his blood, sweat and tears that built this wonderful resort we all love. I'm just the product of fortunate genealogy and the beneficiary of an inherited legacy."

Tom faintly smiled. He knew exactly the self-doubt Faith was experiencing, and the daily struggle that comes with questioning your own worthiness. For the last five years he'd struggled with the nagging question whether he could have made it on his own if his father hadn't tipped the scales in his favor for so long. Should he have been grateful for the assistance he got along the way, even though he didn't ask for it, or resent being cheated out of knowing whether he could have succeeded on his own? It was the same debate he'd been having with himself ever since he learned the truth. When he looked up, he noticed Faith was staring at him.

"You haven't heard a word I've been saying, have you?" Faith said, smiling and wagging her finger.

"Actually, Faith. I was listening. Very carefully. I know exactly how you feel."

Tom took a gulp of coffee and wiped his mouth with a paper napkin.

"But for now there's something else I want to talk to you about. I recently met with the attorney for Phoenix Holdings Group. Anastasia Maine. She made a proposal to settle our case. Just hear me out before you say no."

10

"Castle Ridge isn't for sale."

"I know that, Faith. I mean, I know you probably haven't considered selling it before. But I also know you've never received an offer like this one before. As your attorney, I need to present it to you. The offer may be too good to pass up."

"Tom, let's start over. You're telling me Phoenix Holdings, which owns about seven acres of land adjacent to the ski resort, and that's doing God knows what on its land, is offering to buy Castle Ridge Ski Resort as part of settling the lawsuit we filed?"

"You heard me correctly. Phoenix Holdings is owned by foreign individuals, mainly from Qatar, the United Arab Emirates, and Saudi Arabia. The company owns several blue-chip businesses in the UK and throughout Europe, and it's looking to expand its footprint in the U.S. They've zeroed in on Castle Ridge Ski Resort as their foray into the U.S. leisure and hospitality market. They recognize it's the premier ski and snowboard destination in the northeast, with top-notch amenities on par with the most popular ski venues anywhere in the world."

"Nice to hear. You should consider taking a job in marketing instead of being a lawyer," Faith deadpanned. "How long have you, or they, been practicing that line? Seriously, what do these people from a part of the world that's never even seen snow know about running a ski business?"

"Actually, parts of Saudi Arabia do get snow," Tom said with a grin. "Look, it's a good question, and I'm not sure I know the answer, but I'm certain they have the resources to hire a first-rate management team."

"And they want to buy everything? The entire operation?"

"That's what they're offering. The land, lodges, hotel, townhouses, restaurants, ski lifts, snow groomers, and even the entire inventory of skis, snowboards, boots and poles in the rental shop. All seven hundred and fifty acres and everything in between. Lock, stock and barrel."

"And how much are they offering?"

"I'm glad you're sitting down. Five hundred million dollars," Tom said slowly. "Plus Phoenix Holdings will assume your debt. You'll walk away with the full five hundred million."

Faith whistled, and Tom was certain he had at least piqued her interest.

"And they'll continue to operate it as a ski resort?"

"That's what their lawyer says. I'm sure Phoenix Holdings has its own ideas on how to improve on what you and your family have built, and Anastasia said her client intends to make substantial investments in the surrounding area, from the Thruway up to Castle Ridge to enhance the experience of traveling up to the resort. These folks have deep pockets." He left out the part about Anastasia being a condescending snob.

Tom was certain Faith never thought of selling the resort, and possibly didn't even know what it was worth in the current market. But he did. Based on his research, the land and fixed assets were valued, generously, at two hundred and fifty million. There was probably another twenty-five million in inventory and non-fixed assets. He figured the skiing and riding operations, and the lodging and dining segments, generated about another hundred million a year in gross revenue, but he also knew the resort's operating costs were staggering, and profit margins were thin. Running a business that operated for only half the year, at most, and was heavily dependent on mother nature, made the ski business one of the riskiest around. It was often feast or famine, which is why the industry had such a high bankruptcy rate. He didn't think it was a wise investment for Phoenix

Holdings to purchase the resort, but he wasn't the company's lawyer and no one asked him to provide it with financial advice.

"What is Phoenix Holdings doing with the seven acres it owns? I mean, trucks coming and going at all hours of the day and night dropping off those large crates which are stacked three high in some places. And those tents they erected. Some of them are on the banks of the reservoir. That's part of the conservation easement and an environmentally sensitive area. We can't allow that to continue. As mayor I have a responsibility to the residents to make sure our resources are preserved."

"I agree, and so did the judge. That's the reason she granted the preliminary injunction. Phoenix Holdings is prohibited from doing anything with the land it owns pending the trial in April. And that's probably why it wants to purchase the resort, both as a way to settle the lawsuit and to be free to pursue whatever it's planning to do with the property. When I asked the lawyer what those plans are, she hedged a bit, which I found strange. She said her client was looking at possibly creating a nature preserve, or maybe an animal sanctuary, or even an equine therapy center for children. You know, using horses to help children with physical and developmental challenges. All of those would be permissible uses even within the conservation easement that buffers the reservoir. But I'm sure they'll sort those issues out on their own. Their offer to purchase the resort is obviously contingent on settling the lawsuit. We'd have to document all of this in a written settlement agreement."

Faith looked pensive. Tom assumed she was trying to play it cool and not appear too eager, and he admired her tactic.

"Faith, this is a very generous offer. I'm not counselling you to accept it or to reject it. As your lawyer, I'm just presenting you with the facts. But if you accept it, it will obviously change your life and your family's fortunes forever. Imagine having the ability to do anything you've ever wanted to do and never having to worry again about lift lines, snow base depths, the fickleness of winter, or what global warming might do to your business in ten or twenty years. You'd never have to look at a weather report again and wonder when it'll get cold enough to make snow or whether the natural stuff will fall from the sky. You and your family would be debt free. This is really a once in a lifetime opportunity."

Tom noticed Faith appear more attentive.

"It's sounds like you think I should accept the offer."

"No. My job is to ensure you make the best, most informed decision for you and your family. There are clear pros to accepting Phoenix Holdings' offer. There are also clear cons. We can walk through those if you like."

"No, that won't be necessary." Faith sat up straight and squared her shoulders.

"You're right, Tom. The offer from Phoenix Holdings is very generous and it requires serious consideration. Which is why I already know how I'd like to proceed."

Tom wasn't expecting an answer so quickly. He sat back and met Faith's stare as he waited for her to speak. In the almost five years he'd known her, he'd never seen her look as sure of herself as she did at that moment.

"Tom, I know exactly what I want to do and what's best for me and my family."

Tom anxiously awaited her response.

"Please tell Phoenix Holdings' lawyer there's not a snowball's chance in hell I'd ever sell Castle Ridge Ski Resort. Not now. Not ever."

11

The first flakes started falling as Tom walked to his office after leaving his meeting with Faith. Traffic coming into town was already at a near standstill as city dwellers and locals alike inched their way to the Castle in search of fun on the slopes. The sidewalk was getting slick and the view down Main Street began to resemble a snow globe as Tom approached the century-old white clapboard house that long ago was converted into an art gallery on the first floor and a second-floor office suite that now housed his law office. The gallery was still closed but the white truck belonging to the gallery owners was in the rear parking lot. Chet, who also worked at the resort as head of chairlift operations, was behind the wheel, ready to unload this week's shipment of masterpieces.

The last thing Tom wanted to do was go back to his office, and he considered playing hooky and heading home to build a snowman with Aneilia instead. It was one of her favorite pastimes whenever it snowed. She insisted on different attire for the snowman every time they made one. Last week it was a lawyer snowman, complete with a brief case on one side and a book on the other. When they'd finished piling and carving snow onto their intricate creation, Aneilia had smiled and proudly proclaimed the snowman's name as "Lawyer Tom." As they'd headed inside for hot chocolate, Tom heard her mumble something about wanting to build a

'Barbie' snowwoman next time. He wasn't sure he knew how to build one, but today just might be the day for Barbie's debut.

Before he could think of cutting his workday short, he wanted to call Anastasia with news that Faith had rejected her offer. He was considering what to say to her when he noticed Constable Ozzie's Tahoe parked behind the deputy's car that had been stationed in front of his office ever since his assault. Tom hoped a visit from Constable Ozzie meant a break in his case, or at least a solid lead, so he could stop looking over his shoulder wondering if he was still being surveilled.

Janet glanced up when Tom reached the second-floor landing. She saw him on the security monitors coming up the walkway, entering the house, and climbing the stairs. Janet was on guard for any suspicious intruders. It turned out, she was his best security guard.

"Constable Ozzie is in the conference room, along with the deputy who's been parked outside all morning. He wouldn't say why he wanted to see you, but he said he was willing to wait as long as it took for you to get back. He's been here about twenty minutes."

Tom shed his overcoat in the waiting room and made his way down the hallway to the conference room. A fire was roaring in the hearth and the room was comfortably warm, a welcome reprieve from the freezing cold outside. Constable Ozzie was sitting on the sofa and talking on his phone when Tom knocked and walked in, so he made his way to the deputy first. Tom shared how much Aneilia loved seeing the "police *mens*," and the officer thanked him for the cookies. Tom heard Constable Ozzie's conversation wrapping up so he turned to greet him.

"Constable Ozzie, nice to see you again."

Stuart Ozzie rose from the sofa and extended his hand. Ozzie had been the Castle Ridge Constable for the last dozen years or so. He was tall and lean with a shaved head that gleamed like a shiny pebble. He was elected Constable after spending twenty-three years rising through the ranks in the Castle Ridge Sheriff's Department. He had been the only Black deputy on the force when he started and was still only one of two black members of the department in a town that was as lily white as newly fallen snow. He was reelected after his first term with over seventy percent of the vote, and ran unopposed in the last two elections. Everyone in Castle Ridge either liked Ozzie or at least respected him enough because he was a no-nonsense guy who got the job done. He was a laidback guy who could drape his arm around someone to charm them just as quickly as he'd slap cuffs on them if they got out of line.

He grew up in Georgia and still had a Southern drawl even though he'd lived in northern New York state for the last forty years, since being honorably discharged from the military. Ozzie wasn't a big talker unless it suited him, and then he could chew your ear off. He knew everyone in town and, even better, never forgot a face. He even got to know the strangers, and that was a good thing because there were lots of strangers in the winter, when Castle Ridge's population ballooned from less than two thousand regulars to more than four times that number, including day trippers, seasonal workers, and renters, turning Castle Ridge into a snowy circus. But even with all the hustle and bustle of ski season, when Castle Ridge was bursting at the seams, Ozzie and his deputies maintained the peace and kept things working like clockwork. Although drunk driving and disorderly conduct arrests rose dramatically from December through March, proof of Ozzie's success as the chief law enforcement officer of Castle Ridge was that other crimes were almost nonexistent. In fact, Tom's assault was the first one by an unknown assailant that any of the locals could remember in a long time, and the only case in the Castle Ridge Sheriffs' blotter that remained unsolved. Tom hoped that statistic would change today.

"Sorry to darken your doorstep like this Counselor. Normally, I'd call ahead and ask Janet if you could spare a few minutes. But this visit is official police business, and I didn't have time to make an appointment."

"No worries at all. I hope you have some news about the investigation into my assault."

"Actually, I don't son. We've got nothing on that front. All of our leads have run as cold as the trails on the mountain. I'm in touch regularly with the state police and the FBI, but we're all coming up with goose eggs. On the bright side, the state police tell me they believe you're no longer under surveillance. There's been no suspicious activity anywhere in these parts since your attack and things have been pretty quiet. In fact, we're considering scaling back the watch details posted out front here and at your home. Maybe only schedule it for the overnight at the cabin. We haven't made any decisions yet, and I'll consult with the State Police Superintendent before we make any changes. Some of the townsfolk have been questioning the costs of round-the-clock protection, if you know what I mean. Heck, some are even posting on social media that there're other people we need to protect in Castle Ridge than just lawyers such as yourself. Not that I'm swayed by those whack jobs. But just as a matter of managing our resources and assessing risks, it might make sense for us to pull back a bit."

Tom was annoyed at hearing that some of the townspeople were complaining he and his family were receiving special treatment. He wondered if they'd feel differently if they were the ones who'd been left for dead from a vicious attack. But he also hated being fussed over. He'd be fine fading into the background and liked that the satellite trucks and news reporters had left town. Maybe removing the visible police presence in front of his office and home would get things back to normal quicker.

"Whatever makes sense to you in your professional opinion is fine with me."

"Alright, well, I'll let you know what we decide. In the meantime, you have your own personal protection within reach at all times, don't you?"

It took Tom a second to process what Ozzie was getting at.

"A gun, son? You do have guns, don't you, here and at home?"

"Yes, sorry." Tom hesitated, finally understanding the question. "I have a gun permit."

"Good. It'd be a good idea for you to keep your weapon close by when you're in the office and at home with your family. You know, as a first line of defense."

Tom nodded and smiled, but he couldn't muster the courage to tell Constable Ozzie that having a gun permit wasn't the same as owning a gun. He and Brooke had talked about it both before and after his attack, but Brooke was adamant she didn't want guns in the house. She loved living in the woods on a mountain in a rural town where hunting was a way of life and where gun ownership was as common as owning a car, but she drew the line at having a gun in *her* house. Even after Tom's assault, she thought the constant police presence outside their home made it unnecessary to have a gun inside the house.

"So then," Tom began, sitting up in his chair, "to what do I owe the pleasure of your visit today?"

"Like I said, this is an official police visit." Constable Ozzie pulled a small notebook from his shirt pocket. "At approximately four hundred hours this morning, two of my deputies saw a white, six-wheeled blank-panel box truck driving up Route 52 heading toward town. Two adult males were visible in the truck's cab. Before they got to town, the truck turned left onto a dirt road at which time the driver turned off the truck's headlights."

Tom listened intently and occasionally chimed in with an "uh-huh" and "okay."

"The truck proceeded slowly down the dirt road in the dark. My deputies got out of their patrol car and made their way down a foot path. That foot path leads into the woods and provides a view of the dirt road until it ends."

Tom nodded, paying close attention.

"You know where that dirt road leads to, right?"

"It leads down to Bensonville Reservoir," Tom blurted out as if he had guessed an answer on a gameshow.

"You bet it does," Constable Ozzie said, slapping his knee as if he was swatting a fly. "Well, anyway, the deputies staked out the truck for a while and eventually the two male occupants exited the cab and moved to the rear of the truck. They proceeded to unfold a mechanical loading gate used to lift and lower cargo from the truck."

"I'm familiar with those kinds of trucks."

"Right," Constable Ozzie continued, looking as though he was enjoying recounting his story. "These male occupants were wearing helmets with flashlights on the front, like miners wear. They unfolded the gate, climbed up, and opened the overhead tailgate. They entered the cargo area of the truck and a few minutes later they rolled out a large dolly on wheels onto the lift gate. On the dolly was a huge crate made out of metal and wood. The men lowered the crate to the ground and then rolled it down to the banks of the reservoir."

"As you know, I obtained an injunction on behalf of the town and Faith preventing the owners of that land from undertaking any work on the property," Tom interrupted. "Did you find what's in the crate?"

"Well, I'm fixing to get to that point, son. Just hold on."

Tom smiled and gave Constable Ozzie the floor.

"My deputies were curious why these men were wheeling the dolly to the edge of the reservoir in total darkness. Suspecting they might be up to no good, my deputies announced themselves before making their way over to them. But here's where it gets interesting. When the men saw and heard my deputies approaching, they ran. They uttered something in a language my deputies didn't understand and took off running deep into the woods. My deputies gave chase but couldn't keep up. These guys were fast. Canines have been out all morning, but so far, no luck. We've impounded the truck and state police are checking for fingerprints."

"And the crate?"

"Well, a forensics team is running tests on the contents as we speak. But I'm hoping you'll be able to shed some light on it for us.

Tom scrunched his face. "How would I know what's in a crate being transported in a truck I know nothing about?"

"That's a good question, son, except for one thing." Constable Ozzie shifted in his chair and pulled out a sheaf of papers from his side pants pocket. He flipped the papers while perusing them carefully.

"This is the manifest of the truck's cargo. We retrieved it after impounding the truck. Your business card is stapled to the top of the manifest."

"Okay," Tom said. "I've given out my business card to hundreds of people over the years. I'm not sure what that means."

"Well, you may be right. But perhaps you can tell me why your name is on the manifest as the person responsible for receiving the cargo?"

12

Tom wasn't sure Constable Ozzie believed he had no idea how his name wound up on the manifest. They went over the facts a dozen times, and came at it from different angles, but each time Tom insisted he knew nothing about the manifest. After thirty minutes exhausting various scenarios and playing out the "what ifs," they were no closer to solving the case of the mysterious cargo. They both agreed no crime had been committed and, at worst, the men who fled into the darkness might have violated the court's preliminary injunction, but that was a civil matter for now. Ozzie said he'd inform Tom of the results of the forensics tests when they came in and hinted he might have more questions for him in the days to come. Tom assured him he'd raise the issue of the truck and mysterious cargo with the property owner's attorney, as well as the Court. That seemed to satisfy Ozzie for the time being.

After accompanying him and his deputy to the second-floor landing, and promising to relay any additional information he learned, Tom went to his office and shut the door. He rubbed his temples and wondered how he was going to explain this one to Brooke. Building a Barbie snowwoman with Aneilia started to sound better and better. But before he could frolic in the snow with his daughter he needed to speak with Anastasia.

All he had was her cell number, and given the static on the line when she answered the call, he wondered where in the world she might be. Anastasia asked him to hold for a moment, and when she came back seconds later the connection was crystal clear.

"I'm delighted to hear from you, Tom. I've been anxiously awaiting your call. I hope you have good news."

"Well, I'm afraid I don't."

Tom toyed with the idea of leading with the information he'd just learned about his name being on a cargo manifest tied to a truck that likely violated the injunction, but he decided at the last minute to lead with Faith's rejection of the offer instead.

"Faith McReynolds has no interest in selling Castle Ridge Ski Resort. She was very firm in rejecting your offer."

All Tom heard in response was silence. He thought the call might have disconnected. Just when he was about to ask if Anastasia was still there, she spoke up.

"This is extremely disappointing. Did you explain to Ms. McReynolds the full contours of the offer?"

"I most certainly did. My client is smart enough to understand its significance. But in the end, she was adamant she would never sell."

"Perhaps my client needs to sweeten its offer."

"Your client can try, but I know Ms. McReynolds well, and I can tell you she won't be motivated by more money."

"You may not know her as well as you think."

The comment caught Tom off guard. Anastasia was clearly trying to goad him into saying something hostile, but he decided to bide his time. *It is often better to listen than to speak.*

"Everything is negotiable and everyone has a price, or at least a point at which they'll relent rather than stand on principle. I guess my client will need to determine where that point is for Ms. McReynolds."

"Listen Anastasia, you can posture all you want. The fact is my client is a sophisticated businesswoman, especially when it concerns *her* business. You made a settlement offer and it's been rejected. That leaves us where we were before you made your offer. The preliminary injunction is in place and we're preparing for trial in April. In the meantime, I trust your clients will continue to abide by the terms of the court order and refrain from any activity on the property."

Tom wondered if Anastasia would bring up what had happened overnight.

"My clients have invested much time and resources into their plan. They won't take kindly to walking away. They want the land. All of it."

Anastasia's words were sharp, and Tom heard the brusqueness in her voice. She wasn't backing down.

He decided he'd had enough and returned fire.

"The ploy your client engaged in last night will backfire. I'm preparing a motion as we speak informing the court about your client's intentional violation of the injunction and I will be seeking sanctions and other remedies."

Tom wasn't preparing any such thing. He had a date with Aneilia to build a snowwoman, and he wasn't about to let the violation of a court order derail those plans even if Faith was his most important client. When he was a cub lawyer, just starting out, he wouldn't have thought twice about cancelling dates or visits with friends and family to pull an all-nighter to grind out a motion, but this was the new Tom. Maybe if he had a staff of eager young associates the billing machine would be cranking, but his was strictly a one-man shop for now. He resolved when he opened his practice that his family would always come first. Nevertheless, he didn't mind letting Anastasia think he was still the pit-bull litigator he once was.

"Tom, I have no earthly idea what you're talking about. My client hasn't violated any court order. While we disagree with the injunction, we will litigate that at trial. My client isn't foolish enough to taunt the judge. That's child's play and neither I nor my client engage in such games."

Tom thought her denial sounded genuine. Was it possible she wasn't aware of what happened last night? God knows lawyers are caught off guard all the time by their clients doing stupid things. He didn't think he'd get far getting into a debate with her. She already said she didn't know what he was talking about, and pressing the issue didn't make sense. Nor would raising the cargo manifest with his name on it. He decided to keep his powder dry until he knew more and would spring it on her when the time was right.

"I guess I'll see you in court."

"Tom, your idle threats will not cause my client to back down. This is not about money for the people behind Phoenix Holdings. It's about an ideology, a vision, a movement. It's about shaping the future and a devotion to obtaining re...."

Anastasia abruptly stopped, as if someone cut her off mid-sentence. What was she talking about, Tom thought. What ideology? What movement? If investing half a billion dollars buying Castle Ridge Ski Resort wasn't about making money, then what the hell was the point? It sounded like she was spewing cult-like propaganda. He wondered if Anastasia's client was part of some social or environmental crusade, or maybe some religious order. Whatever it was, Tom didn't care enough to ask for an explanation. Faith rejected the offer and he had to prepare for trial. This conversation was turning into a waste of time, and it clearly wasn't going to settle the dispute between their clients.

"If Ms. McReynolds isn't willing to sell the resort and the land it sits on now, my client will insist I pursue a different strategy. That will be unfortunate for everyone involved. Of that I'm certain."

Tom had had just about enough of Anastasia's antics and threats. His clients were in the right, but he wasn't going to persuade Anastasia of that. He'd have to continue to wage a legal battle and win his case in court.

"Anastasia, this conversation is over. You'll have my motion in a few days, and you can respond accordingly."

"That would be a mistake, Tom," she said sternly. "I suggest you reflect on what I've said."

Before Tom could respond, the line went dead.

He leaned back in his chair. He hadn't realized how tense he'd gotten during the call. He took in a deep breath, let it out slowly, and tried to relax.

He had expended enough energy on Anastasia and Phoenix Holdings for one afternoon. He'd draft the motion next week. He needed to speak to Constable Ozzie one more time and nail down details of exactly what the deputies saw and heard. But this afternoon he had an important date with Aneilia, and he was all too eager to call it a day.

Night descended quickly halfway around the world. His Eminence and trusted lieutenant Waddah were quietly sipping tea in His Eminence's chamber reviewing production reports from the lab technicians. Seventy-five tons of Zincar, the viral agent needed to execute the Grand Plan, had been produced thus far and were ready for use. Half of what was needed. Batches containing the remaining tonnage were being prepared and would be available by early spring, well in advance of the shipment date. The eerie silence was broken by the ringing telephone. Normally, calls would be routed to any one of a half dozen security personnel staffing the communications bunker in the compound. But this call was coming in on His Eminence's private line used only by Anastasia for urgent communications requiring immediate attention. Waddah lifted the receiver, and after speaking to Anastasia, passed the receiver to His Eminence.

"The owner of the resort turned down our offer to acquire the land surrounding our property and to resolve the lawsuit which would allow us to continue our work without interruption—like the one that occurred last night. We will need to increase the pressure."

"You assured us the American lawyer would be an easy target and you'd be able to reason with him. It appears you were wrong on both counts."

Anastasia heard the displeasure in His Eminence's voice. She had looked into Thomas Berte's background when she learned he was the attorney for the resort and the town of Castle Ridge. That was shortly after he filed the lawsuit seeking to prevent Phoenix Holdings from building the necessary infrastructure on the banks of the reservoir to implement the Grand Plan. She quickly concluded Tom was neither highly sophisticated nor exceptionally talented, and that whatever accomplishments and successes he'd achieved in life were the result of his family's influence-peddling and graft. He was, after all, the illegitimate son of a criminal mastermind. And, although he was estranged from his father for much of his life, his father still controlled his destiny and created opportunities for him. But despite diplomas from Ivy league schools, employment at a fancy law firm, and a short stint with the Department of Justice, the fact was today Thomas Berte was a struggling small-town country lawyer, which only served to reinforce her belief he'd be motivated by money and wasn't shrewd or sophisticated enough to uncover her client's true intentions.

Even though Bradley Mitchelson tried telling her otherwise, she ignored it. She assumed the former Attorney General was deliberately trying to undermine Phoenix Holding's plans, and he was turning out to be a liability that needed to be dealt with. She quickly came to the realization that Thomas Berte was too.

"Perhaps, Your Eminence." She was in no position to try to defend herself. "Which is why it is imperative we increase the pressure on the lawyer."

"Proceed as you must. We cannot be deterred from accomplishing the path that has been ordained for us by our messiah, the Almighty. We must carry out the Grand Plan."

"I understand."

His Eminence inhaled from the hookah shisha, holding his breath momentarily before releasing a puff of smoke. He watched it slowly waft toward the ceiling.

13

The bluish-white glow from the computer screen provided the only light in the musty, damp windowless bunker. It was sparsely furnished, with a wooden desk and chair, and a small table in the corner. Across from the desk, on a shelf, sat a framed photograph resting on an easel. An unlit votive candle, a small gold cauldron, and a silver cup containing long matchsticks were haphazardly arranged next to the photograph.

The technician sitting at the desk worked feverishly, forcibly hammering at the keyboard in a rhythmic *clappity clap, tap, tap* sequence. Though his fingers seemed to move in a random pattern, his keystrokes were intentional and his eyes carefully tracked each line of code on the screen.

The undertaking was tedious and time consuming but necessary. Necessary after Faith McReynolds made the fateful decision to reject the generous offer made to her, and necessary after attorney Thomas Berte signaled his intention to continue his pursuit of the lawsuit against Phoenix Holdings. Throughout the compound there was high anticipation concerning the critical function the technician was performing, and a fervent hope it would eventually result in the successful execution of the Grand Plan.

Almost two hours into his assignment, he was nearing completion. His fingers were swollen and numb. A thin line of perspiration wedged itself within the wispy stalks of his scraggly beard. He was barely twenty and had never stepped foot outside the compound. He certainly had never been to America, but he was familiar with his target, having memorized hundreds of images and video clips. He had studied the diagrams and operational notes even though they were written in German, and understood the inner workings of the infrastructure and component parts better than the engineers who put them together. The internet is a powerful tool, allowing a young man who had never attended university to master the intricacies of machinery those far smarter than he spent years building and refining. In a matter of hours, and at an optimal time, the fruits of his labor would be revealed.

After pressing *enter* for the final time, the technician stood and wrapped his head and shoulders with the prayer shawl draped over the back of his chair. He slowly made his way to the shelf next to the door and stared at the framed photograph of His Eminence. The technician reached for a long matchstick and struck it against powdered glass on the side of the silver cup. He slowly brushed the flame against the incense crystals in the small gold cauldron next to the photograph, and then lit the votive candle, casting a hallowed glow over His Eminence's image. The technician knelt and bowed his head. Closing his eyes and inhaling deeply, he allowed the pungent incense to coat his nose and throat. He recited words known only to him, giving praise for the small role he was asked to play in accomplishing the Grand Plan.

When he finished his prayers, he walked over to the small table in the dark corner. He picked up his cell phone and pressed the text icon. He held the phone with both hands just inches from his face and began to type.

Anastasia, with the grace of powers bestowed upon me by His Eminence, and in His Name and in His Glory, I have complied with the instructions given to me. At precisely 10 am Eastern Standard Time tomorrow, Saturday, February 8, the next critical step in the realization of the Grand Plan will occur. Praise and Glory be to His Eminence, and may death and suffering rain down on the infidels and the enemy of our people.

14

Saturday, February 8
Castle Ridge Mountain

More snow fell overnight transforming Castle Ridge yet again into an alpine wonderland with trees draped in white and mountains bathed in the alpenglow of a frosted dawn. Corduroy grooves on the slopes were deeper and straighter and the few icy spots that had formed when temperatures rose slightly yesterday before refreezing with last night's storm were quickly coated with tightly packed white crystals. Weather forecasters had been calling for weekend snow for days, which always excites big city dwellers to trek to the mountains for some action on the slopes. Fortunately, the brunt of the storm's first wave came in late Friday night, ending by Saturday morning, and didn't deter those making the early drive from sticking with their plans. Heavy traffic on the two-lane road from the Thruway to Castle Ridge made for a sure bet today was going to be a red-banner day.

The sky in Castle Ridge always seemed bigger after a snowfall. The parting clouds revealed a deep blue dome as the sun rose over the east peak making the slopes appear crisper and steeper. If there was a downside to the forecast, it was the wind. It began howling early and gusts from the west were expected to top seventy miles an hour throughout the day before phase two of the storm cycled in by early evening. But that just motivated skiers and snowboarders to get an earlier start and ride the first chair.

As she did most weekend mornings at 7:00 a.m., Faith gathered her team leaders in the meeting room in the basement of the main lodge for a briefing. Advance ticket sales had sold out by Thursday, and window sales for the walk-up crowd would likely sell out by 10:00 a.m. Close to five thousand people would be carving tracks on the west and east peaks today, riding nineteen lifts and swooping down ninety-five trails, all of which were open and ready for the seventh sellout of the season so far. Ski patrol leader Terrie reported that her team was fully staffed for the weekend, with EMT's in place and two ambulances and the medevac helicopter at the ready if needed. Chet, leader of the lift operations team, reported that all chairlifts successfully passed their early morning inspections, and all systems were go for normal run rates and capacity turns with no limitations. One by one, each team leader reported all personnel were accounted for and helming their posts. It was the rare day when no issues cropped up at the morning briefing, but today was turning out to be one of those unicorn days where everything pointed to ideal skiing conditions and optimal operations.

When the meeting ended, Faith bypassed the elevator and climbed three flights of stairs to her office on the third floor of the main lodge with a wall of windows overlooking the east and west peaks forming a semicircular bowl around the sprawling base area spread out in front of her. Finishing her third cup of coffee, she sat back in her leather chair and smiled to no one in particular. She loved Castle Ridge Ski Resort and the people who made it shine, and days like today made all the blood, sweat and tears she had invested in her mountain worth it.

By 9:00 a.m. lift lines across the base were already at least ten skiers deep and growing. Faith settled into her office but wasn't staring at the growing crowds. Instead, with her back to the windows, she immersed herself in the spreadsheets plastered across three computer monitors on her desk, studying revenue numbers from daily and seasonal lift ticket sales, food and beverage service, hotel and condominium occupancies, ski and snowboard lessons, and equipment rentals. The columns of data seemed to extend forever, and with a push of her keyboard buttons, Faith sliced and diced the data to see in real time the fruits of her labor. When she was done analyzing the revenue side of the ledger, she moved to the expense side and studied every entry, while jotting down anomalies and making a note to reconcile and adjust them later in the afternoon. The exercise was enough to make anyone's head spin and eyesight blur, but Faith thrived on poring over financial details and crunching numbers.

So engrossed was Faith in analyzing the data displayed on the screens in front of her that she didn't notice the scene unfolding behind her at The Turret high-speed chairlift.

Six at a time, skiers and snowboarders shuffled through the RFID gates which scanned their passes as they made their way to a red line in the lift loading area before turning to await the approaching chair that would whisk them to the summit of Castle Ridge Mountain. Chet steadily directed the skiers and riders through the gates, trying to keep the lines moving briskly. Most everyone appreciated his efforts and good humor as he skillfully and deftly performed his job. Like a ballet-dancing orchestra conductor, he waved his arms with precision and slid and twirled on the snow guiding skiers and riders into tight formations of six patrons at a time, all while keeping a smile on his face and cracking jokes to distract them from the growing lift lines. He kept a close watch on both the crowd and the RFID gate, knowing that if the scanners failed to read just one pass, his carefully crafted line shuffle would descend into utter chaos and create a bottleneck of unhappy skiers and riders.

At precisely 10:00 a.m., just as a group of five kids whose parents had signed them up for a day-long ski lesson sat their bums on the chairlift along with their instructor, The Turret lift came to a grinding halt. Moans and groans were heard along the lines, with more than a few guests, mainly a group of snowboarders, heckling Chet to get the lift moving again. Most in the crowd suspected the wheelhouse attendant at the top of the mountain had stopped the lift because someone fell while getting off or perhaps needed extra assistance. But Chet knew better. Alarms and buzzers weren't blaring and the red light on top of the wheelhouse wasn't flashing. That meant the stoppage wasn't intentional—it was mechanical.

He made his way through the maze of skiers and riders, nudging them to the side, while skipping around the RFID gate. As he approached the attendant shed next to the loading area, he, along with everyone else in the base area, heard the unmistakable sounds of grinding gears and crunching metal. He instinctively ducked while looking up at the giant wheel holding up the lubricated steel cable and lift chairs. The wheel began to spin. His pulse quickened and his heart raced. For an instant he couldn't process what his eyes were seeing. He tried to scream but had no voice. The chairlift wheel was spinning—but in reverse. Instead of chairs ascending the mountain with its passengers facing uphill, the chairs were being sucked backwards as they raced down the mountain in reverse, gaining speed quickly which each successive spin of the wheel. Jolted by screams from terrified passengers, Chet finally swallowed a gulp of air and screamed to clear the loading area as the clatter of twisting metal grew louder.

He ran into the attendant shed where two pimple-faced operators were standing panic-stricken and as pale as the snow. They couldn't stop the lift. None of the controls worked. Chet shoved them out of the way, causing one of them to land hard on the ground. He lunged for the control panel, flipping switches and pushing every lever and button he could lay his hands on. Lights flashed on and off but the wheel kept spinning. The phone rang from the attendant at the summit, but Chet ignored it. He yelled to no one in particular that the lift was out of control. He pounded the panel, but the wheel kept spinning faster and faster in reverse. He stretched his left hand as far as he could to reach the emergency cut-off switch on the far side of the shed, but it proved useless. The power stayed on, and the lift kept spinning, automatically releasing the lap bar as chairs reached the loading area. Looking out the plexiglass window in front of him, Chet saw skiers and riders being whip-sawed against the wheelhouse stanchion and flung and tossed like rag dolls. Anguished cries filled the loading area as desperate parents reached for their children while mangled bodies lay everywhere.

Chet picked up the intercom phone and began screaming.

"Mayday, mayday, mayday. The Turret lift is malfunctioning. It's out of control. Help, help."

The transmission line was dead. The young operators ran out of the shed and were trying to help the injured, but masses of fallen bodies made their task impossible. Some of the skiers and riders in the lift line kicked off their skis and boards and rushed over to help those thrown from the chairs, but they just added to the mayhem and became moving targets for the lift chairs that collided into them with each successive spin of the wheel. A twisted nest of skies, poles, boards, gloves, blood and mutilated body fragments littered the ground under the constant shrill of shredding metal and cries of terror.

The sideways angle of the backward moving chairs became more pronounced as their speed increased. The chairs crashed wildly against the shed and then rebounded into the steel stanchion holding up the wheel as bodies continued to be whipped and thrown. One by one the chairs tumbled into each other crushing anyone who hadn't been flung into the air. As the chairs stacked up, the steel cable line holding the chairs slackened causing them to swing even more wildly. Blood curdling screams echoed as bodies slammed into one another and piled up. Realizing what was happening, a few passengers on the backwards-moving chairs jumped off before they reached the wheelhouse turn, hoping that falling on packed snow would hurt less than being hurtled through the air or being crushed by rushing jagged metal. That may have worked for passengers who jumped first, but those who jumped later landed hard on top of blood-soaked bodies, many impaled by skis and poles strewn about.

Helpless and in shock, Chet saw an even bigger disaster unfolding. An acrid smell began to permeate the loading area. Plumes of turbid, black smoke poured out of the wheelhouse as the friction of grinding and tearing metal caused the lift engine to combust. Agitated by ferocious, howling winds, searing flames shot out of the cowling engulfing everything—and everyone—in their path. Wails of torture and agony caused by burning flesh were soon suffocated by the silence of death.

Chet fell to his knees but managed to keep his head above the control panel. He stared helplessly at the catastrophe occurring just beyond his reach. Dazed and horrified, he forced his eyes shut and prayed for God's mercy to stop the butchery that was massacring innocent men, women and children.

15

The headline in the *Castle Ridge Sentinel* the next morning said it all: *Winter Paradise Turned into Hellish Inferno; Avalanche of Death and Destruction Strikes Castle Ridge Mountain.*

Tom was sitting on the couch next to Brooke, a crackling fire keeping the den toasty warm on a cold and snowy Sunday morning. His heart raced as he read article after article describing yesterday's tragedy causing him to relive the pandemonium he had witnessed in real time. He was standing in his kitchen Saturday morning having coffee with Brooke while Aneilia was attempting to play hide and seek with Bentley, who wasn't cooperating, when his volunteer fire department-issued pager beeped. Listening to the dispatcher's voice, Tom's face went ashen. He heard the dispatcher announce a confirmed structure fire at The Turret high-speed chairlift in the base area of Castle Ridge Ski Resort. Although the dispatcher tried to intone every word without emotion, Tom picked up on the shakiness in her voice. He heard her say there were untold number of victims burned and injured, with likely casualties, and requested mutual aid from surrounding towns.

He bolted for his pickup truck, flicked on the blue emergency lights, and sped to the firehouse.

He spent the better part of the day at the base of Castle Ridge Mountain, initially dousing the flames that had engulfed the wheelhouse and lift attendant's shed. Intense heat from the flames disintegrated the cable holding up the chairs and severed it, causing hundreds of chairs along the forty-six-hundred-foot-long lift line to tumble to the ground, some falling more than ninety feet into the thick snow-covered forest below. Hundreds of bodies were strewn up and down the mountain, from the loading area to the summit.

For hours after the fire was declared under control, as a massive snowstorm hit Castle Ridge, he assisted with triaging the injured. As night fell, he lent a hand with the grim task of carrying dozens of body bags containing the deceased to a long line of idling ambulances and refrigerated vans from coroners' offices dispatched from throughout the region and from as far away as New York City and Boston.

By the time he got home close to midnight, Brooke and Aneilia were already asleep. He tried to sleep, too, but every time he closed his eyes, he saw the images of charred bodies and mutilated remains. And the blood. It was everywhere, along with the stench of death. Reading news articles that following morning made the barbaric tragedy real again and brought it back to life.

According to news reports, as of early Sunday morning, the Constable's office confirmed 319 people had been taken to area hospitals to be treated for everything from severe sprains to multiple compound fractures to lacerations, hypothermia, seizures, burns, and even heart attacks. Over forty of the maimed were in critical condition, with many not expected to survive. The death toll stood at one hundred and nine, thirty-six of whom were children under the age of ten. Still, the articles went to great lengths to highlight that as gruesome as the day's events were, there was a thin silver lining of solicitude. With an estimated eight hundred people riding the lift at the time of the malfunction, it was miraculous there weren't more fatalities and more injuries. Hundreds walked away with nothing more than minor bumps, scrapes, and bruises.

Tom bowed his head when he finished reading the last article and closed his eyes. He said a prayer of gratitude for those who survived, and a prayer of mercy for those who hadn't.

Brooke curled her legs under her and wrapped her left arm around

Tom's chest and hugged him tightly. He lowered his face and kissed her head while inhaling the lavender scent of her hair. They lingered there for a long moment in quiet reflection before Tom gently pulled away, losing himself in Brooke's deep brown eyes. It was only the tender, sweet sound of her voice that lifted him out of his trance.

"How are you holding up after yesterday?"

"I'm okay, just tired. And emotionally drained. All those poor, innocent people were just slaughtered. I can't imagine what Faith is going through. We should go over and visit with her this afternoon."

"I was thinking the same thing. I called her last night before you got home to offer our support and love but got her voicemail. Her sister later told me Faith was out all night visiting hospitals checking on the injured."

"I saw her for a brief second yesterday in the lodge and she looked shell shocked."

"Any word on what caused the fire?"

"The assumption is the lift experienced some kind of a mechanical malfunction, but it might take weeks before a final cause is determined."

"Faith's sister texted me this morning to say that news vans and satellite trucks are parked up and down Main Street and have taken over the main parking lot of the resort. I can't believe this place is going to be the focus of round the clock news coverage again for the second time in a matter of weeks." Brooke's voice trailed off. "I know your attack was brutal and scary, and whoever did it is still out there, but this tragedy affected so many more people, and there are so many fatalities. How much can one small town take? This is going to be devastating."

"I know. The resort is shut down indefinitely and I heard last night that it may not reopen this season," Tom said wistfully.

After a few moments of sitting quietly, the only sound coming from the crackling fire, Brooke got up to check on Aneilia and to get her ready to spend the afternoon at a friend's house while they visited with Faith.

Tom realized he hadn't checked his messages. Given the events of the past twenty-four hours, the last thing on his mind was his work. But he took out his phone anyway and scrolled through his messages. There was an assortment of spam emails, ads, breaking news alerts about the Castle Ridge disaster, texts from friends checking in on him assuming he had responded to yesterday's emergency, and a few messages from clients and from Janet about matters on his calendar for Monday. He almost didn't hear the knock on the door. It was faint, and Tom thought the deputy sitting guard outside his cabin might need to use the bathroom. He got up and walked to the front door. Squinting through the peep hole, he didn't see anyone. He slowly opened the door. No one was standing under the covered portico. He glanced to his right and his left and didn't see anyone either. He craned his head toward the base of the driveway and saw the deputy's car parked there, smoke billowing from its tailpipe, but it was empty. The deputy must be on his hourly patrol around the property, he thought. As he was about to close the door, he looked down and saw something red poking out from under the doormat. He knelt down to get a closer look and noticed it was a red envelope. Pulling the envelope out from under the mat, Tom turned it over in his hands. It was small, about the size of a postcard, and sealed closed. He saw only his name typed on the front of it.

He walked back inside, shutting the door behind him. He held the envelope in his hands and examined it closely. He gently ran his finger through the top flap to break the seal. Inside was a white notecard. He slowly pulled it out of the envelope. His eyes grew wide as he read the words typed in the center of the notecard:

Your assault and yesterday's massacre are just the start.
Phoenix Holdings is behind it all.
Pursue the deal to uncover another horrific plot before the Fourth of July.
I am powerless to stop it, but you must.
Remain silent or Brooke and Aneilia will perish.
YOU ARE BEING WATCHED. TRUST NO ONE.

PART II

16

Darkness had long descended on the compound and the air was still as a nighttime chill settled in. Encompassing over six hundred hectares of desert, the compound was encircled by a steel-reinforced stone wall averaging three meters high which in spots climbed to ten meters. Sentry posts perched atop steel girders seven meters taller than the highest point of the wall were spaced precisely thirty meters apart along the perimeter providing unobstructed views of the surrounding cracked dried-sand plains, crumbling rocks, and wind-worn dunes.

The amber-orange glow cast from light towers mounted above the sentry posts illuminated the perimeter wall allowing guards to detect approaching threats or anyone lurking in the barren fields. The guards didn't rely solely on visual surveillance, however. Inside each sentry post were an array of sensors and monitors capturing birds-eye views from high resolution cameras and from dozens of high-altitude unmanned aerial vehicles hovering above outfitted with night vision technology.

The compound housed thirteen structures, each no more than a single story high, concealing a maze-like warren of rooms and bunkers embedded thirty meters deep into the bedrock. Blast resistant steel-reinforced and concrete-encased superstructures formed the outer shell of the underground fortification supported by high-strength tungsten metal beams designed to withstand aerial missile attacks. From its conception, the compound was intended to be an impenetrable fortress with layers of security to prevent what had happened in the past from ever happening again.

A large contingent of armed soldiers, communications specialists, skilled technicians, scientists, and staff lived and worked in the compound. Many were related by blood, others linked by shared beliefs and a common hatred for the infidels. Although they were survivors, they suffered daily, forced to endure life without their loved ones. The dead, at least, had ascended into glory amid ushering sounds of trumpets and hymns of praise. Peaceful eternity was theirs, and salvation cradled them in a protective balm, healing wounds and mending hearts. But the survivors grieved alone, marking time until they reunited with their loved ones in paradise within the kingdom of rapturous joy. But while they lived, it was contempt that nourished their souls, and a desire for revenge that sustained their common bond. Every supplicant passionately beseeched the Divine Almighty to shower His Eminence with power and courage to bring death to the infidels in the just battle they waged in his name.

Inside the communications bunker, deep below the compound, His Eminence sat expressionless before banks of high-resolution digital screens witnessing the mayhem as it unfolded at Castle Ridge Ski Resort. He watched as The Turret chairlift began its backward march toward devastation. The faces of innocent children being tossed and crushed yielded no emotion. The panic-filled screams of mutilation and death crisply heard via the live audio-feed, and the horror displayed on the screens, registered no remorse in him. As the chairlift's reverse speed increased, multiplying the carnage, His Eminence sat stone-faced, betraying neither satisfaction nor contempt. Finally, as the devastating fire ravaged the wheelhouse structure and everything around it, leaving a path of smoldering destruction in its wake, His Eminence closed his eyes, sighed heavily, and silently recited a prayer of humility and gratitude.

Rising slowly from his throne, His Eminence processed slowly to a photograph on the wall of those who once graced his life. His wife Halima was barely twenty-five when she was slaughtered by hell-fire missiles launched from the sea that obliterated the bedroom where she lay nursing their five-month-old daughter, Zara. His son, Hamza, four, who bore a striking resemblance to His Eminence, slept down the hall. The blast destroyed his room and pulverized his small body. His Eminence's elderly parents, asleep in a small adjacent bedroom, also perished in the midnight attack. His Eminence prayed daily that death had been immediate for Halima, Zara, Hamza and his parents before fires consumed their bodies. All told, nine members of his immediate family, including his younger brother, a niece, and two cousins were butchered. Hundreds of innocent souls who knew no evil were massacred by the barrage of missiles that rained down on their tiny village by the unrelenting assault carried out by the infidels on the orders of the President of the United States. The date was July 4.

By providence of the Almighty, His Eminence had escaped death. A day earlier he had been summoned to an assembly of elders in a neighboring village. When he departed, he hugged Zara and Hamza tightly and softly kissed their foreheads. He embraced Halima and imparted on her a blessing of love and peace. It was the last time he saw his family alive.

Staring at the photograph, His Eminence wiped away tears. He closed his eyes and could almost hear the laughter of his children.

When he returned days after the bombing, charred splinters of wood and stone were all that remained of his home. The stench of death and destruction lingered over his tiny village. He recalled surveying the horrific devastation around him and seeing the sun glint off of shards of munitions strewn across the landscape. He crawled toward a large piece of shrapnel several meters away and scooped the heavy fragment in his hands. It was blackened with soot and punctured with holes. He turned it over and brought it up to his eyes, staring intently at the faint outlines of a United States flag stamped on the edge of the shorn metal. As he cradled the remnants of the enemy's spear that destroyed his family, His Eminence fell to his knees. Grief pierced his soul as surely as the enemies' missiles pierced the souls of his family members. Raising the fragment of metal towards the heavens, His Eminence vowed revenge and retribution and chanted a hymn for the souls of the martyrs.

The phone rang in the underground bunker interrupting his solemn remembrance. It had been almost an hour since the rampage began at Castle Ridge Ski Resort, with scenes of devastation displayed across the screens. His Eminence raised the receiver and heard the voice of Waddah, his trusted lieutenant.

"Great suffering has been thrust upon the infidels. We are one step closer to achieving the Grand Plan."

The smile that had graced His Eminence's face when he heard Waddah's update soon faded. "Death to the infidels," he mumbled after a long pause. "And may eternal peace be granted unto the warriors of our divine cause."

17

Tom's heart raced. He read the notecard three times. Waves of nausea roiled through him and he felt a chill. He swallowed hard and tried to control his breathing. He felt helpless. He wondered if he was dreaming, but quickly realized the notecard was as real as the words typed on it.

Who sent it to him and why, he asked himself. He was just a small-time country lawyer who had gone through his own hell to finally get to a point of serenity, only for his new life to now be turned upside down again, first by a madman who savagely beat him on the mountain, and now by being thrust into the middle of a heinous attack that killed and injured hundreds. How the hell did he wind up in this insanity?

Your assault and yesterday's massacre are just the start. He had never considered the possibility that his attack was connected to the tragedy on the mountain. He was told his attack was a warning. If that was a warning, what the hell was yesterday?

Phoenix Holdings is behind it all. Why would a company run by a bunch of foreign billionaires want to harm him and kill and injure so many innocent lives at a ski resort in a tiny village in upstate New York? Who was really behind Phoenix Holdings and what did they want? And how much did Anastasia Maine know about it? Anastasia was a tough lawyer, but was she a murderer?

Pursue the deal to uncover another horrific plot. Yesterday was just a precursor to something worse. Something more horrific was coming. To uncover it, he had to pursue the deal. The deal Phoenix Holdings made to buy the resort. And the deal to settle the lawsuit. The lawsuit he filed.

He felt lightheaded and thought he was going to pass out. The case against Phoenix Holdings was a small stakes skirmish. Faith considered it important and told him she'd spare no expense to stop Phoenix Holdings from developing its land, but in the annals of landmark litigation, the case was more t-ball than major leagues. Why did that land matter so much to Phoenix Holdings that it would kill and injure hundreds of innocent people and beat him to within an inch of his life? And how did the cargo manifest with his name on it figure into all of this? None of it made sense. If the notecard was real, he had to salvage the deal to uncover the sinister plot to come. But how would pursuing the sale of the resort and settling the litigation with Phoenix Holdings accomplish that? He needed to get closer to Phoenix Holdings. For now, that had to be the strategy because he had nothing else.

The Fourth of July. The significance of that date was obvious, but what did it have to do with Castle Ridge? That was almost five months from now. It was both a lifetime away and practically tomorrow. Especially since he didn't know where to begin or what to look for. Ski season would be long over by then and Castle Ridge would be in summer mode. On July 4, hundreds would be swimming and kayaking in Bensonville Reservoir. Later in the day, families and children would line Main Street to watch fire trucks and marching bands go by. And at night, those families and children would gawk at a kaleidoscope of colors from fireworks bursting in the night-time sky. Tom shuddered at the thought of an attack happening during the Fourth of July parade or the fireworks celebration.

I am powerless to stop it, but you must. Whoever sent him the notecard was on the inside and knew what Phoenix was planning. But he or she couldn't prevent it. They didn't have the power to stop it, but they thought Tom did. It must be someone who knew Tom and knew he wouldn't run from the challenge. That he'd do whatever was necessary to find those responsible for his attack and the attack on the mountain, and to prevent the next one. All he needed to do was warn the authorities; he needed to sound the alarm.

But he couldn't.

Remain silent or Brooke and Aneilia will perish. He couldn't contact Constable Ozzie. Calling FBI Deputy Director Aronson wasn't an option either, even though the FBI was keeping tabs on him. *How fucking ironic* he thought. He used to be the second highest official in the Department of Justice in another life, and he had the FBI director's home number on speed dial, but now he was being threatened to remain silent and refrain from involving the authorities on pain of death to his family. He'd never put Brooke and Aneilia's lives in jeopardy. But what if remaining silent meant hundreds or perhaps thousands would die? How do you even begin to consider whether sparing the two most important people in your life is worth the lives of countless others? Tom felt weak. He dry-heaved and his head throbbed. He re-read the notecard. His eyes glistened at the thought of Brooke and Aneilia being harmed. He loved them beyond measure, and he had vowed to do everything in his power to protect them.

The notecard's last sentence shook him to his core. *YOU ARE BEING WATCHED. TRUST NO ONE.* Aronson warned him he had been under surveillance—and he still was. Tom looked around the den. If he was being watched, there was a better than even chance he was being heard too. He learned a long time ago that no one was secure anywhere. Long range receivers from miles away could likely hear a pin drop in his cabin. And in his office, his car, everywhere he went. He wasn't alone—anywhere. And neither were Brooke and Aneilia.

The enormity of the challenges and dangers facing him began to sink in and he felt overwhelmed. Nothing in his life prepared him for this moment. Not Harvard, not working at one of the largest and most prestigious law firms in the world, and not learning about his family's secrets. Not even taking down the world's most notorious and reclusive criminal mastermind had equipped him with the know-how to prevent a massacre. He was staring at a giant puzzle with a million pieces and no idea how to assemble it. He wanted to open the front door and run as far away from Castle Ridge as he could, and take Brooke and Aneilia with him, but he couldn't. He was mired in quicksand and paralyzed.

"Tom, I've been calling your name for a minute. How did you not hear me?"

Brooke stood in the transom between the kitchen and den. "Are you okay? You look pale."

"Sorry, honey. My mind was wandering. I must have zoned out." He slipped the notecard under the seat cushion. "I think I must be dehydrated from yesterday."

"Was there someone at the door? I thought I heard a knock."

Shit! He had to think quickly.

"Ah, yeah, it was the deputy. Some snowshoe hikers took a short cut across the edge of our property and he wanted to let us know."

"Oh, okay, whatever. I'm going to run Aneilia over to the Hendersons for her playdate with Maddy. I'll be back in a few minutes."

Anelia rushed over and hugged Tom and kissed him on his cheek. "I'm going to go play with Maddy. I love you, daddy."

"Have fun, sweetie. I love you, too."

Tom's eyes followed Brooke and Aneilia as they walked to the garage. Then he slumped back onto the sofa.

He pulled out the notecard and read it again.

He had no earthly idea who sent it to him.

But he knew he had to do something. And the clock was ticking.

18

Tom and Brooke arrived at Faith's house in the early afternoon. He was still shaken from the words on the notecard but tried hard not to show it. Before leaving the cabin, he checked the doorbell video camera link on his phone. He hoped to see who left the envelope under the doormat but came up empty. The battery was dead on the wireless camera, and he must have missed the alerts to recharge it. He also called Constable Ozzie to check whether his deputy had seen anyone, but that was a dead end too. Ozzie told him the deputy was walking along the perimeter of the property at about the time Tom said he heard the knock on the door.

He desperately wanted to tell Brooke about the notecard, but he couldn't risk doing it. *Remain Silent or Brooke and Aneilia will perish. Trust no one.* But Brooke was the only person in the world he could trust. With his life. With his secrets. With the things that scared him most. He needed to find a way to tell her what he knew, but he needed to be smart about it. He had to be one thousand percent certain no one was listening. *You are being watched.* It would need to be at a time and place of his choosing. Even though it would terrify her, he needed to tell her—for his own selfish reasons. She was the smartest person he knew, and he'd need her help to figure out who sent him the notecard and how to uncover the horrific plot to come.

But just then he had another thought. What if the notecard wasn't real? What if it was all a hoax intended to divert his attention away from his real attacker? What if the tragedy on the mountain was, in fact, caused by a malfunction and it wasn't sabotage? He realized he needed to slow down and gather his evidence, just like he did when he prepared for trial. Follow the evidence and he'd find the truth.

Tom pulled his truck onto a snowbank behind a line of cars extending down the road from the gated driveway entrance to Faith's house. Or her mansion. Tom helped her refinance her mortgage when he first opened his practice, so he knew a lot about the property. The main stone and timber living quarters were over eleven thousand square feet spread over three floors with patios, decks and balconies jutting out from every facade. He estimated that his small cabin could fit entirely within Faith's two-story great room with its walk-in size fireplace. Two other chalets on the property were for staff and overnight guests, and the separate purpose-built garage contained more trucks, cars and SUVs than were on the local car lot, in addition to snowmobiles, ATV's and assorted toys. All of it was nestled on five acres of prime, wooded slope-side terrain far enough from neighbors to ensure privacy, but close enough to a blue trail to provide easy access to the network of slopes connecting the east and west peaks of Castle Ridge Ski Resort. It was by far the largest house on Castle Ridge Mountain and the most expensive. At last count, Faith had invested in excess of thirty million dollars building the structures and outfitting them with the latest state-of-the-art gadgets and amenities.

As big as the house was, it felt crowded that Sunday afternoon with so many folks packed in it to support Faith. The old Irish wish that a home should always be too small to hold all your family and friends certainly came true for Faith McReynolds. Neighbors from the mountain and friends who lived in town were there to offer their support and commiserate with her. Her colleagues from the Castle Ridge Town Council were also there, as were staff members from town hall. And her employees showed up in droves. Since the resort was closed, they had nowhere else to be. Most of them had worked at the resort for years, with some dating back to when her father and grandfather ran the resort. The longest currently active employee began working at the resort more than sixty years ago when his job was to grease the first tow rope on the mountain in the middle of the night. Today, his main job was to sit in the break room and regale his coworkers with stories of how things used to be, before snowboarders, half pipes and terrain parks became all the rage, when skiers didn't wear helmets and stepped onto ten-foot-long wooden skis with leather straps to maneuver down steep, ungroomed, icy slopes.

Tom spotted Chet manning the bar in the great room and headed his way as Brooke quickly found Faith's sister and sat with her in the solarium.

"Has it been like this all day?" Tom asked Chet as he took a seat on a bar stool.

"Nonstop since about ten this morning. Can I get you a beer?"

"Make it a ginger ale instead."

Tom could have used something stronger to quell his shaky nerves, but he was never much of a drinker and decided it was best not to start now. Besides, he still felt queasy and hoped ginger ale would settle the backflips his stomach was doing.

"Thanks for your service yesterday at the base, Tom. You and all the other volunteer firefighters were amazing. It seemed like you guys knocked down the fire in seconds. I don't know how you all do it, dealing with some of the things you see on calls, like the horror we saw yesterday. It makes all of you heroes in my book. You guys saved a lot of lives and prevented an even greater tragedy from..."

Chet's voice trailed off and he looked away. Tom took a gulp of his ginger ale and gave his pal the space to collect himself.

"From what I heard you were also a hero yesterday, Chet. The report from the chief said you managed to stop a lot of people from getting closer to the wheelhouse and you moved them away from danger, likely saving dozens of people from getting burned or inhaling smoke. You did a great job, my friend."

Chet looked down and nodded in appreciation.

Tom said all he was going to say about what he saw yesterday and was ready to move on to another subject when Terrie gently tapped his shoulder. He sprung up from his seat to hug her.

"Good to see you, Terrie. Although I wish it were under different circumstances."

"Same here. You look good Tom, and I'm really glad to see you up and about and getting better."

Tom had seen Terrie only once since his assault and that was when she visited him in the hospital in Larange. He'd thanked her then repeatedly for saving his life, but Terrie downplayed what she did for him and appeared to be trying hard to convince him he wasn't in bad shape when she found him. He wanted to speak with her more in the hospital about the condition he was in when she found him, but she looked uncomfortable and said they'd have time to speak about it when he was released and got back home. Brooke was with Tom when Terrie visited, and she later told him her sense was Terrie didn't want to talk about what she saw. Tom was still curious, but it wasn't going to happen today. Besides, given the notecard, what he really wanted to know was what she remembered about his attacker. But he recalled what Brooke said and decided now wasn't the right time to play detective.

"Terrie, I know I've said it a number of times, but I'll never be able to thank you enough for what you did for me. I wouldn't be here today were it not for you."

"Oh, stop," Terrie said smiling. "I was simply doing what I was trained to do. It's my job." Tom knew she was being modest again and he respected her feelings. He recognized what she had done for him, and he was determined to show Terrie his gratitude in small ways and big every chance he could.

"Have you seen Faith?" Tom asked, redirecting the conversation.

"I did, but only for a few minutes when I first arrived. She spent the night making the rounds visiting hospitals and clinics checking on the injured and even went to the morgue. Poor thing, I don't think she's slept a wink. She's going on pure adrenaline. I can't imagine what she's going through."

Tom nodded. "I feel terrible for her."

Just as Tom was about to ask Chet for a refill of his ginger ale, a hushed silence fell over the expansive room even though it was teeming with people. Tom craned his neck toward the kitchen and saw Faith making a beeline right for him. Guests quickly stopped their conversations and stared at Faith who looked drained and haggard, her hair pulled back in a messy bun with strands wildly sprouting from it. She glared straight ahead ignoring everyone. After rounding the billiard table, she stepped right up to Tom and lowered her head to whisper in his ear.

"I need to speak with you. Now. In my study. I received a message. It's about yesterday."

19

Tom felt like he was in a fishbowl. Everyone stared at him as he followed Faith through the kitchen and living room, down a long winding hallway, until he finally reached Faith's wood-paneled study. Walking in past the tall, thick mahogany doors, he was struck by the view. The study rose above King Lair, a blue trail on the west side of the mountain. Through giant evergreen trees tinged with snow, he could see the east peak in the distance. He snapped back to attention when Faith shut the heavy doors behind. Turning away from the view, he noticed a youngish-looking woman with short hair, wearing a black leather jacket, sitting on a couch hunched over a laptop, intently studying the screen and intermittently poking at the keyboard.

"Tom, this is Darryl Stratford. She's head of security for the ski resort. I'm not sure if you two have ever met."

Tom remembered seeing her around the resort. From what he'd heard, Darryl was a former major in the Marine Corps who later spent several years working for the Department of Homeland Security before becoming Faith's head of security. He liked her already.

"Nice to meet you, I'm Tom Berte." Tom extended his hand as Darryl rose from the couch and stood ramrod tall as if she was going to salute him.

"I know, Sir. I'm well acquainted with you."

Tom assumed, based on the work Darryl did for Faith, that she knew he was Faith's attorney and represented her and the Castle Ridge Town Council in the lawsuit against Phoenix Holdings, among other matters he handled for Faith from time to time. He was about to pull his hand back when Darryl excitedly spoke up again.

"It's an honor to meet you, Sir. I learned about your work on behalf of our nation when I was with DHS. Thank you for your service, Sir."

Tom was taken aback. He wondered which part of his past *work* Darryl was referring to. No one had greeted him like that since he moved to Castle Ridge.

"Same to you Darryl. What section were you in at DHS?"

"Counterintelligence Division and Cyber Security Task Force, Sir. I spent four years there after spending twenty years with the United States Marine Corps. And I've been working here at Castle Ridge for the last six months, Sir."

Tom took a closer look at Darryl and did some quick math in his head. The youngish looking woman standing in front of him was maybe a few years older than he was, yet looked like she could be in college. Or at least grad school. Being a lawyer ages you, Tom thought.

"I have the highest regard for the men and women of our armed services and for our veterans. And I know firsthand the important work you and your colleagues at DHS performed for our nation."

Tom knew well the sophisticated work the Counterintelligence Division at DHS handled. It was responsible for thwarting some of the most devastating cyber-attacks carried out against American interests. Most of the time, intelligence officials at DHS posed as hackers and infiltrated the bad guys' operations before they could unleash their malware codes and disable entire networks. Other times, the officials actually did the hacking, something called Project PAWNED, a variant of the slang term 'pwned' which in the cyber world meant a successful cyberattack and data breach. PAWNED was an acronym for Predetermined Access Without Need for Entry Data. In other words, getting in and screwing around without permission. Project PAWNED allowed the Counterintelligence Division to take control of the bad guys' systems and obtain crucial evidence it then used to take down hackers' operations. He was in awe of the talent and technical proficiency of officials like Darryl, and he suspected she held the highest security clearance when she was at DHS. He had worked closely with the Counterintelligence Division and Cyber Security Task Force during his short time at the DOJ on some high-level, top-secret operations the public never knew about, but he never ran across Darryl and wondered if their time working for the government overlapped. He also wondered whether she was at DHS when the Department of Veteran's affairs servers were hacked. He made a mental note to ask her another time.

"Thank you, Sir. And same to you. Your reputation within the DHS is legendary. Your work while you were with the Department of Justice was still heralded long after you left the government, Sir. I'm sorry about what happened to you a few weeks ago. My team and I are working closely with Constable Ozzie and the New York State Police. We'll catch whoever assaulted you. I'm sure of it. If there is anything I can do for you, Sir, please don't hesitate to let me know."

"Thanks Darryl, that's very kind of you," Tom said, trying to act cool. After pausing for a second, he spoke up again.

"Actually, there is something you can do, starting now."

Tom noticed Darryl's face light up and she looked eager to jump into action.

Please stop referring to me as 'Sir' and call me Tom."

"Thank you S..., I mean Tom," Darryl said grinning broadly and nodding her head.

"I hate to break up this *kumbaya* moment, but we have a serious matter on our hands," Faith said, sounding all business as she sat down. "Tom, I asked Darryl to meet with us because I received an email this morning. It concerns yesterday's tragedy."

Tom wondered if the email contained the same message as was on the notecard. But based on his read of Faith and Darryl's demeanor, he guessed it didn't and that neither of them knew that he'd received it. Either way, he planned to do a lot of listening.

Remain silent or Brooke and Aneilia will perish.

"The attack yesterday wasn't an accident," Faith began, in a somber tone. "It wasn't a mechanical failure or a malfunction as news outlets and social media sites are reporting."

At first, even Tom had assumed a mechanical failure in the wheelhouse caused it to spin out of control, and the friction from the spinning cable resulted in the fire. But since receiving the notecard he knew better, and apparently so did Faith.

"We were sabotaged, Tom. It was a cyberattack. Castle Ridge Ski Resort was deliberately targeted by cyberterrorists who killed and injured all those innocent people."

Faith's voice cracked and her eyes filled with tears. She slowly sat back and dabbed her cheeks with a tissue. After a few seconds of silence, Darryl picked up the briefing.

"Faith received an email in her personal inbox at 10:15 eastern standard time this morning. The sender claims to be an entity calling itself Revolutionary Avengers. I attempted to trace the IP geolocation but so far I've come up empty. The resort's entire network is disabled. I contacted DHS and the FBI, and a team of cybersecurity technicians from the FBI's Albany field office are on their way."

Darryl spoke in short declarative sentences with the diction and precision of someone who'd spent years working for the government. It brought Tom back to a time when he worked with people like Darryl, people he respected and admired. Except Douglas Aronson. Tom wondered whether Aronson was aware of the cyberattack and if he'd make a cameo appearance in Castle Ridge again.

"Revolutionary Avengers has taken responsibility for the attack. It launched a sophisticated malware virus that penetrated our security infrastructure and infected the resort's entire computer network. Nothing like I've ever seen. This is full-scale ransomware cyberattack."

Tom was dumbfounded. He knew how ransomware attacks worked. In almost every case it involved a business proposition. Valuable information is hijacked and traded for money. Blood isn't shed and the only casualty is a financial one. No one gets injured, and certainly no one gets killed. But this one was different. This cyberattack broke all the rules. Why kill and injure so many innocent victims if the purpose was simply a payday? As he processed it all, Darryl continued her military-style briefing.

"Software programs that run all of the resort's operations, from the lifts to snowmaking, from reservations to accounting, and even programs that run inventory and equipment rentals, were targeted with malicious code enabling the hackers to gain control of our entire network. Credit card numbers, banking information, and personally identifiable data for every guest that has ever stayed with us or purchased anything at the resort is now in the hands of Revolutionary Avengers who promise to release the information in ninety-six hours unless..."

Faith suddenly spoke up in a trembling voice. "Unless I agree to pay a ransom to unlock the encryption code that's disabling our network. And if I don't, in addition to all of our records being destroyed, sensitive data of anyone who ever charged so much as a dollar at the resort will be exploited and made available on the dark web. This is unimaginable, Tom. This will destroy my business, and it will hurt tens of thousands of people."

Tom hesitated for a moment, then asked the obvious question.

"How much is the ransom?"

"One hundred and fifty million dollars," Darryl answered without hesitating. "Instructions for payment are included in the email. Bitcoin and other forms of crypto accepted."

Faith let out a muffled wail and buried her head in her hands.

"Anything else?" Tom blinked hard and leaned forward. He wanted to know if the email mentioned Phoenix Holdings. "Did the message say anything else?" he shouted before realizing how insensitive he sounded.

"What more do you want?" Faith screamed. "My business is destroyed. Hundreds of people are dead and hundreds more injured. And, if that wasn't enough, the financial information of tens of thousands of people if not more will soon be exposed. What more do you want the fucking email to say, Tom?" Faith shouted through sobs. If she was holding something in her hands besides tissues, Tom was certain she would have thrown it at him.

"I'm sorry, Faith," he mumbled. "I'm just trying to make sense of all of this. Cyberterrorism isn't normally accompanied by acts of violence like the one that occurred yesterday. This is all highly unusual." Tom caught Darryl nodding in agreement and appreciated her vote of confidence. What he really wanted to know, though, was whether the email contained any of the information included on the notecard left on his doorstep.

"There is one more thing," Darryl said.

Tom narrowed his eyes and braced himself.

"The last line of the email says *independence is coming*. We're trying to figure out what that means."

Tom slowly blew out a puff of air while clenching his teeth. He knew what it meant. He rubbed his temples to quell the headache that never went away after he first received the notecard.

"Faith, I have to ask. Do you have the funds to pay the ransom?"

Faith looked dismayed. "Are you crazy? Of course I don't have that kind of money. Who has a hundred fifty million dollars lying around?"

Tom had a feeling he knew who did.

20

The tragedy at the resort put the hamlet of Castle Ridge in the spotlight again. The only silver lining was the town's hotels were fully booked, not by weekend warriors who attacked the resort's slopes, but by cameramen, technicians, producers, and reporters who filled the airwaves with breathless wall-to-wall coverage of the carnage and destruction at the resort. Tom always thought the luckiest criminals were the ones who were arrested on days of big news events. He'd heard that over twenty thousand crimes were reported across America in the twelve hours after the 9/11 terrorist attacks in New York City and Pennsylvania. Not one suspect's name ever appeared in a headline.

So far, news reports were focused on the human tragedy and rising death toll, which had climbed to 121 by Sunday evening. Speculation swirled about possible labor unrest at the resort, and whether the chairlift malfunction was caused by a disgruntled employee. Little did the journalists know that most of Faith's employees had worked at the resort for years, if not longer, and were like family to her. Perhaps it was better for the news hounds to stumble over themselves with speculation of an inside job, rather than learn the truth. Tom wasn't sure the local community, or the world, was prepared to learn the resort was really sabotaged by cyberterrorists.

After deciding to call Anastasia the following day, Tom went to bed early that night in hopes of getting some rest, but he kept waking up every hour to look out every window in the cabin to make sure the deputy was still in his patrol car at the base of the driveway. Brooke offered to sleep in Aneilia's room, so Tom could have the bed to himself, but it didn't help. He tossed and turned, replaying in his head the words he memorized from the notecard while trying to piece together the events of the past month. He was at the center of a high-stakes chess match he wanted no part of. This isn't how things were supposed to play out for him and his family when he left his old life behind and started over in Castle Ridge. He silently cursed whatever gods were in control of his destiny, while at the same time hoping for a miracle that would allow him to protect his family and countless others innocently caught up in the madness enveloping his world.

He finally fell asleep around 4:00 a.m. but woke up in a cold sweat at six. He raced to Aneilia's room. His heart started beating again when he saw Brooke and Aneilia sound asleep, with Bentley peering up at him from the foot of the bed. Wide awake now, he jumped in the shower to get his day started. By the time Brooke joined him in the kitchen, Tom had already prepared breakfast and was on his second cup of coffee. He told Brooke a white lie about wanting to get into the office early to catch up on bills, but, in reality, he wanted to pour over his files concerning Phoenix Holdings before contacting Anastasia. If she and her client were involved in his assault and the attack on the mountain, he needed to learn everything he could about them.

Janet arrived at work at 8:30 a.m. and poked her head in his office.

"You're here early. I guess you couldn't sleep either."

"Hardly a wink," Tom said. "I saw you yesterday at Faith's house and was going to make my way over to you, but I was interrupted."

"I saw. Everyone there did too. You were still holed up with Faith when I left. Anything I can do to help on that front?"

Tom paused before answering, wondering how much to say. Janet had begun working for him part time shortly after he opened his office, and eventually spent more and more time there taking on more responsibility as Millard Jensen began winding down his practice. She had proven herself to be a hard worker, punctual, diligent, and with excellent judgment. She was approaching sixty, cared for her elderly mother who suffered from dementia, and also her husband who was on disability and struggled with emphysema. Her only child, a daughter, was married with a son and lived in the suburbs of Boston. Tom feared he might be asking too much of her if he got her involved in what he was dealing with and he considered keeping her in the dark. She didn't deserve to get caught up in this mess. But then again, if there was one thing he knew about Janet, it's that she never backed down from a fight and would never forgive him if he needed her help and didn't ask.

"Actually, there is. I'd like you to do some research on the Holister matter in Boston. We need to develop a strategy to win that case. Maybe you can visit your daughter and grandchild while you're there."

Janet tilted her head and scrunched her forehead. She was about to speak when Tom brought his index finger to his mouth and opened his eyes wide. He coughed and shook his head slightly, hoping he wouldn't have to do anything more to cue Janet to keep quiet and go along with him. He was worried the walls in his office had ears.

"Whatever you need, Boss, I'm here for you. Everyone in town is. Let's get to work. I haven't seen my daughter and grandson in a few weeks, and it would be nice to visit them."

21

At 11:00 a.m., Tom dialed Anastasia's cell number. On the third ring, she answered.

"Good morning, Tom. I'm glad you called. I've been watching news reports of what happened in Castle Ridge. It's just awful. I trust you and your family are safe and well."

"Yes, thank you, we're fine. Although I'm not sure the town or resort will ever recover."

"The images are just horrific. All those poor souls who perished and were injured. It's just so unfortunate, and a terrible reminder of the vagaries of life and how being at the wrong place at the wrong time can change one's destiny forever."

Tom didn't buy a word of Anastasia's pious act.

"It's a good reminder for all of us," Tom said. "Life is short and everything can change in an instant."

"News reports are pointing to a mechanical failure. Perhaps caused by a disgruntled employee. That would be awful if it's true."

Smooth, Tom thought. She gave no indication she knew anything more than what was publicly reported, and she didn't mention a word about the cyberattack.

"I don't have any information about that. I'm sure the authorities and investigators are looking into every possible cause for the malfunction. I understand that a final report may not be released for months. Perhaps as long as six months."

"Just terrible. My thoughts and prayers are with the injured and the families of the deceased."

Anastasia paused and Tom imagined her dabbing her moistened eyes full of crocodile tears.

"Where does that leave us, Tom? When we last spoke you were about to run to court with some foolish theory that my clients somehow violated the court-ordered injunction. I hope you've reconsidered since then."

Tom had almost forgotten about the empty threat he'd made. He hadn't even begun to put pen to paper and, frankly, didn't have any desire to draft the motion. He hadn't even spoken with Faith about it.

"Look, Anastasia, I think what happened yesterday will have repercussions for a long time. Years, if not decades. The adverse publicity suffered by the resort, and the countless lawsuits that will surely follow in the days and weeks to come, will change the landscape of Castle Ridge and the fortunes of those who live and work here. The economy of this entire area may suffer as a result. The potential devastation shouldn't be underestimated. I think everyone needs to reassess their priorities and decide what's really worth fighting for."

Tom worried he was pouring it on too thick, and overdoing the doom and gloom scenario, but it was part of something he came up with on the fly. He wanted to hear Anastasia's reaction to his dire predictions and see whether she and her clients were still willing to fight for their small seven-acre corner of Castle Ridge.

"You may be right, Tom. As resilient as the town of Castle Ridge is, and indeed the entire region and the state of New York have been over the past many years, through economic downturns and even a global pandemic, yesterday's event may be different. One wonders whether anyone will ever feel safe again climbing aboard a chairlift at the resort. It may take time for scenes of yesterday's tragedy, which have been viewed all over the world, to fade from peoples' memories and for the resort to regain its prominence."

Tom knew Anastasia was a worthy adversary. She sounded like she was choosing her words carefully.

"That's the million-dollar question," Tom said. "Will Castle Ridge ever return to where it was a few days ago and, even if it does, how long will that take? No one really knows, and only time will tell."

Tom cleared his throat and signaled he was ready to move past ruminations about the future.

"So, Anastasia, can we revisit settlement discussions in our case? In light of what's happened, I take it your client's offer to purchase the resort is off the table. Perhaps your client should simply reconsider its position and move on with its business elsewhere."

He didn't want to appear eager to pursue the deal, even though the notecard told him he had to in order to uncover the plot. It was a test to see how she'd react. Line cast. Bait immersed. Would Anastasia bite? Tom held his breath.

"To the contrary. My client is more determined than ever to acquire the resort and the land it sits on. Despite the horrific incident of this past weekend, it doesn't really change my client's plans at all."

He was on the right track. He bit his lower lip.

"If in fact the cause of the tragedy was a mechanical failure or an intentional act by disgruntled workers, current management will suffer the reputational harm inflicted by such circumstances," Anastasia continued. "The public may be loath to trust current ownership in the future. They may fear the root causes of this tragedy may reoccur. As you yourself said, Castle Ridge Ski Resort may never recover from this unfortunate incident."

"I hadn't considered that."

"Oh. Come on, Tom, really? New ownership coming in to acquire the resort may just be the balm needed to salvage the resort's future. A new management team. New policies and millions spent on refurbishing and modernizing equipment and infrastructure. A complete rebranding. My client can wipe the slate clean of past blemishes and provide a fresh start with a clean reputation and a bright future. They'd be able to reposition the resort and restore its luster."

Tom squirmed in his seat.

"A cynic might say your client is only too happy to capitalize on the timing of this weekend's tragedy. The bodies of the dead aren't even cold yet, and you're already considering how your client can profit from the destruction. It sounds all too coincidental."

Tom needed to tread carefully. He risked too much if he pushed too hard.

"Don't be silly, Tom. This is purely a rational business play. Your client owns an asset that is losing value by the day. My client believes it can restore the asset's value and turn around the resort's fortunes. Classic supply and demand paradigm. Your client rebuffed my client's offer once. I hope she doesn't make the same mistake twice."

Anastasia and Phoenix Holdings were still clearly interested in acquiring the resort and were using this weekend's tragedy as leverage to push the deal. To Tom, it seemed Anastasia had no idea he had received the notecard.

"I'll relay your continued interest in purchasing the resort to Faith McReynolds. I know she was adamant in the past she would never sell, but perhaps what happened this weekend has caused a change of heart."

"I hope it has. It would be in everyone's best interest."

"It appears our renewed efforts have succeeded in persuading those in control of the land we covet to relinquish it." Anastasia spoke haltingly to His Eminence.

"They would be wise to accept the generous offer we've made to them. We must be able to work in secrecy and with total control of the land surrounding the water source." His Eminence's voice was crisp and clear as if he was standing in the same room with her.

"I will do everything in my power to see that your wishes are fulfilled, Your Eminence," she responded. "I do find it puzzling, however, that he didn't mention the ransom."

"Why would he? He isn't likely to reveal more than is necessary. His client now has the financial incentive to pursue the sale of the land."

"Let us not lose sight of the Grand Plan."

Anastasia was surprised to hear Waddah's voice. She thought she was speaking to His Eminence privately.

"Acquiring the land will make execution of the Grand Plan easier, but we must not become distracted by the journey. It is the destination that matters." Waddah added. "Certainly, if the infidels continue to refuse to sell the resort, we will increase the pressure. Preparations are already underway should another intermediate step become necessary. But, in the meantime, let us continue to focus all our energies on achieving our goal."

22

Tom drove to the resort to meet with Faith again. Gray skies meant another winter storm was brewing. He could almost smell the coming snow. Acres of gravel and black-top parking lots sat empty. A little more than forty-eight hours had passed since the horrific devastation and fire at The Turret lift claimed the lives of so many innocent souls—the latest casualty occurring overnight after the victim succumbed to infections ravaging her body from third and fourth-degree burns sustained from the massive fireball that shot out of the wheelhouse when the motor that powdered the lift exploded. Almost two hundred more victims were still nursing wounds and recovering from their injuries. While many of the injured were expected to recover—in time—a handful would likely require amputations or long-term care, which meant a life-long reminder of the devastation that rocked the bucolic town of Castle Ridge two days earlier.

The employee parking lot was deserted. None of the hundreds of employees who relied on the resort to put food on their table would be back to work anytime soon. A smattering of satellite trucks and news vans remained clustered in a corner of the lot closest to the main lodge, their generators humming so reporters could transmit live video of investigators combing through the rubble of what was left of The Turret lift while others began the massive task of clearing chunks of charred and twisted metal.

The intense heat from the fire had melted snow and ice in a ring extending a hundred yards from the perimeter of the wheelhouse, turning the base area into a muddy, soot-covered pit. Several fire engine pumpers and at least one ladder truck were still in the base area, stuck in the mud in ruts they carved when they sped from the paved parking area to the lift.

An eerie silence surrounded Tom as he climbed out of his truck, a stark contrast to the blaring sirens and blood-curdling screams he'd heard after he arrived on scene and dismounted the fire engine two days earlier. The quiet now was unsettling. Even the investigators and construction crews near where the wheelhouse once stood worked in silence. But as he walked toward the deserted lodge, Tom thought the calm serenity was appropriate to honor the lives lost. As far as he was concerned, it was now hallowed ground that should be preserved in memory of all those who perished.

Faith was sitting at her desk in her office when Tom walked in. He had been cleared by Darryl who met him at the entrance to the lodge, which was still guarded by state troopers, and she accompanied him to Faith's office. The twin peaks of Castle Ridge Mountain, framed perfectly by the large windows in Faith's office, rose in the distance shrouded in a misty, rolling fog. Their empty, snow-covered trails poked downward like limbs on a headless body.

"Look at this stack of papers, Tom," Faith said when he walked in, dispensing with any greeting. "I've already been served with dozens of complaints from scum-sucking ambulance-chasing lawyers trying to capitalize on this weekend's tragedy. Class actions. Mass-tort actions. These damn lawyers have no shame. There ought to be a law that you need to wait at least until the first burial before you can run to court and file a lawsuit."

Tom heard the frustration in Faith's voice and saw it clearly in her face. He agreed with her but wasn't going to add his two cents to the need for tort reform legislation.

Darryl followed Tom into the office and took a seat in a chair across from Faith's desk.

"Any further word from the hackers?" Tom asked as he took a seat next to Darryl.

"Nothing," Darryl said. "We've had no further communications from anyone on behalf of Revolutionary Avengers. An FBI task force has been trying to track the email, but so far, they haven't uncovered its provenance. A team from DHS is making its way to Castle Ridge as we speak to assist with the investigation."

"It's good to know people in high places, isn't it?"

Darryl smiled. "The DHS Secretary was only too willing and eager to assist when I reached out to him."

"Well, they're the best in the business, and if anyone'll be able to trace the email back to the hackers, the FBI and DHS will," Tom said as he turned to Faith who was still hunched over her desk reading the complaints.

Tom considered calling Aronson, but, frankly, he was annoyed that Aronson hadn't reached out to him. On the other hand, given how he treated the Deputy Director when he saw him in the hospital a few weeks earlier, Aronson was probably smart to ignore him. Besides, there was no way Aronson could know how directly involved Tom was in this whole ordeal.

Your assault and yesterday's massacre are just the start.

But he realized he'd eventually need Aronson's help to prevent whatever Phoenix Holdings was planning for the Fourth of July—as long as Tom was able to uncover it first.

"Darryl, would you mind if I spoke with Faith alone? In private, please."

Tom could tell he caught Darryl by surprise with his request.

"Tom, Darryl is my head of security. She knows everything that's going on. Anything you need to say to me you can say in front of her. I trust Darryl implicitly."

"I understand that, Faith. And Darryl, I mean no disrespect, and I'm sure you're aware of everything that's going on, but I have my reasons which I'll explain in due time. But not today. Please. There are some things I need to discuss with my client in private."

Tom liked and was certain he could trust Darryl, but he wasn't willing to take any chances.

TRUST NO ONE.

"I'm sure you understand, don't you Darryl? Just give us a few minutes," Tom said.

Darryl quickly rose from her chair and nodded.

"Of course. Not a problem. Faith, I'll be downstairs with the FBI agents, and I'll let you know when the DHS personnel arrive."

Darryl had barely shut the door behind her, when Faith tore into Tom.

"What the hell was that about? Darryl is my most trusted employee. She knows everything that's going on. She knows more about what's happening than I do sometimes. That even goes for our lawsuit against Phoenix Holdings. If I want her included in our conversations, you're going to have to live with that. I'm the client after all, right? I call the shots."

"I understand, Faith. And, yes, you are the client. But I'm your lawyer and you're going to have to just trust me on this."

Tom looked around the massive office. The lodge was empty and they appeared to be alone, but he couldn't be sure.

YOU ARE BEING WATCHED.

"Let's go snowshoeing up the mountain. The fresh air and exercise will do us both some good."

More than forty-eight hours had passed since death and destruction were unleashed halfway around the world. He knew it had been planned, but he didn't know for sure when it would occur, or even if it would occur. Just like he didn't know the pure evil these people were capable of when he began working for them years earlier. Back then he was driven by a desire for renewed wealth and proximity to power. The kind of wealth he once possessed but which he squandered over time, and the kind of power he once wielded but which he was forced to relinquish.

He had been promised a fresh start. The opportunity to advise rich and powerful people embarking on a crusade to restore order and bring peace to a region torn apart by centuries of war and terror. Theirs would be a mission to bring freedom and dignity to millions who had known only strife and turmoil. Prosperity would flourish where poverty and famine once ruled.

But disillusionment came quickly. Jubilant chants of salvation soon turned into fervent cries for revenge. Pronouncements of amity gave way to pledges of violence and calls to destroy the enemy. He had been lured with tales of grandeur and rewarded handsomely with immense riches, but it was simply part of a scheme to lend an air of credibility and legitimacy to conceal their real motives. By the time he discovered the truth, he was in too deep. Death would be the least of his worries if he sought to escape the surly bonds that controlled him.

His only hope was for Tom Berte to prevent the unimaginable atrocity that would soon take place.

23

Faith and Tom made it halfway up Drawbridge Path before either of them spoke. It was a narrow blue trail that steadily rose from the base. Tucked beneath towering umbrella pines, it was deceptively easy to misjudge since it didn't appear steep, but with each step of their wide, elongated snowshoes, they rose more than two feet in elevation. With their first three hundred steps, they made it to a glade where most first-time snowshoers declare victory and soak in the views of the town of Castle Ridge and Bensonville Reservoir nestled below. Tom took in a huge, deep breath.

From the clearing, the steeple of First Central Church, the first Presbyterian church established in upstate New York in 1645, was plainly visible, standing sentinel over Castle Ridge. It was the tallest structure at ninety-five feet. The town's forefathers had long ago ordained that no other man-made edifice within Castle Ridge's borders could rise to more than half its height.

The town was still, unusually so even for a midday Monday. Only two cars snaked along Main Street. The parking lot of Peak's Perk Coffee Chalet sat empty as was the lot in front of Castle Ridge Public Day School. The school board held an emergency meeting Sunday night and decided to cancel classes on Monday as a sign of respect for those who were killed at the resort. Although none of the deceased were locals who lived in Castle Ridge, a number of the injured were kids who attended the school. It was a small gesture, but it felt like the right thing to do. A stupor had fallen over the tight-knit community, and dozens of anguished faces filled the pews at Sunday's church services.

Tom admired the view of Bensonville Reservoir in the distance, its cobalt blue waters now encased in brilliant, white snow-covered ice stretching out like a vast, pristine plain protected by a forest of thick, bare trees along the mountain slopes surrounding it. From that vantage point, it looked tranquil, a serene reminder of the raw, cold beauty of nature when it pauses for the winter sojourn, as if time itself had slowed. Never could Tom imagine the outsized role the reservoir would soon play in one of the most barbaric crimes the world would ever witness. The only hint of its intended purpose was the scarring of a small portion of its banks where Phoenix Holdings' evil warriors had clear-cut trees and set up an encampment of equipment under tarps and white tents as they eagerly awaited the coming spring thaw.

Faith barely appeared to be laboring from the climb when she stopped to look at Tom. He came to a stop in a glade a few feet behind her and was still catching his breath.

"What do we need to discuss up here that we couldn't discuss in my office?

"You need to reconsider the offer from Phoenix Holdings to buy the resort," Tom finally said in between huffs, as he wiped sweat from his forehead.

"Like hell I do. Selling the resort is the last thing on my mind, as is Phoenix Holdings or its plans for the property it owns. I have the families of 122 people who died on my mountain to think about, not to mention the hundreds more who are nursing injuries. And on top of that, there are the hundreds of people who depend on me for a job they no longer have. Oh, and let's not forget the little matter of all the sensitive information that's going to be made public in about two days thanks to the animals who hacked our network."

"That's my point, Faith. You need to come up with the hundred and fifty million dollars for the ransom. Phoenix is prepared to offer you five hundred million dollars for the resort. If we move quickly, I'm sure I can get them to put up a hundred and fifty million as a downpayment that you can use to pay the ransom and prevent the disclosure of financial and personal data of everyone who's ever visited the resort. Phoenix Holdings has a vested interest in preventing that information from getting out as much as you do if they're going to take over and run this place."

Tom figured that if Phoenix Holdings was behind the cyberattack as part of its plan to convince Faith to sell the resort, it would be eager to pay the downpayment to move one step closer to acquiring the land it coveted. And Faith would be able to use Phoenix's money to prevent the disclosure of her customers' personal financial information. It also meant Tom would be one step closer to making it look like he was pursuing the deal—in hopes of learning more about Phoenix Holdings' intentions. It was a win-win in his view, as long as he uncovered the plot before Phoenix Holdings insisted on actually exchanging money for title to the resort. But first he needed Faith's buy-in.

"How are you going to get Phoenix to part with a hundred and fifty million dollars so quickly? If you tell them about the cyberattack and the ransom, they'll run from the deal in a hot second. Come on, Tom, you're not making sense. None of this makes any sense."

If Faith only knew how many things didn't make sense.

"Look, I know this all sounds crazy. But you need to trust me on this one. I can't tell you everything I know. Or even what I don't know. Which is a lot. But I'm following my gut and I need you to take my advice. There's no other way out of this mess. The clock is ticking on the ransom and if the time expires, thousands upon thousands of people will be financially devastated. Many of them are your friends and people you've known for decades, and I know you want to protect them. I hate to say it, but the prospects of you running this resort as a successful enterprise ever again are slim to none. You have to be realistic. Even if you get past the ransom issue, which you can't, the chances of reopening the resort and regaining the reputation it had before this weekend are almost nonexistent. Businesses don't come back from these types of devastating tragedies. It's like

Pan Am after the Lockerbie crash, or TWA after the bombing in 1995. The brand is tarnished—likely forever. The only real option you have is to sell the resort. New owners can wipe the slate clean, re-brand it and start over. If you care about this town and the people who live and work here, you have to sell the resort. It's the only way you can help this place."

Tom didn't believe a word he was saying, but he needed to convince Faith to accept Phoenix Holdings' offer.

Pursue the deal to uncover another horrific plot before the Fourth of July.

"If Castle Hill is forever tarnished as you say it is, then that'll be true for the new owners as well. That's what doesn't make sense, Tom. Why would Phoenix be willing to plow that kind of money into this place if it's destined to be forever known as the epicenter of death and..."

Faith cut herself off. Tom noticed a look of surprise stretch across her face, as if she had just discovered something. She set her jaw and glared at him.

"Phoenix Holdings is behind the cyberattack." She punctuated her words sharply as if slicing the air between them. "They're the one who hacked into our systems and caused the malfunction and murdered all those innocent lives." Faith's eyes opened wide. "They did it so they could force me to sell my mountain to them, didn't they? Didn't they, Tom?" Faith was bristling with anger and seething. She had gone from zero to sixty in a nano second and was staring wildly into Tom's eyes. "They did this! Phoenix did this! And you want me to sell my mountain to them! This is bullshit." Faith continued shouting. Her face was flushed with anger as she stomped the ground with her snowshoes. "You're not denying it. Are you complicit in their plan? Are you part of the goddamned ploy to take my resort and give it to those fucking mass murders?"

"Stop right there, Faith. Listen to yourself, damn it," the intensity in his voice matching hers. He knew she'd figure out Phoenix was behind the cyberattack. She was too smart to ignore the facts. But he didn't expect her to accuse him of being complicit in it. That came out of nowhere.

"Faith, you need to lower your voice and listen to me." Although they were alone, he was certain their voices would carry in the still air. He wanted to speak with her outdoors, on the mountain, because he was worried her office was bugged. Now he worried their voices would echo throughout the valley and would be heard even without listening devices.

"Look, I don't know for sure what's happening, or why," he said through clenched teeth, "but I'm one hundred percent on your side. Don't accuse me of working against you ever again."

Tom stopped himself, giving his words a chance to sink in.

Then he continued in a hushed, softer tone. "I'm on your side, Faith. You need to trust me on this. There are things that are happening that I can't tell you about."

Remain silent or Brooke and Aneilia will perish.

"Not yet anyway. You hired me to be your lawyer to represent you against Phoenix Holdings and that's exactly what I plan to do. I'm going to do everything I possibly can to find out what Phoenix is up to. And part of my plan is to make it *look* like we're going to sell the resort to them. I need you to go along with it and let everyone think you're selling. But I won't let that happen. I promise. I just need you to believe me and follow my advice."

Faith lowered her head. Her shoulders slumped and her face, which had been a ruddy cauldron, was now drained of color.

"This is all I've ever known my whole life," she said quietly. "This land has been in my family for generations." Her trembling voice caught as tears welled up in her eyes. "I was given this land as an opportunity and a test to see if I could handle it. My grandfather Earl was certain I could. I think he wanted me to run this business even more than I did. I never thought I had earned the right to carry on his legacy."

Tom pinched his eyes shut. His chest tightened and a knot formed in his throat. Her words hit close to home for him.

"And now I've failed, Tom. I failed the test. The business he left me is in ruins and so many lives have been destroyed because of me." Tears streamed down her face. She sobbed and her chest heaved as she tried to catch her breath.

Tom straightened his back and slowly made his way over to her and gently clasped her hands.

"I promise you, Faith, on the souls of Brooke and Aneilia, I'll help you get through this," he said softly. "I'll find out why Phoenix Holdings did this, and you'll get to keep your mountain. I give you my word."

As the two made their way down Drawbridge Path back to the base area, Tom wondered if he'd be able to keep the promise he just made. He wasn't sure how he'd do it, or how he was going to keep Brooke and Aneilia safe in the process, but he was determined not to fail.

24

The conclave of elders concluded their meeting, and after bidding farewell to His Eminence, filed out one by one. The table was still strewn with maps and drawings the men had analyzed for the umpteenth time. On the wall opposite where His Eminence sat during the meeting was a poster-sized photograph of Bensonville Reservoir which took up nearly the entire upper half of the wall. Charts indicating the reservoir's depths from shore to center point were taped off to the right, as were graphs measuring historical water temperatures and flow rates. The presentation was crude and rudimentary, with highlighting and intersecting black marker lines, but the data was precise, calculated by a team of engineers and scientists who had been specifically recruited and trained for three years to assist with execution of the Grand Plan.

No detail had been overlooked and each data point was measured and calibrated. Mock tests had been carried out in a laboratory in the compound for a year before the experiment migrated to lakes and streams. Six months earlier, the tests were moved to locations within a one-hundred-mile radius of Bensonville Reservoir to mimic similar real-world conditions. And then, three months ago, the first tests took place within Bensonville Reservoir itself. The plot of land Phoenix Holdings had acquired, which provided easy access to the reservoir itself, was finally put to its intended use.

Canisters with semi-permeable membranes filled with harmless dye and distilled water had been lowered into the water countless times. The dye was scientifically engineered to mimic Zincar, the real viral agent sourced from a laboratory in Switzerland. Tiny sensors measured the rate at which the dye seeped out of the canisters upon detonation as well as the rate of dilution. Once the dye was dispersed, additional sensors measured speed, rate, distance and direction, with the data transmitted to a bank of computers deep within the compound's subterranean control and command center. From there, the data was analyzed and studied and adjustments made to the volume, titration, and concentration levels. The protocol was now greenlit for final execution.

Hanging on a wall to the right of the photograph of Bensonville Reservoir was a color map eight feet high by five feet wide. In contrast to the crude charts and graphs detailing conditions in the reservoir, this color map was digitally reproduced with exact markings enhanced by satellite images. The banner across the top announced the map depicted the New York City Water Supply System. It contained a detailed lineation of the numbered water tunnels and trunk mains carrying drinking water from Bensonville Reservoir into the homes of 8.5 million residents of New York City. In the center of the map were a series of concentric circles forming a bullseye. The bullseye was centered over the island of Manhattan.

Repeated studies confirmed the elapsed time from immersion of capsules in Bensonville Reservoir to the catastrophic results was just under seventy-two hours.

Above the map stood a countdown clock. It was set to hit zero hours at 9:00 a.m. on July 4.

The legal proceedings commenced by attorney Thomas Berte to enjoin Phoenix Holdings' use of its land in Castle Ridge threatened to derail the Grand Plan. A warning was sent, followed by an opportunity to course correct. Both he and his client failed to do so and a second warning was delivered, this one more intense and its destruction more widespread. Now, His Eminence had directed that the American attorney and his client be given one final opportunity to alter their conduct.

The elders rejoiced in their sacrifices. The Almighty had answered their intercessions on behalf of the suffering masses. His Eminence, who had led his followers to design and implement the Grand Plan they had worked on for so long, was hailed for his vision, courage and strength. Nothing would stand in their way.

Not even Thomas Berte.

25

"Anastasia, this is Tom. I've spent a lot of time meeting with Faith McReynolds and she's reconsidered your client's offer to settle the litigation and purchase Castle Ridge Ski Resort. In light of what's happened over the last several days, she has decided to sell the resort. But there's one catch, and you'll need to move quickly if your clients are as serious as you say they are. Faith wants a good faith deposit of one hundred and fifty million dollars within forty-eight hours, with the balance due at closing."

There was a long pause. Anastasia finally spoke up. "Agreed."

Tom turned his desk chair so he could stare out onto Main Street. He was waiting for Faith to arrive at his office and bring with her the paperwork needed to prepare the contract and related documents for the sale of the resort. Faith insisted Darryl accompany her to the meeting. Tom also wanted Faith to be present when he received the wire from Phoenix Holdings for the downpayment, which could occur at any moment. His bank was going to call Janet on her cell phone to confirm the transfer. She was on her way back from Boston and promised to let him know the minute the money hit the account. The large old-fashioned clock with Roman numerals hanging on the wall in Tom's office was about to strike 4:30 p.m. Thirty minutes until the deadline he'd given Anastasia.

Every few minutes Tom rose and paced around his office, not because Faith and Darryl were late, but because it gave him something to do to keep busy while waiting to learn if Phoenix Holdings would actually transfer the money.

Winds howled from the west, and the sun, which had shone brightly earlier, was slowly receding behind dark clouds gathering over Castle Ridge. A polar vortex was expected to descend over northern New York state from the arctic with temperatures dropping to the low single digits and well below zero at the summit of Castle Ridge Mountain. As Tom looked out his office windows again, he noticed the town looking deserted except for a local or two headed to the hardware store and the market, likely to stock up on provisions before the next storm barreled through. Three restaurants and two inns had already shut their doors for the season after their business all but dried up after the tragedy at the resort. A couple of ski rental shops followed suit and hung banners announcing storewide clearance sales. While tourists and locals would normally descend like vultures on these sales to gobble up practically brand-new equipment at deep discounts, today the sidewalks were empty and cash registers sat idle. If folks had forgotten how dependent ski towns like Castle Ridge were on resorts nestled within them to attract visitors and fuel their economy, they were about to get a rude reality check. The cruel irony was that this winter's weather had been perfect, the best in years, both for snowmaking and for the real stuff falling from the skies. Global warming had taken a siesta and upstate New York was the epicenter for abundant snow measured in meters, not inches. The resort was on track to break all-time attendance records until the unimaginable happened, resulting in the mountain shutting down and threatening the economic health of the entire region.

Faith and Darryl arrived a little after four-thirty and Tom showed them to his office where they took seats across from his desk.

"The FBI is adamant that we not pay the ransom," Darryl began. "Their theory is that it will only embolden the hackers, and there's no guarantee they'll give us the decryption keys to unlock our files. They might take the money and release the data anyway."

Tom knew full well the FBI's strategy for responding to cyberattacks. Do nothing. Let the hackers churn through the electronic data. Let them release it and sell it to the highest bidders because everything they do leaves a marker of electronic breadcrumbs that, in theory, makes it easier to track their activities. It also provides more opportunities for the hackers to screw up and for the feds to find the weak link, swoop in, and catch them red handed. Not a bad strategy, and Tom agreed with it most times. But not this time. He suspected Phoenix Holdings and Revolutionary Avengers were one-and-the-same, and given how quickly Anastasia had agreed to pay the hundred and fifty million dollars and wire the funds within forty-eight hours, it just cemented what he knew to be true.

"It's the same FBI playbook. I'm sure you saw it a million times when you were at DHS," Tom said.

"I sure did. And I hated it. I used to tell those spineless paper pushes to go back to Quantico and let my team find the hackers in the holes they crawled into, but they never listened."

Tom let Darryl's words bounce around his mind for a bit before he filed them away in his memory bank.

As they waited, Tom continued to formulate his strategy for uncovering what Phoenix Holdings was up to. The hacking, and the death and destruction that resulted from it, was part of Phoenix Holdings' plan to get what it wanted, and it was the secret weapon used to convince Faith to part ways with the thing she valued most and vowed never to sell. Agreeing to pay the hundred and fifty million dollars was an easy decision for Phoenix. As soon as the funds would hit Tom's attorney escrow account, he'd wire the money to the hackers and it would ultimately end up back under Phoenix's control, only in an untraceable offshore account. It's as if the money vanished into thin air, resulting in the cleanest money laundering operation ever. It also dropped Phoenix Holdings' cost to purchase the resort from five hundred million down to three hundred and fifty million, since it would get back the downpayment in the form of the ransom payment, giving it a nifty discount without having to negotiate. The only financial loss would be suffered by Faith, who'd net one hundred and fifty million less from the sale. But the goal of Tom's plan was for there never to be a sale. Tom was determined to find a way to keep his promise. To do that,

Tom had to figure out why Castle Ridge Ski Resort was a prize worth killing for.

"I just hate that we're giving into the hacker's demand without exhausting every tool in our toolbox to find what they're up to first. Those fuckers don't deserve to get a god damn penny," Darryl said. She was bubbling with anger. "I also think selling the resort is a mistake," she added. "I know you two are in agreement, but I don't understand why you would do that. We can come back from this tragedy and turn things around."

Darryl was in attack mode. The former marine and DHS official was right of course, and Tom admired her grit and determination. But he wasn't ready to share what he knew with her. Not yet anyway.

Tom shot Faith a look and saw her bloodshot eyes watering.

"Darryl, it was my decision to sell," Faith said. "Tom counselled me as my attorney and we discussed our options. I ultimately decided to make the deal to sell the resort and pay the ransom, case closed."

Faith sounded fiercer than Tom expected. He was seeing her fortitude, the one that made her the successful business owner she was. She had bought into Tom's scheme and hadn't shared details of what they were planning with Darryl. She was putting her blind trust, and her future, in his hands. Now all he had to do was deliver on his promise.

Pursue the deal to uncover another horrific plot before the 4th of July.

Darryl's shoulders slumped and she slowly made her way back to her chair.

"The Deputy Director of the FBI, Douglas Aronson, is on his way to Castle Ridge," Darryl said without looking at Tom or Faith. "He'd like to speak with both of you. He should be here by six. Can you at least hold off paying the ransom until you speak with him? The deadline isn't until tomorrow at 10:00 a.m. You still have almost eighteen hours. Faith, as head of your security team, I strongly urge you to meet with Deputy Director Aronson before making a decision you won't be able to undo."

Tom's pulse quickened hearing Aronson was returning to Castle Ridge, but he wasn't entirely surprised. The massacre on the mountain made headlines all over the world and the FBI would be involved even if it wasn't tied to a ransomware cyberattack. But since it was, it significantly raised the incident's profile and grabbed the attention of the FBI's second in command, and likely the Director himself. And since it also occurred in the same place where the FBI's former prize possession lives, it was a no brainer Aronson would be involved.

Faith turned toward Tom. He knew she'd look to him for guidance whether to meet with the FBI.

"Faith as CEO of Castle Ridge Ski Resort, you should meet with the Deputy Director. Hear what he has to say. But I need to work on the contract for the sale of the resort. My time is better spent here." Tom spoke the last part very slowly, careful to clearly enunciate every word, in case anyone was listening.

That seemed to satisfy Darryl for the moment. Tom knew she meant well and had Faith's best interest at heart. But she was playing chess with only half the pieces on the board. He might need her help one day, but only after he figured out where the rest of the chess pieces were.

Tom was looking at Faith and Darryl with a steely resolve when he heard the sound of a car pulling into the parking lot. He walked to the window and saw Janet returning from the errand in Boston he had sent her on concerning the Holister matter. He stood there while she made her way into the foyer and up the stairs to his office. She knocked before slowly opening the door and walking in.

"Tom, I just received confirmation that the funds hit your trust account. The bank manager called me five times in the last few minutes to confirm the accuracy of the wire. He said he'd never seen such a large transfer of money. Should I prepare the outgoing wire based on the instructions you gave me?"

"Yes, Janet. Faith is going to meet with the FBI this evening, but I expect the meeting will not change anything. We'll send the wire out first thing tomorrow morning."

Tom made sure that his words were clearly audible. He and Janet had worked out a plan before she left for Boston. When they were in the office and wanted to discuss the sale of Castle Ridge and didn't care if anyone was listening, they'd speak loudly and clearly. Anything else that wasn't for public consumption would be mouthed, conveyed with hand signals, or written on notes that would be quickly flushed down the toilet. Janet said she looked forward to playing charades.

"Janet, also please bring me the file for the sale of Castle Ridge Ski Resort. I want to finalize the contract tonight."

"Yes, right away."

Janet remained standing staring at Tom. After a few seconds he noticed she hadn't moved. He looked up and remembered there was something else he wanted her to report on.

"When you get a moment," she said, "we should discuss the Holister case from Boston. I found some information you might find interesting."

26

At six o'clock sharp, Tom pulled into the muddy, pockmarked driveway in front of Janet's house, a modest two-story clapboard bungalow on the outskirts of Castle Ridge. Ever since Tom received the notecard, he was convinced his home and office, and his telephones and computers, were bugged. He wasn't going to take any chances by having sensitive discussions he didn't want anyone else to know about in those places. He was in stealth mode

YOU ARE BEING WATCHED

He resorted to in-person meetings as far away from prying eyes and itchy ears as he could get. He sorely missed the SCIF he used when he worked at the DOJ—a sensitive compartmented information facility—that contained encrypted phones and computers, used to review top-secret information and communicate with members of his team who had security clearances. Now, he'd have to improvise and do it old school.

That's why after Faith and Darryl left his office, he inquired about Janet's husband, Hank, and fished hard for an invite to visit with him. Janet caught on and invited her boss to a home-cooked dinner. Judging by the pies, brownies, and leftovers Janet occasionally brought to the office, he knew she was a pretty good cook, but he wasn't interested in dinner, even though he hadn't eaten much the last three days. Nor was he interested in visiting with Hank, a swell guy who'd been a harbor pilot in the port of Albany until ten years ago, when his two-pack-a-day smoking habit caught up with him and destroyed his lungs, leaving him in need of an oxygen tank to nurse his centrilobular emphysema. Dinner and visiting with Hank would have to wait for another day. This meeting was strictly business. He was there to learn about the Holister case.

"So, was Claire helpful?"

"Was she ever," Janet said. "She's clearly still very fond of you. She gushed how you were the smartest student in your law class-and the handsomest."

"She's in her eighties now, so it sounds like her memory may be failing," Tom said, grinning.

Claire Holister was the head librarian at Harvard Law School and a long-time friend to Tom and Brooke. When Tom had arrived at the law school, he was still surprised he was accepted and felt like he didn't belong, even though he had graduated first in his class from Harvard undergrad.

Claire sensed Tom's uneasiness and befriended him during orientation, even before his 1-L year started, and made sure his Introduction to Legal Process seminar went smoothly. Before coming to Harvard, Claire and her husband, Phillip, lived on Long Island, close to where Tom grew up, and that connection led her to take Tom under her wing. She never had children of her own and thought of all the law students as her family. Tom was so appreciative of Claire's kindness that he invited her and Phillip to dinner with him and Brooke. Even though they were considerably younger than Claire and Phillip, a close friendship blossomed that had lasted almost eighteen years. The four of them celebrated anniversaries, birthdays and holidays together, and Claire and Phillip were the first to congratulate Tom and Brooke when they announced they were moving to New York after Tom's clerkship in Boston. And when Tom received the offer to work at the DOJ, Claire and Phillip flew to New York for a celebratory dinner. They also wasted no time flying to Washington, D.C. to comfort Brooke and Tom when his life was turned upside down with the revelations of his family's secrets.

Now, Tom needed another assist from his trusted friend.

Janet laid out a number of large accordion folders on her dining room table.

"Claire was only too happy to help with research on Phoenix Holdings. She said the winter term was off to a slow start and she appreciated the distraction."

"Good to know." Tom was anxious to see what Claire had uncovered.

"Folder one contains general business information about the company. Certificates of Formation, organizational charts, copies of by-laws, charters, resolutions, and things like that. There's also a list of subsidiaries and affiliated companies. No surprise, Phoenix Holdings is a huge multi-national corporation and has its hand in almost every industry, including construction, real estate, shipping, and manufacturing. Nothing terribly exciting and all pretty routine stuff."

Tom glanced at the documents but wasn't impressed. He had done his own homework on Phoenix Holdings when Faith first retained him and was familiar with its organizational structure.

"There's mention of former Attorney General Mitchelson having acted as an outside advisor to the company some years ago."

With all that had happened in the last few days, Tom almost forgot about Mitchelson's connection to Phoenix Holdings. He was angry at himself for his lapse and made a mental note to call Mitchelson again as soon as he could. He hoped Mitchelson wouldn't know anything about what Phoenix Holdings was up to in Castle Ridge. He wasn't sure how much Mitchelson would share, but he had an inkling he'd learn more about the company after he spoke with him.

"Here's something I found interesting," Janet continued. "Your pal Anastasia Maine isn't just Phoenix Holdings' lawyer, she owns ten percent of the company."

Tom raised an eyebrow. Perhaps it explained why Anastasia seemed so personally offended that Tom had filed a lawsuit against Phoenix. But whatever Anastasia's relationship was with her client, it wasn't interesting enough to derail Tom's attention from wanting to find out what was in the rest of the folders.

"Folder number two contains a list of organizations, charities and entities Phoenix Holdings has supported over the last ten years or so. Many are well-known household names, the kind of groups you'd expect a company like Phoenix to support. But others are more obscure. Some are international non-governmental actors whose purpose and mission are hard to decipher. Others are private organizations associated with supporting religious, political, and social causes around the globe. A real mixed bag."

Tom fidgeted in his chair and was getting antsy. He wasn't hearing or seeing anything that brought him closer to understanding why Phoenix Holdings was fixated on Castle Ridge Ski Resort, his assault, the massacre on the mountain, or what the hell was going to happen on July Fourth. He was starting to think that sending Janet to meet with Claire was a waste of time. The Holister case was turning out to be a bust.

Janet must have sensed Tom's disappointment.

"Not seeing anything of interest yet?"

"You read my mind. I hope the remaining three folders hold something more exciting."

"I can't wait to show you."

Tom sat back in his chair, hoping to be surprised.

"I don't know how she did it, but Claire was able to search parts of the internet I never knew existed. She found a cluster of small organizations that are affiliated with and financially supported by Phoenix Holdings. And they all have something in common: hatred for America, and rantings and posts calling for death to America and the infidels who call it home. And we're not talking about just one or two postings. Hundreds and hundreds. How-to videos on making bombs to destroy American cities. Videos praising the 9/11 attackers. Recruiting videos for terrorist organizations whose sole purpose is to destroy our country. Manifestos declaring war on the United States and urging death and destruction. Much of it is chilling and scary to watch. The common thread connecting many of the postings is talk of retribution against the United States for the bombing of the village of Al-Kharabi about a decade ago. You can see how someone can get quickly radicalized against the United States by watching and listening to all that crap."

Tom shifted closer to the edge of his chair.

Janet stuck her hand into folder number three and pulled out a set of papers held together with a binder clip. "Leaders of these organizations have direct ties to Phoenix Holdings and its subsidiaries by virtue of being board members, officers, and managers. For example, the CFO of Phoenix Holdings, a gentleman named Waddah, appears to spend his nights and weekends on the dark web spewing venom against Americans and describing conspiracy theories of how America is responsible for famines and pandemics, including the coronavirus, as a way to eradicate Muslims and other ethnic and religious minority groups so it can gain world dominance. Just insane rantings and nonsense."

Tom paid close attention. If Phoenix Holdings was a financier of terrorist organizations whose aim was to destroy the United States and kill innocent Americans, it could be the motivation for the massacre on the mountain. Was Phoenix Holdings intent on carrying out a terrorist attack? But even if it did, it didn't answer the question of why it wanted to purchase the resort for half a billion dollars? And why go to the trouble of carrying out a ransom cyberattack? Surely it could undertake a terrorist attack and wreak havoc without the huge financial investment and time needed to pull off the hacking? Something still didn't add up.

"But wait, there's more, as they say on TV," Janet said. Tom knew she was trying to lighten the mood, but he wasn't interested in jokes. And if she knew about the notecard, she wouldn't be either.

"Last year, a subsidiary of Phoenix Holdings acquired a controlling interest in a chemical manufacturer located in a small village outside of Bern, Switzerland. A company called Societe Robolex. It's a small company, and it apparently goes to great lengths to conceal its true purpose. In the 1990's it was sanctioned by the UN and the international Court of Justice for selling war grade chemicals disguised as purified distilled water. The chemical was eventually used in the war in Bosnia and Herzegovina. And in the 2000's, it manufactured sarin and other nerve agents that were used in Syria to poison thousands. Throughout its existence, Societe Robolex has been on the wrong side of history and aligned with autocratic regimes intent on mass poisonings and destruction."

Tom reached for the Societe Robolex documents and spread them on the table. He studied each document intently while Janet continued with her briefing.

"Claire was really thorough. Phoenix Holdings' tentacles reach far and wide, and it's clearly funding several organizations with an anti-American bent," Janet said when she was finished.

"But none of this tells us why Phoenix Holdings is interested in acquiring Castle Ridge Ski Resort."

"Can't you scuttle the deal? We can't have a company with ties to terrorists in this town. If Faith knew about this, she'd never sell her business. You need to tell her."

Tom considered Janet's words. He needed to find the missing link. He needed to understand why Phoenix Holdings was so intent on acquiring the ski resort and the land it sits on. And he needed to uncover whatever Phoenix Holdings was planning for the Fourth of July.

Tom rubbed his eyes and exhaled slowly. He hadn't slept much in the last couple of days and was tired. His mind was in a fog and he wasn't able to focus. He needed to go home and get some rest.

"Janet, keep these documents here. Remember, let's not discuss any of this when we're in the office. In the meantime, I'll speak to Faith about what we've learned."

Tom was about to get up when he realized there was a fifth folder on the table that Janet hadn't mentioned.

"What's in that fifth folder?"

"Oh, just some maps about the property Phoenix Holdings owns in Castle Ridge and clippings from social media posts that Claire found during her research. They look to be marketing materials for some of Phoenix's subsidiaries. I don't think any of it is particularly useful."

Tom reached for the folder anyway. It was the slimmest of the bunch and only seemed to contain a few sheets of paper. He pulled them out. The first was a color brochure of Bensonville Reservoir, with a heading announcing that it was the largest man-made reservoir in New York state. Tucked under the brochure was a diagram of several aqueducts leading from the reservoir to New York City. The legend indicated that Bensonville Reservoir was the single largest source of drinking water for residents in the city. Next was a photo of fireworks bursting at night against a backdrop of the New York City skyline in the far distance. The photo was post-dated July 4 of the current year, some five months from now. Tom read the caption.

Independence Day is Coming! New York City Is Pleased to Announce the Completion of the Rebuilding of a Vital Aquifer and Water Tunnel by a Subsidiary of the Phoenix Holdings Group.

27

After leaving Janet's house, Tom headed home to have dinner with Brooke and Anelia just as snow started to fall again. It was taco night, one of Aneilia's favorite foods. He tried to be cheery, but all he could think about was that Phoenix Holdings was funding terrorist organizations whose sole purpose was the destruction of the United States. And it wanted to gain a foothold in Castle Ridge. Heck it was already there, owning seven acres of wetlands and looking to acquire more. Did Bradley Mitchelson know what it was up to? Tom was worried. Especially after seeing the brochure of Bensonville Reservoir and the diagram of the New York City aquifer system, and the photo about Independence Day in New York City. It was all hitting too close to home and it was chilling.

Faith called around eight to fill him in on her meeting with Deputy Director Aronson, who, she said, was disappointed Tom didn't attend. They agreed to meet the next morning at her office at 9:00 a.m. at which time Tom would authorize payment of the ransom from his escrow account to Revolutionary Avengers. Just in time to meet the hacker's deadline.

The drive from Tom's cabin to the base lodge at the resort took longer than usual because the roads were still slick from last night's storm. Tom went the long way so he could pass through town. The streets were deserted. Even the hardware store and market were desolate this time. Without the resort, the town would die a slow death. By the looks of things that morning, Castle Ridge was already on death's door.

Three vehicles occupied the "reserved" spaces in front of the lodge. Tom pulled his pickup truck in between Faith's Yukon and Darryl's smaller SUV, but he didn't recognize the third vehicle, a nondescript gray Chevy Impala. It didn't have studded tires, so Tom guessed it didn't belong to a local.

A state trooper opened the door to let Tom in. He took the stairs up to Faith's third-floor office. Walking down the hallway, he stopped at a large window overlooking the base area with the twin peaks of Castle Ridge Mountain in the distance. The remnants of the blackened chairlift, encircled in yellow caution tape, looked out of place amid the blanket of freshly fallen snow. Winter was Tom's favorite season, but with the resort shuttered and desolate, he hoped spring would arrive soon.

Faith was sitting at her desk when Tom knocked on the door. Darryl was in her usual spot on the couch hunched over her laptop. And sitting across from her was FBI Deputy Director Douglas Aronson.

"Come in, Tom." Faith waved him in.

Darryl stood tall and immediately extended her hand.

Aronson remained seated and nodded in Tom's direction.

"Full house I see," Tom said as he took a seat across from Faith's desk.

"Deputy Director Aronson asked to meet with us this morning. He wants to try to convince us not to pay the ransom," Faith explained.

"Good to see you again, Tom. I'm glad to hear you're doing well," Aronson said.

Tom frowned and didn't offer to shake Aronson's hand.

"I see some things haven't changed, so I'll get down to business. You know the government's policy is to refrain from paying ransom to hackers. It just encourages them to keep doing what they're doing," Aronson said with a by-the-book manner.

Tom smirked. "I recall at least one instance where our government didn't follow the playbook and paid out a huge ransom. You may want to check your files. You must have forgotten that one."

It happened when Tom was at the DOJ. Hackers accessed the computer system of the Department of Veterans affairs. They threatened to expose personal information of everyone who ever served in the military and wore a United States uniform. Politicians ran scared and the President of the United States authorized a ransom payment of five hundred million dollars to the hackers. He wasn't consulted on the strategy back then, but the Attorney General was in the thick of it. As was the FBI. The hackers were eventually caught, and Tom later learned they were part of the syndicate controlled by his father.

Tom tried to clear his mind. This wasn't the time for a stroll down memory lane.

"Those circumstances were different," Aronson said, sounding frustrated. "There were specific reasons the government did what it did back then. This is a whole different ballgame."

"Why? Because what's at stake now isn't the well-being of politicians, but a family's business built over decades? And the livelihood of thousands who live in this town and depend on that business to put food on their table and a roof over their heads?" Tom's voice grew louder. "Paying the ransom is the right thing to do. We need to protect the information of the tens of thousands of people who've patronized this resort over the years. We have the funds in place and we're going to transfer the money."

Tom glanced at Faith who nodded.

Darryl looked like she was about to speak up when Tom cut her off. "If the FBI isn't able to trace the funds back to the hackers, that's on you. The government needs to get better at its job. But it's not a good enough reason for Faith to give up on trying to protect innocent people who've been loyal to her and her business over the years."

Tom wanted to say more but couldn't. If Aronson knew what he knew, he'd agree with Tom's plan. Pay the ransom, buy some time, and *pursue the deal*—for now. The lives of countless people could depend on his strategy succeeding.

At 9:45 a.m. sharp Tom called the bank manager at First Hudson National, which held his attorney escrow account. By 9:47 a.m., one hundred and fifty million dollars was wired to a numbered account at a bank in Guernsey, a spec of land in the English Channel near the coast of France. Tom was certain it wouldn't remain there for long and would soon be transferred out to parts unknown and ultimately wind up back in the coffers of Phoenix Holdings. Aronson frowned and shook his head.

At precisely 10:00 a.m., just as promised, an encryption code was emailed to Faith's personal email address. Darryl punched in the code as Tom and Faith looked over her shoulder. An hourglass filled the screen as the sands of time virtually drained into the lower chamber. After a few seconds, the hourglass flashed green. With a few more clicks of the mouse and keyboard, Darryl was able to access Castle Ridge Ski Resort's entire computer network. Bank files, ticket sales data, rental records, control of the snow-making equipment, customers' credit card information, databases of the resort's historical operations, tax files, it was all there. The resort's computer system was up and running again—even if the resort itself wasn't.

For the first time since the tragedy days earlier, Tom saw Faith smile. She had regained control of her business and protected the confidential personal information of thousands upon thousands of people who had made her success possible. Her eyes glistened as she high-fived Darryl and hugged Tom. He wondered if she was thinking the same thing he did: given all that had happened in the last week, would Castle Ridge Ski Resort ever return to its former glory and luster?

Waddah paused at the entrance to His Eminence's chamber before entering. There he saw His Eminence reading from the Book of Glory while inhaling gently through the mouthpiece of the hookah shisha.

"Your Eminence, the fund transfer is complete. The infidels have been granted access to their records, but the purpose of their endeavor has been dismantled. Our effort to convince them to part ways with the land has succeeded. Anastasia is working to finalize the transaction. She believes we will take ownership of the property within a very short time period and the lawsuit commenced by the American lawyer will be dismissed. That will give us sufficient time to transport the remaining viral agent to the reservoir for release on July 1 without anyone interfering with our endeavors. We will control all of the land required to carry out the Grand Plan."

His Eminence placed the hookah hose on the table beside his chair and closed the Book of Glory, taking pains to secure the satin ribbon to save his place.

"And work on the aquifer?"

"It is nearing completion, Your Eminence. Repairs to the viaducts have been made and Water Tunnel Two is expected to commence operations on May 1. Water from the Bensonville Reservoir will be diverted to the tunnel beginning in the middle of May. By the end of May, Water Tunnel One will be shut for repairs, meaning that Water Tunnel Two, which will carry water from Bensonville Reservoir, will be the only source of water for New York City. Zincar will be released on July 1, and by July 4 it will be flowing into every home in New York City."

His Eminence smiled as he closed his eyes. More than a decade of careful planning and the investment of billions of dollars had brought him to the precipice of finalizing the Grand Plan and avenging the death of his wife and children, not to mention the souls of all the martyrs who perished in the village of Al-Kharabi in the attack by the infidels.

Waddah was the first to devise the Grand Plan. During his years of engineering study in the United States he became fascinated with the water supply and distribution system of New York City. After graduation, he worked in the City's Department of Environmental Protection for many years, eventually becoming Chief Engineer of the Bureau of Water Supply which manages, operates, and protects the City's water supply system. It was his job to ensure the delivery of high-quality safe drinking water to more than eight and a half million residents. While in that job he developed an encyclopedic knowledge of the system of reservoirs, aqueducts, water tunnels, and distribution pipes that supplied fresh drinking water. Despite it being one of the largest water systems in the world, its ingenuity was based on the simplest of concepts: gravity. Over 95% of the drinking water used in New York City is supplied by gravity fed by water flowing downhill from man-made reservoirs in mountainous regions to the north of the metropolitan area, including the Bensonville Reservoir in the town of Castle Ridge. Waddah was amazed when he learned the reservoirs were unguarded and open to the public for recreational use, including boating, swimming and fishing. More importantly, in a raw display of hubris by the infidels, and in effort to conserve funds, the water supply of New York City is largely exempt from mandated filtration requirements. Less than ten percent of the water is filtered, and the water flowing from Bensonville Reservoir is excluded from the filtration system. Although chlorine is added to the entire water supply, and ultraviolet disinfection is used to control certain microorganisms resistant to chlorine treatment, the viral agent created by Waddah and his team of scientists was resistant to both. One of the largest water systems in the world, supplying drinking water to one of the largest urban centers in the United States, was thus largely unguarded, providing an ideal opportunity to exert maximum retribution against a great many people in the United States.

"Through the power of the Almighty, and the brilliance of our colleagues, we will soon reclaim the glory our long-suffering people deserve," His Eminence proclaimed, bowing his head. "Contact Anastasia immediately and direct her to proceed to finalize the transaction without delay."

28

Deputy Director Aronson promised to stick around town for a few days while FBI field agents continued to investigate Revolutionary Avengers in hopes of tracing the ransom payment back to the hackers. Tom wasn't holding his breath, but he didn't mind having Aronson close by this time, just in case things got out of hand again.

It was close to noon when the meeting in Faith's office wrapped up. Faith, Darryl and her team were busy poring over electronic files on the resort's electronic storage system to make sure all of their data and records were intact. Tom wasn't adding much to the effort, so he said his goodbyes and slipped out without anyone asking him to stick around. It was just as well because the Holister files Janet brought back from Boston gave him several leads he wanted to follow up on. With his afternoon calendar clear, Tom decided to get to work.

First on his agenda was a visit to Constable Stuart Ozzie.

"I'd like to see Constable Ozzie. My name is Tom Berte."

Tom was pretty certain the young deputy manning the lobby desk in Castle Ridge Constable's headquarters knew who he was, but he identified himself anyway. She asked him to take a seat. A few seconds later Sheila, Constable Ozzie's assistant, came out to greet Tom and escort him to the back of the stationhouse. But first Tom had to go through the metal detector. He emptied his pockets into a small plastic tray, passed it through the x-ray machine, and walked through the upright detector. After clearing security and walking down a hall and making a left, he arrived in Constable Ozzie's office.

"Good morning, Constable. Thanks for seeing me."

"Happy to welcome you in, son. Have a seat. Can I get you anything?"

"Some water would be great."

Ozzie poured Tom a cup of water as Tom took a seat in a chair adjacent to the desk. Tom marveled at how meticulous the office looked. No clutter, and nothing out of place. Photos of the Constable's family lined the credenza next to a printer behind the large desk from where Constable Ozzie kept the people of Castle Ridge, and its visitors, safe—up until the last month anyway.

"How's Faith holding up?" Ozzie asked.

"As best as can be expected." Tom wasn't sure how much Ozzie knew about the cyberattack or the ransom payment, and he wasn't going to spill the beans. From his time at the DOJ, he knew the FBI was often stingy with information and didn't like sharing what it knew with local law enforcement agencies. His guess was that Constable Ozzie was in the dark.

"The resort's closed until further notice as you might expect, and Faith is figuring out how she can keep paying her employees. She's going through some tough times, no doubt about it," Tom said.

Constable Ozzie clasped his hands and let out a sigh. "The whole town is suffering. The Business Association is calling a special emergency meeting next week to see what it can do for the shop owners in town that depend on the resort. Many of 'em may not survive."

Tom had spoken to a number of business owners already and knew how scared they were. He pledged to help anyway he could.

"I assume there've been no developments in my assault?"

"Nothing. All of our leads, the few we had anyway, have all dried up. And to be honest with you, since Saturday all our resources have been devoted to the tragedy on the mountain."

Constable Ozzie made no mention that the two events might be linked.

"Tom, in light of all that's going on in town, our resources are spread thin. Since we haven't uncovered any evidence connected to your assault, I'm going to have to pull the details watching your house and office."

Tom wanted to protest. He needed protection now more than ever. But he couldn't share what he knew, and without that, he'd have no way to convince Ozzie to maintain the police presence.

"Can't say I like the idea, but I understand. Aneilia has gotten used to seeing the cars with flashing lights every day."

"If there's ever a need to restart the details, I won't hesitate. But hopefully there won't be."

Tom hoped for the same thing, but he knew better. He had a target on his back. And time was ticking.

"Constable, the reason I'm here is because I was hoping I can get a copy of the manifest you recovered from the truck you impounded last week by the reservoir. The manifest that you said had my name on it. I think it could be useful in the litigation I'm handling for Faith and the town against the owner of the property."

Since Faith was the mayor of Castle Ridge and Ozzie's boss, he figured it wouldn't hurt to invoke her name.

Ozzie's chair squeaked as he leaned back. Tom could tell he was troubled by the request.

"The manifest is evidence in a criminal investigation. You should know better than anyone that I can't just give it to you. It needs to remain in this office so we can maintain chain of custody."

Tom couldn't argue with him and decided to change course.

"Did the investigators ever uncover what was in the back of the truck? Faith asked me about it this morning." Tom was on a roll and decided to double down. A little white lie, or two, never hurt anyone. Besides, he was certain Faith would have asked about the cargo if she wasn't preoccupied by a hundred and fifty million other things.

Ozzie chuckled. He probably realized Tom was fishing for information and trying to shortcut his way to it.

"The truck was carrying crates of small capsules containing a liquid. Lab tests conducted by the state police revealed the liquid was just distilled water with a plain food dye in it. But the capsules are interesting. It appears they contain tiny electrodes that could be used to dissolve the capsules.

Lord knows what they're used for. Maybe they're a tracking device. State Police are sending the capsules to Buffalo for forensic testing, but the lab is so backed up it's anyone's guess when they'll get to it."

"Where's the truck?"

"Sitting in a warehouse in Albany. Fingerprint results came back negative and no one's claimed it."

Tom considered telling Ozzie to get the FBI to examine the capsules, but decided to wait until he knew more. He saw Ozzie reach for a manilla folder on the credenza behind his desk. Ozzie flipped it open and stared at it for a few minutes. Then he stared at Tom. He bit his lower lip, smiled, and put the folder back on top of the credenza.

"I'm sorry Tom. I just realized I'm late for a meeting. You should feel free to stay here and use my office if you like. Make yourself at home. But I need to leave."

Ozzie rose from his chair and headed for the door. When he was next to Tom he stopped and extended his hand.

"Thanks for all you're doing for Faith and the folks of Castle Ridge. I hope you find what you're looking for."

In a flash Ozzie slipped through the door and closed it behind him. Tom smiled as he heard Ozzie lumbering down the hallway, the sound of his footsteps becoming fainter with each step.

He quickly made his way around the desk and reached for the folder Ozzie had been holding. Opening the cover, he looked at the single sheet of paper. *Cargo Manifest* was written in large black letters across the masthead, and his business card was stapled to the left corner. He sighed in relief.

The name of the shipper was typed in the box under the heading *Consignor*. It was listed as Societe Robolex, the chemical manufacturing company with a deadly reputation that Phoenix Holdings acquired last year according to Claire's research. The recipient's name was typed in the box marked *Consignee*, but it was crossed out and Tom couldn't make it out. In its place was a handwritten name: *Thomas Berte, Esq., c/o Phoenix Holdings*. Why in the world would someone write his name as the consignee of the cargo?

The address listed for the consignee was also curious. It was simply *Bensonville Reservoir, Castle Ridge, New York*. There was no street address or even a name for a brick-and-mortar structure. Just the name of the reservoir—the same reservoir described in the brochure Claire found when she was investigating Phoenix Holdings.

The description of the cargo was blank as was the weight and value. It had arrived at JFK International Airport two days earlier via a charted flight on an airline Tom had never heard of. The cargo was then turned over to Manatee Trucking for its final destination—Castle Ridge. On the bottom of the page, in small block type was the word *essai*. At first Tom thought it was an abbreviation or an acronym. He tried sounding out the letters, but nothing made sense. He looked at the date on the manifest. *4 February*. The date preceded the month, the way dates are written in most European countries. Societe Robolex was a Swiss company with a French name. Tom concluded *essai* must be a French word. He had taken French in high school but that was a long time ago and he remembered little of it. He pulled out his phone and was about to type in the word, but thought better of it. He was in stealth mode. Sitting on Ozzie's desk was his computer. *You should feel free to stay here and use my office if you like.*

Tom toggled to the search engine icon and typed in the letters.

The French word essai has multiple meanings in English, including trial. For example 'a l'essai' means "on a trial basis."

Trial basis? A trial basis for what? To test something. A test run. The manifest was for cargo shipped for a test run. More of it would be coming. Probably right around the Fourth of July, he assumed.

Scanning the manifest again, he noticed a code containing five numbers and four letters in a box marked *C.O.D.* The code could mean anything, but at the moment it didn't mean a thing.

Tom turned and saw the printer on the credenza. He hoped it doubled as a copier. He propped open the lid and smiled. He was in luck. He copied the manifest, stuck the copy in his jacket pocket, and put the original in the folder. He returned the folder to its place on the credenza as if he had never touched it.

Tom walked out of Ozzie's office onto Main Street and quickly realized he had no idea where to go. His office was off limits, as was his home. Both places were likely bugged.

The Castle Ridge Courthouse had a law library with computer terminals, but everyone who worked there, and most of the lawyers from surrounding towns who had business there, knew him. He'd be eyed with suspicion, or worse, peppered with questions from his friends and colleagues about why he was working in the law library instead of his well-appointed office just down the street. He could stay in Ozzie's office and work, but this was a police station, open to the public, and at any given time all sorts of unsavory characters from around the region could be perp-walked in and booked into the holding cell. He needed someplace quiet and off the beaten path.

After a few seconds, he thought of the perfect place. And it was right next door.

29

The law office of Millard Jensen wasn't open for business anymore, and it hadn't taken on a new client in over five years, but you wouldn't know it from the looks of Millard's office visible from Main Street through large first-floor windows. The view consisted of hundreds of file folders piled high to the ceiling, covering every square inch of the place, including the windows, which made it difficult for Millard to see what was happening along Main Street. But since he'd been practically blind for the last few years due to glaucoma, he wasn't missing much.

Millard was almost eighty-nine years old and looked every bit of it. Years of hard drinking, mostly in the private chambers of judges throughout the county, and long hours spent working on almost every type of case imaginable in his long and illustrious career, finally caught up with him. His hands were ravaged by arthritis and he could no longer even hold a pen. He decided to call it quits for good when his eyesight got so bad he needed a magnifying glass just to read his mail. Some of his long-time loyal clients tried to convince him to hold on longer and stave off retirement, but Millard was too proud to hang around beyond his expiration date. He quickly referred all his clients to Tom. Without much fanfare, and without a retirement party, he paid for a notice in the *Castle Ridge Sentinel* that simply read:

Millard Jensen, Esq., Counselor at Law, proud alumnus of Fordham University School of Law, former Chief Judge of the Third Judicial District of New York Supreme Court, humbly announces his retirement from the active practice of law. Clients wishing to retrieve their files are kindly requested to contact Janet to make appropriate arrangements. All clients are invited to contact Thomas Berte, Esq., for their legal needs. God bless the Town of Castle Ridge and its residents.

Born in Castle Ridge to a family that traced its roots in upstate New York back to the Revolutionary war, Millard was one of those rare lawyers who found success on every rung of his career climb. From his service with the Army JAG Corps after graduating law school, where he rose to the rank of lieutenant colonel, to practicing at a white-shoe New York City firm, to his appointment as a judge by the Governor of New York, and then finally when he returned to private practice helming his own firm, first in Albany, and then eventually back in Castle Ridge for the last twenty years or so.

When Millard retired, he was only too happy to pass the torch to Tom, who never forgot the assist he received from Millard when he opened his solo practice. Tom welcomed Millard's sage advice then, and he knew it would come in handy now.

Tom walked up the driveway and rang the doorbell to his office which sat smack in the middle of town, on Main Street, in between the Castle Ridge Courthouse and the Constable's headquarters.

"Thomas, is that you? What a pleasant surprise, please come in."

Millard's wife, Phyllis, met Tom at the door. The Jensens lived in an apartment upstairs from Millard's law office, the same home Millard was born and grew up in. Phyllis accompanied Tom to Millard's office, where they found him sitting behind his large, antique oak desk. Millard still spent several hours a day in his dimly lit office listening to the news and enjoying opera music.

Tom maneuvered around several folders and cleared some space on a leather chair opposite Millard's desk. Sagging shelves lining the wood-paneled walls teemed with books covered in thick dust that had long settled over every crevice. The air was musty, giving Millard's office the smell of an unkempt locker room. Tom took a seat in a worn armchair whose springs had lost their tension long ago causing him to sink almost to the floor.

"Millard, you're looking well. I hope I'm not disturbing you."

"At my age any disturbance is welcomed. It tells me I'm not dead yet."

Tom enjoyed Millard's acerbic wit.

"I'm in between hearings in court next door and needed a quiet place to make a few calls and use a computer. I'm having work done in my office and can't go there. I was hoping I can use your guest office for an hour or so."

Tom was upset with himself for not having called Janet before leaving Ozzie's office to get his story straight with her, but his office phone line was off limits, so Tom would need to check in with her in person later.

Millard's silence before he responded told Tom he wasn't buying his story.

"Oh? Must be some serious work you're doing in your office if you can't get any work done there."

It was vintage Millard—always quick with a quip or a comment that set you back on your heels.

"Yeah, I guess. In any event, is it okay if I set up shop here for a while? I promise to be quiet and stay out of your way."

"Certainly, Thomas. I'd welcome the company. It'd be good for these old walls to come alive again with the sounds of a lawyer practicing his trade."

Tom was about to stand up and make his way to the guest office when he turned back toward Millard and sat back down.

"Millard, did you ever face a situation in your career where you questioned whether the law provided enough tools to find the truth?"

Millard frowned and pushed his chair away from his desk.

"How do you mean?"

Tom shifted in his seat, causing him to sink even lower.

"I'm not sure," he said as he was searching for the right words. "As lawyers, our work is governed by so many rules. Often times those rules prevent us from doing what's necessary to find the truth. Yet, it's ingrained in us since the earliest days of law school that our justice system is the greatest tool ever created to uncover the truth. It just seems to create a conflict that's hard to reconcile."

Tom wanted to say so much more. He wanted to share what he knew—

about Phoenix Holdings, about the massacre on the mountain, about what he suspected was being planned for the Fourth of July. He wanted to tell Millard everything and get his advice on what to do. He'd been thinking about a plan, a way to find out exactly what Phoenix Holdings was up to. But the law put constraints on him. It was as if he was shackled. He was a lawyer and had to work within the system he swore to uphold. But what if that same system prevented him from learning the truth and prevented him from potentially saving the lives of millions?

Tom could tell Millard was considering his question. Millard closed his eyes, clasped his hands together in a pyramid, and brought them under his chin while resting his elbows on the arms of his chair. After a long pause, he was ready to speak. He began in a soft whisper.

"Thomas, the precept that countless wide-eyed students are taught in law school every year, that our justice system is a search for the truth is, in a word, bullshit."

Millard's frankness surprised Tom.

"Our judicial system is set up so the factfinder makes probability determinations for reasons that oftentimes have nothing to do with truth-seeking. When I was a judge, I often excluded relevant evidence even if it proved the truth. Hell, our system of justice protects against self-incrimination unless certain warnings are first given even though those confessions are often times the best measure of truth. The reason for this is because our system was devised as a means to preserve the *appearance* of fairness and to satisfy a higher moral stricture. One where innocence is presumed for all, and where the burden to prove guilt beyond reasonable doubt rests with the sovereign. But a judicial system guided by a moral code works only when both sides abide by that same morality. Both sides need to play by the same rules. The system works only when the need to punish is met by a willingness to accept responsibility. But if someone is unwilling to be deterred, or if deterrence comes too late or doesn't occur at all, then the protections afforded by our system of justice are for naught. In those situations, the search for truth becomes a fruitless exercise and the noble goals of justice and righteousness are never attained." Millard paused as if he was collecting his thoughts. "I've come to learn in my career that the law has its limits. And that's why, Thomas, a lawyer's true purpose is to prevent injustice, not merely to seek the truth. And, sometimes, preventing injustice, and preventing evil, requires a higher justice. The difficult question, even for lawyers, is not in determining if a higher justice is necessary. But when."

Tom allowed Millard's words to sink in. If his true calling was to prevent injustice and evil from taking countless lives, then he had to move forward with the plan he'd devised. It was risky and could jeopardize his career and all that he had worked so hard to achieve. But what choice did he have? What good was the law, and a license to practice it, if following it meant millions of innocent lives were in jeopardy? This wasn't a time to think about himself. Whoever sent him that notecard trusted him to do whatever was necessary to prevent evil. He wasn't about to back down now.

"Thomas," Millard said in a somber voice interrupting Tom's thoughts, "I'm glad you've recovered from your...attack. The whole town is. And everyone is immensely proud of the work you're doing to help Faith face her ordeal. I can't imagine what's she's going through. If there is anyone who can assist her, and find out what really happened and why, I know you can." Millard bowed his head for a moment and sighed. He then looked straight at Tom. "Remember, there are occasions where idealism must give way to practicality. There are times in this world when there are simply too many laws and not enough justice."

"Thank you," Tom said in an equally somber voice that matched Millard's. "That's good advice. I'll be sure to keep it in mind." For a second, he wondered if Millard knew more than he was letting on.

Tom considered Millard's words carefully and reflected on their meaning. He'd been living in darkness for the last month, but a glimmer of light was coming into focus. He needed to put his plan into action. He needed to turn gloom into glory.

30

Tom walked into the guest office down the hall from Millard's office, switched on the light, and shut the door. He could hear the soundtrack to Mozart's *The Magic Flute* coming through the walls. It would be soothing background music to his covert reconnaissance—or so he thought. He blew dust off the phone and got to work.

"Claire, this is Tom. I have a follow-up assignment concerning Phoenix Holdings I'm hoping you can help me with."

After updating her on his recovery and passing along greetings from Brooke, he asked Claire to research the construction project involving the aquifer and water tunnel awarded to the subsidiary of Phoenix Holdings. He needed to learn everything he could about the project and Phoenix's involvement in it, and how it figured into the warning he received about the Fourth of July.

He heard Claire pecking at the keyboard. After what seemed like an eternity, she came back on the line.

"I've found quite a bit of information about the construction project and its connection to Phoenix Holdings Group. Would you like me to email it to you?"

"No, our computers are down in my office. Maybe you can quickly skim what you've found and give me a summary."

"Okay, but I'm not sure what you're looking for. It may not be the most efficient way to go about this."

"I know, Claire." Tom was fumbling for an explanation. "Maybe you can just hit the highlights."

"Okay, here goes."

She proceeded to speak slowly.

"The reconstruction of the second water tunnel, as well as several adjoining viaducts and aquifers, was awarded about a decade ago. The cost of the project was estimated to be about ten and a half billion dollars."

Claire paused and Tom heard more typing.

"According to recent published reports, the cost of the project increased significantly in the last three years due to delays, material shortages, and disputes over terms of the contract. Cost overruns were expected to be about thirty percent of the original estimates."

Tom fidgeted, hoping Claire would get to the good parts soon.

"Oh, this is interesting."

Tom's heart beat faster.

"The contract was originally awarded to a U.S. based contractor that worked on the project for three years. But that contractor filed for bankruptcy and the project sat dormant for a year. Until the project was rebid and awarded to a company called Eagle Industries, a subsidiary of Phoenix Holdings Group, based in Gibraltar.

"This article says the second water tunnel will bring more than 1.1 billion gallons of fresh drinking water daily to eight and a half million residents of New York City. The water comes from reservoirs in upstate New York, and ninety seven percent of the water reaches homes and business in the city through gravity alone."

"That's all very interesting. What can you find out about Eagle Industries?"

The line went quiet again except for the rhythmic clatter of keys being punched on the keyboard. After a few seconds, Claire spoke up.

"Just before Eagle Industries was awarded the water tunnel construction project, it was acquired by Phoenix Holdings Group. Eagle Industries claimed it had special expertise to complete the project because of its experience working on similar projects in Iraq and Afghanistan after large areas of those counties were destroyed by the American forces. It appears funding for those projects came from the United States government as part of their rebuilding efforts in that part of the world. Isn't that something, first our government destroys those countries and then it spends billions rebuilding them."

"Can you find the name of the reservoir that feeds the water tunnel that Eagle Industries is constructing?"

"Let's see. Give me a second. Here it is, yes. It's Bensonville Reservoir in Castle Ridge, in upstate New York. Why, that's where you now live, isn't it?"

Tom broke out into a sweat. If Claire kept talking, Tom wasn't listening. His eyesight blurred. He quickly tried to piece together what he'd learned so far. Phoenix Holdings desperately wanted to acquire the ski resort and was prepared to pay a king's ransom for it. The same resort that buffered land Phoenix owned on the banks of the Bensonville Reservoir that he succeeded in stopping Phoenix from developing. Now, he learned a Phoenix subsidiary was rebuilding a water tunnel intended to bring drinking water from Bensonville Reservoir to the residents of New York City. And Phoenix Holdings also owned Societe Robolex, a company that manufactured war grade chemicals disguised as purified distilled water—the same cargo contained in the truck headed to Bensonville Reservoir before it was impounded by Constable Ozzie—with a shipping manifest with his name on it. He felt his face flush. The office was getting hot, as if someone had opened a furnace door.

"Tom, did you hear what I said?"

He barely heard Claire and quickly realized she was still on the line.

"Tom, are you still there?"

"Yes, sorry Claire. I think we lost our connection for a moment."

"I said it's interesting, isn't it, that the former Attorney General of the United States, Bradley Mitchelson, played a role in Phoenix Holdings Group acquiring Eagle Industries and later being awarded the project in New York City."

Tom's stomach churned and he felt weak. He would have fallen over if he wasn't sitting down.

"Claire, are you able to find anything about July Fourth? Is there anything in the documents you've pulled about the Fourth of July?"

"Well, there's a photo I found of a fireworks display over New York Harbor celebrating the completion of the construction project that is dated July Fourth. I think I included that in the folders I gave Janet."

"I know, I saw that. Is there anything else connected to July Fourth?

"Well, let me see."

Tom closed his eyes.

"Okay, here's something."

Tom's heart raced.

"According to the document I'm looking at, Eagle Industries expects that water from Bensonville Reservoir will begin flowing through the water tunnel and out the taps of the eight and a half million residents of New York City on July Fourth, just in time to celebrate Independence Day. It appears Eagle Industries is planning a huge party to take place in New York City on the Fourth of July."

Tom said he had another call coming in. He thanked Claire and slowly placed the phone in its cradle. His mouth was dry and his throat burned. He reached into his jacket pocket for the bottle of water Constable Ozzie had given him, twisted off the cap, and was about to take a swig when it hit him. He stared at the water. On July Fourth, millions of people will do exactly what he was about to do—innocently take a sip of water. Only they'll die doing it. He needed to tell someone, but who?

Remain silent or Brooke and Aneilia will perish.

His body shook and he felt numb. After a few seconds, he decided to make another call.

Mitchelson's assistant Hope answered.

"No, I'm sorry, Mr. Berte, Mr. Mitchelson has been abroad for the last several months. May I take a message and let him know you called?"

Tom debated what to say. He needed to speak with Mitchelson and find out what the hell he knew about Phoenix Holdings.

Tom opted to probe a little.

"Say, Hope, I'm working on a matter involving Phoenix Holdings. I understand Bradley did some consulting work for that company. Do you know the last time Bradley met with anyone from Phoenix Holdings?"

Hope paused.

"I don't recall exactly, but Mr. Mitchelson worked extensively with

Phoenix Holdings Group until about a year ago. He's had only sporadic contact with the company since then."

"Do you know if he's done any work with entities called Eagle Industries and Societe Robolex recently?"

"It doesn't ring a bell."

"Do you know the nature of the consulting work Bradley was engaged in for Phoenix Holdings Group? Did it have anything to do with a large construction project in New York City?"

Tom didn't actually expect Hope to answer his questions. Any executive assistant worth her salt who'd been around as long as Hope had knows the secret to that longevity is saying as little as possible to anyone outside the organization unless authorized to speak.

"I'm sorry, Mr. Berte, I don't have that information. But I'll be sure to let Mr. Mitchelson know you called."

Deep within the bowels of the compound, the chief security officer monitored the call made to Bradley Mitchelson's office. He immediately recognized the voice as belonging to the American attorney, although he didn't recognize the phone number the attorney was calling from. After a few clicks of the tracing software, he identified the number as belonging to a Millard Jensen, Esq. in Castle Ridge, New York. He listened carefully to the inquiries being made about Phoenix Holdings Group, Eagle Industries, and Societe Robolex.

Within seconds he pulled up the access log he had just analyzed detailing online access to the family of companies that made up Phoenix Holdings. It showed a spaghetti string of intersecting lines, codes, and time stamps of searches. Much of the activity occurred the day before, between 3 and 6 p.m. eastern standard time, and also a few minutes before the American attorney called Mitchelson's office today. The searches were made using the same desktop computer. The username for the computer was cholister1942, and the computer was registered in the name of Langdell Hall. Using geospatial vector tracking software he quickly determined the computer's location as Cambridge, Massachusetts. With a few more clicks, he learned the user known as cholister1942 was Claire Holister, Head Librarian at Harvard Law School in Cambridge, Massachusetts. The purpose behind the searches into Phoenix Holdings' web of companies, and Janet's unplanned visit to Boston for the Holister case, now made sense.

The chief security officer picked up his phone, pressed the encryption app, and began typing:

Waddah/Anastasia: Attorney Berte has made inquiries of the former attorney general concerning PH, EI and SR. He is using an agent at Harvard Law School, which Mr. Berte attended, to further his investigation. They have in their possession information that could lead them to discover the Grand Plan. Recommend immediate measures be taken to discourage further reconnaissance. Also recommend continued sequestration of Bradley Mitchelson.

31

Tom stumbled out of Millard Jensen's house onto Main Street. His pickup truck was still parked in the lot behind the Constable headquarters, but he needed to walk. He needed fresh air. He needed to think. He headed in the direction of his office, pulling up the hood on his coat to guard against the blustery wind. The days were getting longer, but it was still dead of winter in Castle Ridge. Although Tom cursed the ground hog who saw his shadow a few days earlier, the wind felt good against his face and he inhaled deeply, clearing his lungs of the leftover musty smell from Millard's office.

He was annoyed Mitchelson wasn't available again. Despite having left several messages for him, his former boss hadn't yet deigned to return any of them. What he'd learned over the last two days shook him to his core. He shuddered at the thought Mitchelson was in on it. But did he have sufficient evidence of Phoenix's involvement in a conspiracy to bash his head in, blow up The Turret lift, and engage in a mass poisoning? The best evidence, of course, was the notecard, but it was hardly a smoking gun. Until he knew who sent it to him, he couldn't prove its authenticity. He couldn't even get it admitted in a trial against Phoenix Holdings. Heck, he wasn't sure he'd even be able to get an indictment in the first place. If a line attorney at the DOJ brought this type of evidence to him when he was second in command, he would have told the lawyer to come back when he had more hard evidence

—the type of evidence a grand jury could sink its teeth into and that a prosecutor would salivate over. The kind of evidence he had uncovered against the Benedetto Syndicate years ago. Without it, it was all still too circumstantial. Until he knew more, he didn't know enough.

He concluded he had more work to do to refine the details of the plan he'd formulated, and he needed to be smart about it. One false move, like going to the authorities too soon, and Brooke and Aneilia would be in grave danger. He'd never forgive himself if anything happened to them.

After walking for several minutes he looked up and realized he was just a few feet from his office. A perfect time to call Anastasia.

As he walked up the side driveway, he noticed the white truck belonging to the art gallery parked in the rear lot. He thought of Chet and hoped the gallery had enough work for him to make up for his lost salary from the resort. Then again, he wondered whether even the art gallery would survive the shutdown. Without the resort bringing city dwellers to Castle Ridge, owners of those multi-million-dollar chalets dotting the mountain wouldn't need artwork adorning their walls.

As he reached the second-floor landing of his office, he spotted Janet in her familiar spot, sitting at her desk in the reception area.

"How are you coming along on the contract for the resort?"

"All finished," Janet said loudly. "I've stacked five duplicate copies on the sideboard in your office. Each stack contains all the exhibits and required forms, and stickers indicate where Faith and the buyer's representative will need to sign. We're just waiting for some final documentation from the county and title company. You'll likely be able to close on the sale in a few days."

Tom entered his office, popped the cap off a bottle of *Yoohoo* he grabbed from the mini fridge, and picked up a copy of the contract. The document was several inches thick and weighed at least half a pound. Special binder clips held the bundle together. Janet was nothing if not fastidious and organized. He was sure she double and triple checked every page, calculation, and mete and bound contained in the deed and survey. Despite Janet saying the closing could take place in a few days, there was no way he was going to let that happen. He had to stall and buy himself more time.

Anastasia picked up on the first ring.

"Tom, good to hear from you. Is the contract ready for signature?"

"Almost. The contract has been drafted and duplicates made. I'm waiting for some final documentation. I should have it very soon."

"Splendid. Shall we go ahead and schedule the closing for Monday next?" Tom heard Anastasia's eagerness, no doubt so she and her colleagues could get a head start on whatever diabolical plot they were planning.

Tom paused.

"We can pencil it in. But before we can transfer title to the resort, I need some additional information about Phoenix Holdings."

He expected Anastasia to ask some questions but instead she remained silent. He decided to forge ahead.

"Because it's such a large transaction, Faith's bank requires additional information to satisfy its internal federal Know Your Customer requirements as well as newly enacted FINCEN requirements. You know, the Financial Crimes Enforcement Network. It's general information concerning the beneficial owners of Phoenix Holdings and the source of funds used to acquire the resort. I can have my assistant send you a list of the requested information and documents."

He imagined Anastasia frantically scribbling notes and wondering how to gather the information. The truth was Faith's bank hadn't asked for any such information, and FINCEN's newly enacted regulations didn't apply to commercial transactions, but he was hoping her eagerness to acquire the resort and the land it sits on would cause her to just give him what he was asking for instead of questioning it. He didn't know exactly what he would do with the information if he got it, but he decided to ask for it anyway as a stalling tactic to delay the closing for as long as necessary until he found proof of Phoenix's involvement in the unfolding conspiracy. Information is power, and the more of it you have, the more powerful you are.

He was ready for some pushback from Anastasia, but her response surprised him.

"No."

Tom looked up and stared blankly out the window.

"Excuse me? What do you mean, no?"

"I'm not sure what games you're playing, but I've done many deals for amounts far greater than the purchase price of the ski resort. I've never provided the type of information you're requesting."

Tom had to think quickly.

"It sounds like you're seeking to delay the transaction. That would be a grave error on your part," Anastasia added, sounding angry.

Tom didn't like being put on the defensive so he decided to go on offense.

"Now hold on there, Anastasia. I've bent over backwards to get this deal done. May I remind you that Faith had no interest in selling the resort to your client until I persuaded her to change her mind. I've done everything possible to make this deal happen."

"The malfunctioning chairlift and the resulting devastation of Faith's business had something to do with it as well, I'm sure," Anastasia said. Her words were chilling.

If Tom could have reached through the phone and choked her, he would have. Phoenix Holdings was behind the tragedy and had blood on its hands, and damn it, he was going to prove it.

"Perhaps you're distracted by what you believe should be other priorities, Tom. Other investigations. You should redirect your energies and focus on finalizing this transaction and nothing else. It should be of the utmost importance. For you and everyone concerned."

Her words and tone stopped Tom in his tracks. What *other investigations* was she talking about? Could she possibly know what he'd been up to and what he'd learned?

You are being watched.

Tom looked around his office. He was certain his office was bugged. Perhaps cameras had also been installed. He tried to take precautions and thought he'd been careful by using Constable Ozzie and Millard's office. But how much did she know?

Maybe he was just being paranoid. Maybe Anastasia was making idle threats to show how tough she could be. Maybe she didn't mean *his* investigation into Phoenix Holdings?

"My client is already paying a premium for the resort, and it agreed to your demand for an initial payment of one hundred fifty million dollars, which is far more than is customary. Some might say the deal isn't worth it.

But my client thinks it is. Either way, the time has come to complete the purchase of the resort. Now. And to resolve the baseless lawsuit you filed."

He was playing a game of chicken, and running out of options. If what he believed was going to happen on the Fourth of July actually occurred, the lives of eight and a half million people would be at risk—and the world would never be the same.

Pursue the deal to uncover another horrific plot before the 4th of July.

"Let me see if the information Faith's bank is requesting is really necessary. Perhaps there's another way. I'll get back to you. I assure you I'll do whatever it takes to resolve this situation."

He braced for Anastasia's response.

"Good. Because my client will do whatever is takes to accomplish its goal without any further delays."

She hung up as quickly as she uttered those words. He was certain she was on to him. He had to work twice as fast to prevent Phoenix Holdings from reaching its goal. He couldn't go to the authorities, not yet, and not with the threat of harm to Brooke and Aneilia hanging over him. He was quickly running out of time.

Tom heard a knock on his office door. Janet opened it halfway and peered in.

"A letter just arrived for you. I saw someone on the monitor coming up the walkway to the front entrance. The person was bundled up so I couldn't see a face. Whoever it was knocked gently then knelt down and placed something on the ground, under the doormat, and walked away."

Tom froze.

Janet was holding a red envelope.

"It's addressed to you. There's no indication who it's from. I assumed you'd want to see it right away."

Tom nodded slowly and motioned for her to come in. She handed him the envelope and he waited until she closed the door behind her before looking at it. It was the size of a postcard, the same as the red envelope left under the doormat at his home. He turned it over several times to inspect it, but there were no markings. Just his name typed on the front of it, like the other one. This one was also sealed. He slid his finger under the flap. When he lifted it, he saw the same type of white notecard inside. Before taking it out, he glanced around his office. He looked up at the corners of the walls and ceiling half expecting to see cameras. He instinctively looked over his shoulder. A chill came over him. He slowly pulled out the notecard and saw the words neatly typed in the center.

Phoenix Holdings is aware of your investigation.
If you go to the authorities now your family will be in grave peril.
Devastation is coming unless you prevent it.
Godspeed.

32

His Eminence was in his private chamber reciting evening prayers when Waddah tapped on the door, entered, and sat next to him.

"I have spoken with Anastasia. It appears she is encountering some resistance again on the part of the American lawyer. He has been curious about our plans and has been investigating our activities, including looking into Eagle Industries and Societe Robolex. He's also attempted on several occasions to contact Bradley Mitchelson."

His Eminence cast his eyes upward at hearing Mitchelson's name.

"Are we certain our guest has not communicated with the lawyer?"

"He remains sequestered and is under constant observation. I am certain he has not spoken with anyone."

"And what are your plans for the lawyer?"

"We are implementing another phase of our strategy. I am confident the results will cause him to discontinue his inquiries and alter his conduct."

His Eminence rose from his chair and spoke in an angry voice.

"The American lawyer has proven more resilient than you or Anastasia anticipated. Your efforts thus far have failed to dissuade him. These distractions trouble me greatly and I am beginning to wonder if I've placed too much trust in people who are incapable of carrying out the mission."

"Your Eminence, I can assure you that is not the case. It is true that we've had to implement additional steps to ensure the lawyer's compliance, but I fully expect the next phase of our strategy will cause him to change his ways. We're confident he will now do what is expected of him."

His Eminence considered Waddah's words but wasn't satisfied.

"Proceed as you intend with the American lawyer, but I am concerned about what he knows and what he may do with the information he's learned. Our people have labored too hard and sacrificed too much for our efforts to be jeopardized. The lawyer has done much to thwart our use of the reservoir. Let him continue to focus his efforts there. But I want us to move expeditiously to implement the Grand Plan now, without further interruptions."

Waddah looked at His Eminence in confusion. "But how will that help us? The lawyer will continue to delay the sale of the land we covet?"

His Eminence turned to Waddah and raised his right palm to his heart.

"We must modify the point of access. Instead of immersing Zincar in Bensonville Reservoir, we must utilize the back-up site to the north of our target area. We already have Zincar pre-positioned there in mobile tank vessels. The effects will not be as widespread, and fewer victims will be sacrificed, but our goal will still be achieved. I will not allow the American lawyer or his client or any official instrumentality of the infidels to derail our plans. Death must come swiftly and our prayers must be answered. I command that Zincar be immersed at the alternate site as soon as possible. Keep me apprised of all developments immediately as and when they occur."

Tom re-read the notecard several times. Phoenix Holdings knew about his investigation. But how? Who had sent him the notecards?

Devastation is coming unless you prevent it.

Tom closed his eyes as pangs of nausea roiled his stomach. He thought he might vomit. He kept what he'd known secret, even from Brooke, and this is where it got him. Brooke and Aneilia were in more danger now than ever and would be until Phoenix Holdings was stopped. But he couldn't involve the authorities. He considered his alternatives but quickly realized he had only one. It was the only way to save his family and prevent the death of millions. Time was ticking and his back was against the wall. It was now or never. He was dealing with evil. And some evils require a higher justice.

He dialed the number to Darryl's office. He knew his call would be monitored.

"Darryl, I need information to complete the sale of the resort to Phoenix Holdings. Let's meet at Peak's Perk Coffee Chalet in an hour. Yeah, it'll be good to patronize a business in town. God knows they need our help. Oh, and bring your laptop."

He was determined to bring an end to his fifteen minutes of gloom.

33

Tom asked Janet to give him a ride back to the Constable headquarters to pick up his truck, and in return he gave her the rest of the afternoon off. Business had declined since the resort shut down and his office was quiet. His phones weren't ringing, and several real estate deals he'd been working on were put on hold due to the economic uncertainty caused by the resort's closure. In fact, the only active deal he was working on was the sale of the resort. With such a steep drop off in his business, he'd normally be scared out of his wits about the future of his firm, but Tom had bigger things to worry about.

By the time Darryl arrived at the coffee house, wearing her signature black leather jacket, Tom had already set up shop in the back speakeasy lounge. He was certain it would be available, and the owners were only too happy to generate some extra cash by letting him rent it.

"I didn't even know this space existed," Darryl said after Tom ushered her into the back room and she took a seat across from him. "I thought we got our wires crossed when I walked into the place and it was deserted out front. I guess you need to be a regular to know about this hideout."

"Or just friends with the owners. Anyway, thanks for seeing me on such short notice." Tom was eager to get down to business.

"It's not like much is going on at the resort. Faith is down in the city meeting with lawyers and insurance agents, and I'm happy for the distraction. So, what are you looking for to complete the sale of the company I work for, which will result in me being unemployed and unable to feed my family," Darryl said, smirking and sounding bitter.

Tom stared straight at her. He wasn't about to let the place she and her fellow employees loved and called home be sold. Not now, not ever.

He took a deep breath. He was about to ask for help to undertake the most important work of his life.

"When you were in the Counterintelligence Division at DHS and on the Cyber Security Task Force did you ever work on Project Eradicate Aifam?

Tom noticed Darryl twitch ever so slightly. It was a small tell, nearly imperceptible, but he already had his answer.

"I did, at the tail end of it. I started at DHS a month before you departed the DOJ. That's how I learned about your dedicated service to our country which folks at DHS still talk about to this day. Project Eradicate Aifam was one of my assignments for the first year of my tenure there, until it was officially closed."

"Tell me about Project PAWNED. You employed it to catch the hackers of the Department of Veterans Affairs, the Benedetto Syndicate, right?"

Darryl squirmed in her chair, clearly uncomfortable.

"Ah, Tom, I'm sorry, that information is highly classified and as far as I'm aware you no longer have security clearance. Plus we're not in a secure location. What does this have to do with the sale of the resort to Phoenix Holdings anyway?"

He paused and took another deep breath. He was about to venture into unknown territory, and he hoped Darryl was willing to play ball with him.

"I need your help. Faith needs your help. I have reason to believe Phoenix Holdings is behind the attack on the resort and is planning something even more sinister in the months ahead. I know this all sounds crazy, but I need you to trust me. I need to find evidence about what Phoenix Holdings is planning in order to prevent it from happening."

Tom noticed blood drain from Darryl's face and he feared she might pass out.

"Darryl, I need your help to find that evidence."

Darryl's mouth fell open. If she intended to say something, words were failing her. She sat stone silent for several seconds.

"Ah, sorry, I mean, ah...why wouldn't you go to the police with this? Deputy Director Aronson is still in town. I'm sure he'd be able to help. I—I can even put a call into DHS for you."

"Darryl, listen to me very carefully. My wife and daughter, and me included, are under threat of imminent danger. My attack on the mountain a few weeks ago wasn't a random event. I was purposely targeted by someone working for Phoenix Holdings. I've received a message, two of them actually, likely from someone inside Phoenix, warning me not to tell anyone what I just told you and not to trust anyone—or my wife and daughter will die."

Darryl's eyes opened wide.

"But you're telling me?" she asked haltingly.

"I am, because I trust you. Because you're the only person who can help me gather evidence against Phoenix Holdings so I can uncover what it's up to. Listen to me very carefully. I have reason to believe Phoenix Holdings is planning to kill millions of people. You and I swore the same oath to uphold the constitution of this country and to defend our nation against all enemies, foreign and domestic. We may not be wearing a uniform anymore, and our paychecks aren't coming from the government, but I never forgot the oath I took, and I'm willing to stake my life, and the lives of my wife and daughter, that you didn't either. Now, I've already told you enough to get me and my family killed." Tom paused. His voice was shaky and his hands trembled. Beads of sweat traced down his face. "Darryl, will you help me, and Faith, and this town, and our country, by helping me hack into Phoenix Holdings' computer system to find evidence that we can turn over to the authorities?"

Tom braced for her answer, but Darryl remained silent. Seconds passed. He saw her lips quiver and her breathing quicken.

"What you're planning to do is illegal. I don't need to tell you that. You're putting your career at risk. You can't do that. You'll be disbarred." Darryl spoke rapidly.

Tom slumped backwards. He knew Darryl was right and he expected her reaction. But he had weighed the consequences of his plan and was prepared for whatever happened to him. Nothing else mattered if Brooke and Aneilia were harmed. And nothing else mattered if millions of innocent lives were in peril. Although he believed in the rule of law, he also knew there are times the law needs to be sacrificed to catch bad guys. It needs to take a back seat to doing whatever is necessary to save lives because sometimes there are simply too many laws and not enough justice. Just like Millard said to him.

Some evils require a higher justice.

If the ends ever justified the means, this was it. His law licensed be damned.

He thought of giving Darryl another patriotic speech and invoking the founding fathers, but it turned out that wasn't necessary. What she said next told him he was right to bet on her.

"Tom, I can't let you risk your career. Tell me what you need, and I'll do it. I'm all in, but keep your hands clean."

Tom smiled.

"No way. We're in this together."

34

The email arrived in the inbox of the production manager at Societe Robolex just after midnight. It provided instructions for a shipment of ten tons of viral agent, to be disguised as children's clothing, to be expedited later that morning for delivery to JFK, New York. The instructions directed the manager to utilize the same information contained on the cargo manifest from the first shipment several weeks earlier, but this time the instructions made clear this was *not* an *essai*—it wasn't a test run. This shipment was for the actual viral agent the scientists in Societe Robolex's lab had been working on, not for distilled water. It was the viral agent needed for execution of the Grand plan.

The timeline was tight and would require his men to work through the night, but the cause was just and sacrifice was necessary. His Eminence had promised eternal glory to the men who accepted this role. They had bid farewell last year to what family they had left and departed the compound for this tiny village outside Bern, Switzerland.

The direction for immediate shipment of the viral agent was consistent with an email Waddah had sent the production manager earlier that morning advising that His Eminence had instructed his followers to proceed with all deliberate speed to redouble their efforts to implement the Grand Plan. The production manager was surprised Waddah's earlier email did not instruct him to prepare the shipment of Zincar, and that he was receiving a second email so soon after the first. He was also surprised by the instruction to disguise the shipment as children's clothing, something he'd never done before. But he recognized that Waddah and especially His Eminence possessed superior knowledge and power and must have their reasons for proceeding in the way they did. He did not dare question the instructions received in this second, late-night email.

Those instructions detailed that upon arrival at JFK, the cargo was to be handed off to the driver of a white truck, similar to the one that was used for the last shipment which unfortunately was seized by local authorities in Castle Ridge, New York. The production manager thought it odd that Waddah would arrange for the same type of vehicle as was used in the unsuccessful test run, but it was not his province to question the wisdom of His Eminence's strategy.

The workers began assembling three pallets of Zincar contained in tiny capsules with semi-permeable membranes and tiny electrodes, just like the last shipment. The pallets were carefully bundled in specially manufactured cellophane wrap designed to mask any scent so dogs used by customs and border agents wouldn't deem the shipment suspicious. Stickers indicating the cargo consisted of children's clothing were slapped onto the sides of the cellophane wrapped pallets, just as the second email instructed.

By early dawn, the pallets had been loaded and were on their way to Bern Airport. The workers turned off the lights in the warehouse and the computer in the production manager's office, and then they headed to the safe house for much needed sleep.

At a few minutes past 11:00 a.m. local time, after customs agents cleared the shipment they believed contained children's clothing, the private charter cargo plane that had sat idle in Bern Airport awaiting instructions for just such a flight, taxied down the runway with its precious cargo aboard. Eight hours and twenty-two minutes later, the plane was expected to land in New York's JFK airport after crossing the skyline of New York City with cargo that, in a few short months, would ultimately wind up in the New York City water system.

At least that's what the production manager at Societe Robolex believed.

At precisely the same time the cargo plane was roaring down the runway of Bern Airport, Chet was waking up in his cluttered apartment in the employee housing complex of Castle Ridge Ski Resort. He prepared two thermoses of hot coffee and two sandwiches of bologna and Swiss cheese, which he thought appropriate given his job today. He drove his Honda in the dark to the parking lot behind the art gallery and Tom's office on Main Street. Tom's second-floor office was dark, as was the art gallery. The only illumination came from the fixture attached to the top of a light pole in the parking lot, brightly shining on the white truck owned by the gallery.

He climbed aboard the truck, secured his lunch bag, strapped his seat belt across his chest and lap, and keyed the address that had been sent to him last night into the navigation system. Seconds later, a color map with a blue route line popped up. His time of arrival was estimated to be 8:52 a.m.

His destination: the international cargo arrivals warehouse at JFK airport.

35

Chet didn't require much convincing. With the resort shuttered, he had a lot of extra time on his hands. And with business slow at the art gallery, his weekly round trip to Albany, Toronto and Rochester to pick up new pieces of artwork had been cancelled. He was all too happy to earn some extra cash picking up a shipment of children's clothing at JFK Airport coming from Switzerland that would be donated to victims of The Turret lift fire. The owners of the art gallery, Tom's landlord, were also happy to donate their truck for Chet to use. They offered to pay for gas and tolls, but Tom insisted he'd be picking up the tab.

Project PAWNED was in full swing within an hour of Darryl going all in. At the outset, Darryl didn't have much luck bypassing several defensive barriers designed to isolate and protect different segments of Phoenix Holdings' computer network. She made several attempts to penetrate the multi-layered Intrusion Prevention Segmentation Partition, but each time came up against an anomaly detection system requiring a decryption code made up of a series of five numbers and four letters to unlock the VPN encryption key. Darryl was growing frustrated, until Tom had an idea.

"Take a look at this." Tom decided to show Darryl the cargo manifest with his name on it that Constable Ozzie conveniently left unattended in his office earlier that morning. "I've wondered what this sequence of numbers and letters in the box marked *C.O.D* means. Could it be the decryption code?"

Darryl raised her eyebrows. "Why didn't you give this to me when we were preparing the instructions to the production manager instead of just telling me to reference it?"

"Because I didn't want to have to tell you how it came into my possession."

"Are you going to tell me now?" Darryl asked.

"Nah. Let's just say I found it lying around. Dumb luck." Tom shrugged his shoulders. "Is this information useful?"

"There's only one way to find out."

Tom watched Darryl intently as she typed in the code, applied mathematical operations to the ciphertext decryption algorithm which automatically created several permutations and re-ordering of the data, and maneuvered through several digital signatures. After a few minutes of punching the keyboard and clicking through hypertexted links, Darryl uttered the words Tom prayed he'd hear.

"We're in."

Tom was dismayed that an enterprise as sophisticated and well-financed as Phoenix Holdings, with the ability to spend half a billion dollars acquiring a ski resort as a front for a terrorist organization, would be careless enough to include a decryption code on a cargo manifest. But Darryl surmised the code was likely needed by engineers at Societe Robolex to access an encoded file with instructions confirming release of the viral agent. Whatever the reason, in the end, Phoenix Holdings' security infrastructure proved no match for Darryl's years of training. Once she applied the code, she described breaching the firewalls like cutting through butter with a hot blow torch, unlike Revolutionary Avengers' network which was much more sophisticated and still hadn't been cracked. Within minutes Darryl located the files that provided her with access to Phoenix Holdings' entire computer network. From that moment forward, Darryl masqueraded as employee PH10488.

Tom was also lucky the production manager at Societe Robolex had received an email hours earlier from Waddah to undertake preparations to quickly execute something called the Grand Plan. Tom didn't know what the Grand Plan was, but he was certain it was connected to whatever Phoenix Holdings was planning for the Fourth of July. He remembered reading Waddah's name in the files Janet brought back from her visit with Claire. Reading his rants in those files, Tom thought he sounded like a maniacal zealot intent on annihilating the United States. If he had any lingering doubts about what he and Darryl were doing, recalling Waddah's pure evilness confirmed he'd made the right decision.

As soon as Darryl found the email from Waddah to the production manager, Tom decided on the spot to send the second email directing the manager to prepare a shipment of product needed to execute the Grand Plan, using the same capsules with tiny electrodes as used in the earlier shipment, and referencing the same information from the cargo manifest he "found" in Ozzie's office. He didn't know what the product was called, but he made sure to clarify he wasn't interested in distilled water this time. He wanted the real deal. He and Darryl hoped to capitalize on the sense of urgency Waddah had created with the first email so that the second one—directing that ten tons of product be shipped to JFK—didn't raise any suspicions. He crossed his fingers the production manager would ship the deadly chemical Phoenix Holdings was planning to use to carry out the Grand Plan.

The next piece of the puzzle was arranging for transportation of the shipment after it arrived at JFK. That's where Chet and the art gallery's white truck he saw daily in the rear parking lot of his office came in handy. The fact that it looked similar to the truck Ozzie had impounded weeks earlier carrying distilled water to the edge of the reservoir for the "test run" could prove problematic, but what other choice did he have? He needed a truck, and Tom's landlord was willing to let him borrow his. When he called Chet, he was only too happy to help. All Tom told him was to head to JFK Airport in New York City to pick up a shipment of children's clothing to be donated to victims of the chairlift fire. Tom wasn't going to share any more information with him than he had to. He had already shared enough with Darryl.

After arranging the shipment to JFK, Tom and Darryl shifted to phase two of Project PAWNED. This one was going to take more time and require more effort. The goal was for Darryl, or PH10488, to penetrate each of the subsidiary companies that make up Phoenix Holdings and duplicate the network files onto an external hard drive. Although it might take more time to do it this way, it made sense to copy everything and comb through it later for evidence of Phoenix Holdings' crimes, instead of going through the files piecemeal now looking for select incriminating evidence.

By the time Darryl gained access to the critical infrastructure that allowed her to duplicate the files, it was almost 8:00 p.m. Peak's Perk had long since closed for the night, but Tom persuaded the owners to allow him and Darryl to remain in the back room for a few more hours. He promised to lock up and asked them to send him the bill for renting the space.

"It's going to take several more hours, at least, to duplicate and download all the files to the hard drive. It doesn't make sense for both of us to stare at a bunch of code lines on a computer screen for the next few hours," Darryl said. "Why don't you call it a night and go home to your family? I'll take care of the rest."

Tom had called Brooke earlier with a white lie, saying he was working late on a brief that was to be filed the next morning. Brooke was fine with it because Aneilia had rehearsals with her dance class for an upcoming show. Still, the rehearsal ended an hour ago and Tom was eager to get home to his girls in hopes of seeing Aneilia before she fell asleep.

"Are you sure?" Tom asked. "It's my life and my family's life on the line here. Maybe I should stay until the work is finished."

"You've been through enough. Go home to your wife and daughter. By tomorrow morning we'll have a duplicate copy of all of Phoenix Holdings' electronic files. I'll call Constable Ozzie in the morning and arrange for us to use one of his conference rooms so we can begin reviewing the information. That way we can transmit what we find directly to the FBI."

"Sounds like a plan," Tom said.

"Does 11:00 a.m. work? By then, Chet should have possession of the cargo and be on his way back to Castle Ridge."

"That works," Tom said. "Hopefully we find what we're looking for."

"I hope so. I want to nail these mother fuckers. There's no way I'm letting Faith sell her mountain to those bastards," Darryl griped, her voice sounding sharp and forceful. Tom was about to walk out of the old speakeasy when he heard Darryl mumble something.

"What'd you say?"

"Oh, just that this is interesting."

"What is it?"

"A file containing information relating to the wire transfer to your escrow account for the downpayment for the resort, and the wire back to an account controlled by Revolutionary Avengers for the ransom payment. It's all here. Account information. Routing numbers. Passwords. The money was received into an account owned by Phoenix in a bank located in Guernsey and then transferred to another account Phoenix controls."

Tom stopped.

"This is proof positive Phoenix was behind the ransomware attack," Darryl said with a look of satisfaction.

"Let me see that."

"I thought you were going home?"

"I will, but I just thought of something."

Tom took control of the mouse and keyboard and started poking around. After a few minutes, he found what he was looking for.

"Darryl, when you said that you're 'all in', how serious were you?"

Darryl shot him a quizzical look.

"All in means all in, Tom. There's nothing I wouldn't do for Faith and the town of Castle Ridge."

Tom smiled.

"Good. I have a plan. And if it works, we're gonna help a lot of people."

By the time Tom pulled into his driveway, his cabin was dark and quiet. He left Darryl at the coffee house to finish duplicating Phoenix Holdings' network. He was looking forward to tomorrow when he could dive into the files and hopefully find the smoking gun he was looking for.

It had begun to snow again, and a few inches were predicted to fall by the morning. He expected to see the deputy's car still parked at the entrance to his driveway, but then remembered Constable Ozzie pulled the detail. He shut his eyes tight and shook his head. After what he did tonight, he knew he'd need police protection now more than ever.

The first floor of his cabin was quiet and dark, so he slowly climbed the stairs to the second floor, the steps creaking underfoot. He passed Aneilia's room and cracked open the door and peeked in. His little angel was already sound asleep under a blanket, cuddled with her favorite teddy bear, as Bentley lay in the corner keeping watch over her. He blew her a kiss

He then walked a few paces to his bedroom, where Brooke was already asleep too. He quickly changed into his pajamas and, as quietly as he could, slid under the covers and lay next to her. The sound of her breathing made him rest easy. His wife and daughter, the two most important people in his life, were safe at home.

He had had a long day and had accomplished much. Receiving the second notecard earlier in the day jarred him. On an impulse he'd decided it was time to implement the plan he came up with after he first met Darryl. He debated the wisdom of including her in his scheme, but he had no choice. She had the skills he needed to hack into Phoenix Holdings' computer network, and his gut told him she'd be willing to help. He was right on both fronts.

He thought long and hard about the consequences of his actions. He took his obligations as a lawyer to be a steward of the rule of law seriously. By hacking into Phoenix Holdings' network he'd be breaking the law and, on some level, he'd be equating himself with those he was pursuing. He'd become just like them, and just like.... The hypocrisy wasn't lost on him. He wondered just how far the apple had fallen from the tree.

He was beginning to realize what love of family meant, and the extent to which he'd go to protect and provide for those who meant everything to him. He thought of Mary, his mother, and the choices she'd made in her life and the lies she perpetuated to protect him from the truth about his father. He felt a gnawing twinge of guilt and remorse and debated whether it was time to make amends and forgive.

In the end, despite the doubts and concerns and potential for disbarment and criminal prosecution, Tom was at peace with the choice he'd made. His decision was an affirmation of his love for his family which would always come first. He was doing what he needed to do to fulfill the promise he made to protect them. No matter the cost.

His eyes were heavy and he was tired. Tomorrow would be an important day, he thought. He prayed he'd find evidence to prevent the horrific plot he'd been warned about.

36

Last night's snowfall didn't live up to expectations. With the mountain off limits, snow was now just another nuisance instead of the lifeblood of the region. Only a few inches coated the roads, which were mostly clear by early morning. The sun was already shining brightly and temperatures were expected to climb well into the upper forties. Despite the light dusting of snow, Brooke received an email that morning from Aneilia's preschool informing her that recess would be outdoors today, on the covered playground, something the school hadn't done since the fall.

Tom was already at the office when Brooke eased her Subaru out of the driveway and down King's Court Drive with Aneilia safely buckled in her carseat in the second row. It was part of their morning ritual. On Mondays, Wednesdays, and Friday mornings, Brooke dropped Aneilia off at Regal Preschool at 8:30 and then headed to her office on a small side road off Main Street down the block from Tom's office.

For weeks she'd been speaking with Aneilia about school buses in preparation for pre-K next year when Aneilia would finally be able to ride a bus to school on her own. Aneilia was so excited about taking the bus "like the big kids" that she asked Brooke if they could ride on one to "practice." Brooke promised to surprise Aneilia one day soon with a bus ride. The two had also started singing *Wheels on the Bus*, and it quickly became Aneilia's favorite song. She would sing it again and again in the morning while dressing, and again on the drive from the cabin to preschool. They sang it so often, every day, for weeks, that the song played in Brooke's head all day and night. She even started dreaming about yellow school buses.

They began singing it again that crisp Friday morning as soon as they got into the car. Maybe that's why Brooke didn't give any thought to the minivan that began following her when she turned off King's Court Drive onto Duke's Pass and followed her for the three-mile drive to the preschool.

Brooke walked Aneilia into the classroom and briefly spoke with Ms. Plessy, one of Aneilia's teachers, before hugging her daughter and giving her a kiss.

"See you at 1:30 my sweet girl."

"OK, mommy. I love you."

"I love you too. Have tons of fun!"

The recess bell rang at 10:45 a.m. With the sun shining, the children were springing with excitement about having recess outside on the covered playground. Aneilia put on her coat and walked with her classmates in a single file to the playground.

Aneilia and her friends giggled and shouted as they ran and jumped and chased each other while climbing the monkey bars, sliding down the slide, and riding the merry-go-round. Aneilia grabbed Ms. Plessy's hand and pulled her toward the swing set. She raised her arms and all but pleaded with Ms. Plessy to pick her up and put her on the low hanging seat, which was only a few feet off the ground. Aneilia pulled down on the safety bar and placed it on her lap while Ms. Plessy started gently pushing the seat. Aneilia pumped her little feet and legs to and fro, and within seconds was gaining momentum, swinging forward and back and climbing higher with each pump.

As Aneilia shouted with joy and kept pushing her legs forward and pulling them back, two girls playing tag in the corner of the playground next to the school building began screaming. Ms. Plessy looked over in the direction of the girls and ran over to the edge of the building to see what had gotten the girls' attention. As she approached, she noticed a rolled-up blanket. Something in the blanket moved, startling the girls who shrieked. Ms. Plessy looked down and saw a tiny kitten poke her head out from under a corner of the blanket. The girls were either frightened or excited, or both, because they immediately began screaming and pointing at the blanket. Hearing their classmates' squeals, other children ran over and formed a semi-circle around Ms. Plessy who had knelt down and carefully unfolded the blanket. She scooped up the tiny kitten, which was waving its paws and opening its mouth, and gently cradled it for the children to see.

Anelia heard her friends screaming and saw them running toward the corner of the playground and she wanted to join them. She stopped pumping her feet and legs to slow her momentum, but she had climbed so high and was moving so fast that the swing kept rocking for several more seconds before it finally began to slow. Just as the swinging was coming to a halt and she prepared to lift the safety bar, Aneilia saw the yellow school bus slowly drive up the street and park along the fence next to the covered playground, close to the swings, on the opposite end of the playground from where Ms. Plessy and the children were gathered around the kitten.

The side door of the bus opened and a young woman who looked to be in her late twenties wearing a baseball cap and sunglasses, with a dark ponytail poking out from the back of the hat, walked off the bus and strode over to the fence. Aneilia stared at the yellow bus as if in a trance. The young woman smiled, knelt down on one knee, and through the links in the fence, waved Aneilia over.

Aneilia hesitated for a moment and then slowly let herself out of the swing and walked toward the bus. She stopped a few feet from the edge of the fence which was just a little taller than she was.

"Hi, you must be Aneilia. My name is Suzy. Your mommy Brooke is surprising you today and asked me to show you this yellow school bus. Your mommy is going to be here any second and then we can all go for a ride."

Aneilia's face lit up and she grinned from ear to ear.

"My mommy promised me we would go on the bus. I can't wait."

"I know, I can't wait either. I'm so excited. And your mommy is, too. She called me and said she'll be here in just a few minutes. Come closer so you can see the bus."

Anelia's mouth fell open as she stared intently at the yellow school bus. She slowly walked right up to the fence.

"I love school buses. My mommy says I'm going to ride one to school every day."

"Yes, you will. Just like all the big girls and boys."

As soon as she uttered those words, the young woman stood up and put her hand over the fence as if she wanted to shake Aneilia's hand.

Aneilia smiled and looked up. She raised her right arm and grabbed the woman's hand.

Aneilia's screams caught Ms. Plessy's attention. Still kneeling, she turned while cradling the tiny kitten in her left hand and used her other hand to move the children out of the way so she could see where the screams were coming from. It was then that she saw the woman in the baseball cap and sunglasses lift Aneilia up and over the fence. In an instant, the woman turned her back and sprinted for the bus's open door. She quickly muffled Aneilia's screams and climbed the bus's stairs as the door swung closed behind her.

Screeching tires were the last thing Ms. Plessy heard as the yellow school bus sped away.

37

Brooke was wrapping up her second appointment of the morning when her cell phone vibrated on the small table next to her. She had a policy of never interrupting her sessions to answer her phone, but something caused her to glance at it while listening to her patient recount a messy story about a childhood fight from long ago. She saw the name Regal Preschool on the phone's tiny screen. That's unusual, she thought. She almost never received calls from Aneilia's preschool during school hours—unless Aneilia wasn't feeling well.

Apologizing to her patient, Brooke said it would only be a minute but she needed to take the call. She pressed the 'talk' button and immediately heard sirens and people yelling.

"Mrs. Berte, ah, I'm calling from Regal Preschool. Ah, would you be able to come over to the school?"

Brooke heard the caller's voice quake but she could hardly make out the words amid the background clamor.

Brooke cupped her other ear in hopes of hearing the caller better.

"What? Is everything okay with Aneilia? What's going on?"

"Ah, we have a bit of a situation, ah, hold on."

Brooke heard more sirens and several loud shouts, but she couldn't understand what they were saying.

"What's happening? Is everything alright? Where's Aneilia?" she yelled into the phone.

Brooke felt her pulse quicken as her mind raced to a dark place.

The caller wasn't back on the line yet, so Brooke yelled into the phone again. "Hello? What the hell is going on? Where's Aneilia? Is she okay?"

She finally heard the caller's voice.

"Ah, Mrs. Berte, I'm sorry. I'm told a deputy is on his way to your office to bring you to the school. He should be there any moment."

Brooke thought she heard the sound of another siren in the distance, but she wasn't sure if the sound was coming through the phone or from outside her office.

"What? Why? What's happened? Please tell me." Tears began to well up in her eyes as fear took control of her mind. Her throat tightened and her voice wobbled as she tried to catch her breath. "Where's my daughter? Where's Aneilia? Is she alright?"

Just then she heard the wail of sirens getting closer and the sound of screeching tires. Within seconds she heard a loud bang on the front door. As she sprinted out of her office, she screamed again into the phone.

"What the hell's happened? Where's Aneilia?"

Brooke collapsed to the floor when she heard the caller's response.

"Aneilia's been kidnapped."

Constable Ozzie was in a meeting when Sheila, his assistant, burst into the conference room interrupting the gathering.

"Constable, there's been an incident at Regal Preschool. A child has been abducted. The 911 call came in a few minutes ago. Two deputies are on their way to the scene. State police are enroute and a SWAT team has been dispatched."

Ozzie put down the coffee cup he'd been holding and began walking out of the room.

"Do we have a description of the abductor? Was the person on foot or in a vehicle? Do we know the name of the child?" Ozzie kept up his rapid fire, clipped questioning as he headed to his office.

"The child was taken in a vehicle. A yellow mini school bus," Sheila answered just as quickly. "Heading west away from the preschool. An all-points bulletin is being issued and we're in the process of putting out an amber alert. I wanted to bring this to your attention as soon as possible."

"Are there any reports of a stolen school bus anywhere in the area? Were there any casualties or injuries in the course of the abduction?" Ozzie was steps away from his office when Sheila stopped behind him. He spun around and noticed she was pale as a ghost and breathing heavily.

"What is it?" he demanded.

"The child who was abducted is Aneilia Berte."

"Fuck!" Ozzie cursed loud enough that deputies throughout the station-house heard him. He began to bark out orders as he swung behind his desk "Tell the command staff to meet me in the Sit-Opp Room stat. Arrange to patch in the superintendent of the state police. Establish a direct line with the deputy in command at the preschool. And call in all available personnel and cancel all leaves." He looked up at Sheila who was furiously jotting down his orders. "But first, get a hold of FBI Deputy Director Aronson and ask him to get here asap!"

Tom was in his office preparing to head over to the Constable's office to review the material Darryl had downloaded at the coffee house. He had spent the morning writing a letter he'd been thinking about ever since he came up with his own plan. Last night, after he decided to put his plan into motion, writing the letter became a matter of urgency. He needed to hand-write it—something he wasn't used to doing anymore—and wanted to finish it before he and Darryl reviewed the hard drive, just in case he didn't make it back.

He placed the notecards he'd received in a separate sealed folder and was handwriting the address on the outside of the envelope when his cell phone rang. Brooke's name and picture popped up on the screen. He answered the call but had a tough time making sense of her words. Between her uncontrollable sobs and the blaring sirens, he could barely hear her.

"Tom, Aneilia's been kidnapped. She's missing! She's missing!" Brooke screamed into the phone. "She's been kidnapped! I'm on my way to the school."

"What? What are you talking about?"

"Aneilia's been kidnapped" Brooke yelled again. "She's been kidnapped! Our baby is missing! Someone has taken our baby! God help us! Get to the preschool. Oh, my god!"

Her screams were steady but becoming muffled. He heard static and then a thud, as if the phone had fallen to the ground. He yelled Brooke's name, but she didn't respond.

Shooting up from his desk, Tom raced from his office and barreled down the steps two at a time. A sense of dread took hold of him. He yelled at Janet to mail the letter on his desk and get the police to Aneilia's preschool. He was still gripping the phone. He yelled Brooke's name again, but she didn't respond. He felt lightheaded and thought he was about to pass out. His knees buckled and he stumbled when he got to the front door. He gasped for air and began to gag and dry heave. He flung the door open and willed his body to sprint toward his truck, fumbling for the key fob in his pocket. When he finally clicked the unlock button and jumped into the driver's seat, he sat there for a moment in shock, cold, and alone.

Suddenly, he realized there was something he didn't know. It hit him like a lightning bolt. He dry heaved again. At that very moment, for the first time ever, Tom didn't know if his precious baby girl was alive or dead.

PART III

38

Deputy Director Aaronson was having an early lunch alone in a quiet restaurant on the outskirts of Castle Ridge. He'd been bored out of his mind the last few days waiting for developments in the ransomware attack on the resort, but there hadn't been any. With no reason to stay in Castle Ridge, he was planning to head back to Washington early the following morning. He'd had enough of his winter sojourn in the mountains and was looking forward to seeing his family. His ringing cellphone interrupted his boredom.

"Deputy Director Aronson. This is Sheila from Constable Stuart Ozzie's office in Castle Ridge. Constable Ozzie requests that you immediately meet him at his office. There's been a kidnapping at the preschool in town."

Aronson wondered why the hell Ozzie was calling him about a kidnapping instead of the head of the FBI's Albany Field Office. He soon got his answer.

"A child has been abducted. Her name is Aneilia Berte. Thomas Berte's daughter."

By the time Aronson got in his government-issued Chevy Impala and sped out of the restaurant parking lot to meet Constable Ozzie, he'd gotten a quick debrief from his first assistant. Aneilia Berte, age three, was abducted at approximately 11:00 a.m. from the playground of the Regal

Preschool in Castle Ridge. Witnesses identified a young woman, likely in her late twenties or early thirties, wearing sunglasses and a baseball cap with a dark ponytail extending out the back of the cap, as the abductor. The vehicle seen fleeing the preschool with Aneilia in it was a yellow school bus. A mini school bus, not one of those full-sized ones. It was headed west out of the town of Castle Ridge—in the opposite direction from which Aronson was driving on his way to Castle Ridge.

He turned on the Impala's red and blue emergency lights, but so far hadn't needed them to clear traffic. No other cars were on the road and the hills and valleys around Castle Ridge Mountain were deserted. He was about thirteen miles away from the Constable station when he pressed down on the accelerator, reaching ninety miles an hour along a winding two-lane country road. The police radio on his dashboard screeched with non-stop staticky chatter from the county dispatcher, Castle Ridge deputies, state police, a county SWAT team, and a contingent of FBI agents from the Albany Field Office who were enroute to Castle Ridge. Updates were coming in fast, with local witnesses reporting conflicting sightings of anything that looked yellow along several routes heading west out of town. An amber alert had been issued, but so far, no confirmed sightings of a yellow mini school bus. He heard state police transmit a command for at least three choppers to get airborne immediately.

Cresting a hill, Aaronson was on a long straightaway. In the distance he saw a vehicle approaching from the opposite direction with its headlights on. It was the first vehicle he'd seen in the last few minutes. His navigation indicated he was ten miles west of his destination. As the vehicle hurtled toward him, Aaronson noticed it wasn't a car. It was larger, like a truck, and it took up the entire roadway. Aaronson took his foot off the accelerator thinking he might need to make way for the oncoming truck.

As the truck got closer, Aronson realized he wasn't staring at a truck after all. It was a bus. A mini school bus. A yellow mini school bus. And it was barreling toward him in the opposite direction.

Aronson blasted his horn, switched on his siren, flashed his high beams, and swerved his car back and forth across the double yellow line hoping the bus would slow down. But the bus kept coming, and it looked to be gaining speed. Aronson had to react quickly. If the bus bypassed him, he might never catch up to it. He couldn't risk letting the bus, and whoever was on it, get away. With seconds to spare, he pressed down on the accelerator, gripped the steering wheel, turned it hard to the left, and stomped on the brakes while bracing for impact. The minibus careened into the passenger side rear door area of the Impala, deploying the side airbags, exploding the side and rear windows, and crushing the rear seat like an accordion. The force of the impact nearly sheared off the back of the Impala, splitting it in two, and spun it around clockwise. The nose of the Impala was now behind the mangled school bus as Aronson watched it skid off the shoulder and careen down a forested embankment. Amid the sounds of crunching metal and breaking glass, Aronson thought he heard the agonizing screams of a child before he blacked out and lost consciousness.

Brooke arrived at the preschool at the same time heavily armed tactical units from the SWAT team arrived. The officers quickly entered the school ahead of her and secured each classroom. Brooke saw Ms. Plessy and ran toward her, begging for information about Aneilia. When she couldn't get a straight answer, she fell to her knees and broke down in tears. Two deputies raised her up and whisked her to a small building next door to the preschool that used to house a church but was now a community center. Today it would function as the command center for the Regal Preschool kidnapping.

"Where's my baby? Where's my baby?" Brooke kept shouting as the deputies escorted her into the large main room. Her body went limp, and the deputies grabbed her by the arms and more or less carried her over to a metal folding chair next to a makeshift desk set up in front of the elevated stage. She was sobbing uncontrollably and trying to catch her breath. "Please find my baby, please find my baby."

"Mrs. Berte, my name is Detective Samantha Kaplan. Please try to remain calm. I'm with the Monroe County Sherriff's Department. I'm in charge until the state police and FBI arrive."

"You need to find my baby. You need to make sure she's okay."

"Mrs. Berte, we are doing everything we can to find your daughter and bring her home. Based on our preliminary review of security video footage from the preschool, it appears your daughter was not harmed when she was carried into the school bus."

Brooke let out a shriek causing everyone in the room to stop what they were doing and turn toward her.

"Mrs. Berte, listen to me. The video shows that your daughter's abductor placed her in a seat and fastened a child safety restraint around her as the bus sped away. We have every reason to believe your daughter is unharmed. We have a description of the bus and a partial license tag number. Every law enforcement officer within a fifty-mile radius is looking for the school bus your daughter is in. We're doing everything we can to find her. I promise."

"School bus?" Brooke said, gasping for air. "Aneilia was infatuated with school buses. That's all she ever talked about. She wanted to ride on a school bus." Her voice was raspy and she was shaking. "Please find her! Please!" Brooke buried her head in her hands as she let out a guttural scream.

Another commotion at the entrance of the hall caught everyone's attention. Tom raced in, looked around, saw Brooked curled in the chair, and sprinted over to her. He fell to his knees and wrapped his arms around her.

"She's gone, Tom, she's gone! Someone took our baby!" Brooke screamed while crying and gasping, her chest heaving and convulsing. They rocked together and cried out in grief, their howls of pain and anguish made some seasoned police officers avert their eyes, and more than a few wiped tears and coughed to avoid choking up.

Tom slowly lifted his head and stared blankly at Brooke.

"I'm sorry, I'm so sorry. I did this. This is all my fault. I'm so sorry." Tom's words were barely audible as he tried to catch his own breath in between sobs.

"What do you mean?" Brooke screamed. "We need to find her! We can't let anything happen to her. We need to find her." Tom grabbed Brooke and hugged her tightly as they cried in each other's arms. They held their embrace for a long while, rocking back and forth, loudly sobbing.

After a few unbearable minutes watching Tom and Brooke grieve over their missing daughter, Sam motioned for a female deputy to assist Brooke to the ladies' room. She knelt down next to Tom and whispered that she needed to speak with him. He stood and tried to compose himself, wiping his face with his sleeve and running his hands through his hair.

"Mr. Berte, I'm Detective Samantha Kaplan. We believe your daughter is physically okay and was unharmed when she was abducted. As I explained to your wife, footage from video cameras outside the preschool show her abductor buckling your daughter into a safety seat on the school bus. Bad guys don't do that if they intend to harm their victim."

Tom's eyes widened.

"She was taken away on a school bus?" he asked dismayed. "Aneilia's been wanting to go on a school bus forever. She's fascinated by them. They must have heard us speaking about it. It's all she ever talked about."

"Sir, I know you've been under surveillance and that someone or some group has been tracking you, and I know Constable Ozzie had a watch detail posted at your home and office after your assault. The person who took your daughter onto the bus is a woman. With dark hair. Possibly in her late twenties or early thirties. Does that description fit anyone you know?"

Tom was dazed and confused. Anastasia? Could she be the one who took his baby girl?

Phoenix Holdings is behind it all...You are being watched...Trust no one...If you go to the authorities now your family will be in grave peril.

Just as Tom was about to speak, several walkie-talkies began squawking in the community center with staticky chatter he couldn't understand. His attention was suddenly drawn to a side door. Through tear-stained eyes he saw Constable Ozzie lumbering into the community center accompanied by two heavily armed deputies. Ozzie held a phone to his ear and his face was scrunched. He was shaking his head. He spotted Tom and darted for him.

"Word just came in." Ozzie was panting heavily. "A yellow mini school bus was involved in an accident on Route 532. It went down an embankment and overturned. It landed in the woods. We believe it's the bus Aneilia is in."

39

Aronson forced his eyes open and blinked several times. He tried lifting his head and strained to hear. Silence filled his space. His head ached. A piercing pain seared across his skull from ear to ear. His vision was blurry. He tasted something frothy. He spat. It was red and dribbled onto his chest. He looked around and realized he was in a car. The window closest to his head was shattered but intact. White fabric from the deflated airbags made it difficult to see out the passenger side of the car. He shifted his weight but couldn't move. He was tied down. A strap tight across his chest cinched him back. It was his seat belt. He remembered seeing a bus and hearing sounds of the impact. He remembered hearing cries from a tiny voice.

He tried to move his arms but the pain in his shoulders was too much. He looked at his left hand. It was bloodied and mangled. He mustered enough energy to bring his right hand down to the side of his waist, but his chest seized in pain. He knew what pain from busted ribs felt like and this was that kind of pain. Times ten. He tried to keep his breathing shallow. He closed his eyes, clenched his jaw and moved his right hand a few inches. He searched for the buckle. He knew it was close. It had to be close. Just a little bit more. He pressed down with as much force as he could muster and snapped it, loosening the strap. He hoped it would relieve the pain in his chest, but it didn't. Breathing hurt. He slowly nudged the strap off him with his right hand and felt the bulge on the left side of his chest under his jacket. It was still there.

After a few seconds, his vision began to clear which allowed him to focus better. His thoughts were becoming clearer too. He'd been in a car accident. His car was broadsided and it spun him around. He lifted his head higher and stared out the windshield. He was in the middle of nowhere. All he saw were snow-covered barren fields and stalks of leafless trees. Snow-capped mountains rose in the distance. An endless kaleidoscope of white, brown and gray. He saw no one. He heard nothing. He was alone.

But he remembered. It was a school bus. A yellow school bus hit his car. He tilted his head. It still ached but he was remembering more. He looked around for his cell phone but didn't see it. He remembered placing it in the cup holder, but it must have been flung about in the crash. He looked at the police radio on the dashboard. Its lights weren't on. He grabbed for the corded mic with his right hand and pressed the talk button. "This is FBI Deputy Director Douglas Aronson." Talking hurt but he needed help. He took in a deep breath as pain seared through his chest like sharp daggers. He let it out slowly. "Is anyone there. Dispatch, can you hear me?" Nothing but dead air. Dropping the mic, he jerked his right hand across his belly and grabbed for the door latch, pushing it open. His legs were heavy and he winced in pain, but he clenched his teeth, groaned loudly, and rolled himself out of the car.

The cold air stung. He opened his eyes wider. He was on his knees but awake. He must have passed out from the impact. He craned his head from side to side but didn't see the bus. He was more awake now and lucid. There was a kidnapping. Aneilia Berte. She was kidnapped and taken away on a school bus. Was she on the school bus?

He put his right hand on the bottom sill of the door frame and mustered all his energy to push himself up despite excruciating pain. He clenched his teeth again and grunted but managed to stand up. He had to find the bus. He had to find Aneilia. He looked up and down the road. On his left he saw an opening in the tree line. Some of the treetops were crooked and toppled, leaning on other trees. He thought he heard a hissing sound coming from the woods below. He couldn't see the base of the trees because they were down the embankment, but he saw a thin layer of fog rising up from the steep ravine below. He shuffled to get closer to the edge of the road. He peered down and that's when he saw a yellow bus lying on its side shrouded in a haze of gauzy white smoke.

"Is anyone there?" he shouted. "Aneilia, are you down there? Yell if you can hear me."

The bus was maybe thirty yards down the embankment. It had cleared everything in its path and taken out several trees before coming to rest on its side, its front end crushed against a wall of trees. The tires had gouged out a muddy rut down the embankment. He looked around one more time. Still no one. He thought he heard sirens in the distance, but when he arced his head and forced himself to listen, he heard nothing. He was still alone.

He considered his next move and decided he had no other choice. With his right hand, he reached for his shoulder holster under his jacket and pulled out his Glock 9mm. Pressing the safety button off, he secured it tightly in his hand. He crouched down on his ass. For a moment he thought he was going to pass out from the pain. He pulled himself with his heels and pushed with his one good hand and began to slide down the snowy, muddy rut. After a few long minutes, he was just a few feet away from the bus. He slowly steadied himself while listening. Silence. He crawled to the front of the bus which was unrecognizable and strained to look through the cracked windshield, but couldn't see anything except beams of light coming through the bus's closed side door and windows that were facing skyward. He retraced his steps and shuffled past the tires and underbelly of the bus toward the back and saw the emergency door. He reached for the handle and, summoning all his strength, turned it, but it didn't budge. He tried twisting the handle up and down, but it didn't move. He cursed loudly but quickly cut himself off fearing someone in the bus might hear him. He slowly made his way around the other side of the bus and stared at its roof. That's when he noticed the open roof hatch. He crawled to the hatch and lifted his Glock to eye level. If anyone was going to pop out, he'd pop them first. He thought he heard faint rustling coming from inside the bus. He inched closer, gripping the gun tighter in his hand. He made it to the edge of the open hatch and peered in.

That's when he heard the whimpering cries of a child.

40

As dusk fell late that afternoon, Tom and Brooke sat clutching each other's hands in a darkened room at Mercy Hospital in Larange, the same hospital Tom had been rushed to after his vicious attack. They were quiet and deep in thought, counting their blessings, while they stared at Aneilia sleeping comfortably in the bed in front of them.

Shortly after Aronson found Anelia alive and safely strapped in her seat in the flipped-over school bus, a swarm of first responders descended on the scene. Medics removed her from the bus and rushed her to a waiting medevac helicopter that landed on an empty field on the other side of the road from where the bus went down the embankment. Her vital signs were stable and she looked alert. One of the medics, a pediatric nurse, made Aneilia giggle when she brought out Mr. Fuzzy Puppy.

Tom and Brooke rushed to the scene with Constable Ozzie. They had been told their daughter was stable and doing well, but it wasn't until they saw her in the back of the waiting helicopter and held her that they exhaled and thanked God for reuniting them with their baby girl. Even though she was stable, the decision was made to airlift her to Mercy Hospital for a full evaluation. Brooke and Tom were invited to join her for the flight to the hospital. Brooke immediately said yes, but Tom took a step back. He felt nauseous and his heart pounded as fast as it had hours earlier when he feared his daughter was gone forever. It was the first time he'd been this close to a helicopter since his life changed forever five years earlier. He swore then he'd never ride in one again. But things were different now. It was his daughter who was in that helicopter now, and he wasn't about to let her out of his sight.

The ER doctors gave Aneilia a clean bill of health. Still, out of an abundance of caution, and because the hospital was the safest place for the Berte family to be for the time being, Constable Ozzie and the state police arranged for Aneilia to remain overnight for observation.

Aronson was also taken to Mercy Hospital. He had several broken ribs, a concussion and a sprained shoulder, and numerous cuts and abrasions on his face and hands, but was expected to make a full recovery. Tom and Brooke hadn't seen him yet, but Constable Ozzie recounted the events of the afternoon after he spoke with Aronson. He told them Aronson had spotted the bus as he was speeding toward Castle Ridge, veered at the last minute in an effort to stop the bus from getting away, and took the full brunt of the crash, with the bus colliding into the side of his car and spinning it around. The bus then careened down a wooded embankment and flipped onto its side. He explained that Aaronson's actions likely made the difference between the bus being found and it speeding away to Lord knows where. A local farmer in the distance heard the accident while clearing snow from his horse's hay feeder and called 911. Despite his injuries, Ozzie explained that Aronson had managed to slide down the embankment, crawl on his hands and knees around the mangled bus, and notice the opened roof hatch. He found Aneilia unharmed and strapped in her seat.

Tom smiled when he learned of Aronson's heroics. Maybe it made up for Aronson's strong-arm tactics years earlier in D.C., he thought to himself.

As for the kidnapping, Ozzie told them that Aneilia was the only person on the bus when the deputies arrived. There was no driver and no sign of the person with a ponytail who had grabbed Anelia as seen on the video from the preschool. But a wig, baseball cap and sunglasses were recovered at the scene. Preliminary DNA testing thus far failed to return a match. They had no leads, but that wasn't stopping them from scouring the area and looking for any trace of evidence.

Tom wanted to tell Ozzie everything he knew, including about the notecards and Project PAWNED, but he needed to tell his best friend first. After Ozzie left the room, Tom draped his arm around Brooke and held her for a few minutes. Without looking at him or unlocking their embrace, Brooke finally broke the silence.

"You said something earlier today, at the community center. You said this is all your fault and you were sorry. You said 'I did this. It's all my fault.' Why did you say that?"

Tom took a deep breath and pulled away. He choked up as his eyes filled with tears. He had never lied to his wife about anything that mattered, and he wasn't about to start now.

"There's something you need to know that I haven't told you." He paused to collect his thoughts. He took another deep breath and glanced around the room as if looking for someone, but he knew they were alone and safe, for now. He stared into Brooke's eyes. "I know who kidnapped Aneilia."

41

Anastasia hated calling His Eminence with bad news. She tried calling Waddah first, but he was in a prayer meeting in the compound with other senior leaders and would be unavailable for several hours. She couldn't delay informing His Eminence about what had happened. He had demanded to be informed of all developments immediately.

"Your Eminence, our activities today did not go as expected. We intended to teach the American lawyer a lesson, to punish him for his investigation and reconnaissance into our activities so we can continue to execute our Grand Plan without further interruption. Unfortunately, there was an accident. There were no fatalities, but the target of our activities was not captured."

Anastasia heard His Eminence sigh.

"Poor planning results in poor execution," His Eminence said in a gruff voice. "There must be consequences for those involved who failed in this mission."

Anastasia stiffened her back. She knew what that meant and wondered if she'd be among those facing consequences.

"How does this affect our strategy for the lawyer?" His Eminence inquired.

"Therein lies a greater problem. With today's development, I suspect he may go to the authorities and reveal what he knows. Any such actions will impede our efforts for implementing the Grand Plan."

His Eminence was silent. Anastasia imagined him considering his alternatives and plotting his next move. She was about to offer a suggestion when he spoke up.

"Do we suspect Bradley Mitchelson of playing a role in the lawyer's activities?"

Anastasia was taken aback by the question. As far as she knew, the former Attorney General was sequestered and under twenty-four-hour surveillance by His Eminence's security forces. Surely, His Eminence had access to better intelligence than she did regarding Mitchelson's actions and ability to communicate with the outside world. Perhaps she was being tested. She was becoming concerned His Eminence suspected her of being a traitor and an impediment to the pursuit of their cause.

"I have no reason to believe Mitchelson is involved in any way, Your Eminence. Waddah and others have repeatedly assured us that he has had no contact with anyone outside the compound and his activities are monitored round-the-clock. We would know if he was communicating with the American lawyer or others. I'm much more concerned with carrying out the Grand Plan. Our people have fought too hard for Your work to be derailed now. Our goal is just, and our destiny is ordained by the Almighty. Your people deserve retribution for the suffering they have endured. May peace and mercy be with you always, Your Eminence."

Anastasia hoped she sounded convincing. She knew they needed to work quickly to accomplish their goals. She had underestimated Thomas Berte's determination, and they couldn't let him stand in their way any longer. She waited for His Eminence's response. After a long pause, he spoke the words she longed to hear.

"We are not waiting any longer. We must execute the Grand Plan now, without any further delay."

Tom told Brooke everything. He began with the notecard left on the front porch of their cabin the morning after The Turret lift fire. He told her the note confirmed the catastrophe was connected to his attack last month.

She began to cry and shake, but he soldiered on.

He told her the malfunction and fire resulted from a cyberattack. It wasn't a mechanical failure but an intentional act of sabotage.

Brooke closed her eyes and tried to control her breathing.

He explained the attackers demanded a hundred-and-fifty-million-dollar ransom or they would disclose sensitive financial information about everyone who ever visited the resort.

Brooke shook her head in disbelief.

Tom had never spoken about his work for his clients with Brooke before, but today he was breaking his golden rule.

He told her about Phoenix Holdings. That it owned a small parcel of land on the banks of Bensonville Reservoir that extended to the border of the ski resort, and that Faith and the Castle Ridge Town Council retained him to obtain an injunction to prevent the company from developing the land. He told her about Phoenix's offer to purchase the resort as part of a global settlement to do away with the injunction and resolve the litigation, and Faith's rejection of the offer. He explained that Phoenix was behind the ransomware attack as a way to persuade Faith to sell the resort because she would need the funds generated by the sale in order to pay the ransom and protect thousands of families from having their financial information disclosed on the dark web.

Brooke paid rapt attention, a stunned look crossing her face.

He returned to the notecard and said it made an ominous reference to something horrific happening on the Fourth of July. Whoever sent it said he had to pursue the deal to sell the resort, likely as a way to gather more information that would allow him to prevent whatever was planned for July Fourth. He explained the notecard warned him to trust no one, that he was being watched, and that Brooke and Aneilia would be harmed if he told anyone what he knew. He'd been trying to protect them all this time. That's why he hadn't gone to the authorities.

Brooked cupped her mouth and gasped. She looked at Aneilia, sleeping in her bed.

He grabbed Brooke's hands and held them tightly.

He explained that he finally convinced Faith to sell the resort to Phoenix Holdings but he never intended to go through with the deal. He was trying to come up with ways to stall the deal so he could find more evidence.

Brooke looked confused and finally spoke up.

"Why does Phoenix Holdings want the resort so badly that it sabotaged the business and killed so many people in the process?" She paused to catch her breath again. "What the hell is it planning for July Fourth and what does the resort have to do with it?"

Brooke was asking all the right questions, the same ones he had tossed around in his mind ever since he received the first notecard. That's when he shared with her his investigation into Phoenix Holdings, with Claire's help, and that Bradley Mitchelson had been a consultant to Phoenix Holdings Group.

Brooke was shocked Bradley figured into this. They hadn't seen him since they left Washington, D.C., five years ago. Tom could see the wheels spinning in her head. She was trying to figure things out, just like she always did.

He told her about Phoenix Holdings' interest in the Swiss chemical company and the venture that was rebuilding a massive water tunnel in New York City, and the maps and diagrams of the City's water supply system that Claire uncovered. At last, he told her about the second note-card, the one delivered to his office yesterday morning, before Aneilia's abduction, telling him Phoenix Holdings knew he was onto them and that his family was in peril. An hour later Aneilia was kidnapped.

"Phoenix Holdings kidnapped Aneilia," Brooke whispered angrily. She buried her head in Tom's chest. "I can't believe this is happening," she continued. "Not after everything we've been through. Let's leave Castle Ridge. For real this time. Before Phoenix Holdings follows through on its plan."

Tom put his hand under her chin to raise her head and look into her eyes. He was about to tell her what he believed Phoenix Holdings was planning when he saw Brooke's eyes widen. She shifted in her chair and sat up straight. She cleared her throat and took a deep breath and looked as though she'd just discovered the earth was round.

"Phoenix Holdings is planning to poison New York City's water supply, isn't it? That's why it wants to purchase the resort. So it can control the land around the Bensonville Reservoir without anyone interfering with its plans to poison the water. Oh, my God. It's going to kill millions of people in New York City,"

Tom leaned back. He didn't need to say it. She had figured it out.

"We need to stop this. We need to figure out who sent you the notecards. Whoever it is knows what's happening and wants you to stop it. We've got to find a way to stop it from happening!"

Tom was relieved and frightened at the same time. Brooke was now aware of the nightmare he'd been living ever since his brutal attack. She knew almost everything he did.

"Listen to me very carefully. There's one more thing you need to know. I need to tell you what else I've done."

42

Chet didn't immediately make it back to Castle Ridge after Aneilia's kidnapping.

It was early evening and he was a few miles from the Castle Ridge exit on the Thruway. Aneilia was safe at Mercy Hospital and being checked out by doctors, but Chet didn't know anything about that. His phone was securely stowed in the glove compartment of the art gallery truck and he didn't hear the pings meant to alert him to the dozens of text alerts about what had happened. He saw overhead signs at several points along the way indicating an amber alert had been issued for a yellow school bus, but he had no idea who was onboard or its connection to Castle Ridge.

The first indication something wasn't right was when he saw flashing lights of a sheriff's deputy vehicle in his side view mirror. Chet took his foot off the gas and immediately looked at his speedometer. It only read sixty, well enough below the speed limit, he thought. When the state trooper didn't pass him and stayed on his tail, he knew the flashing lights were meant for him. He slowly drifted to the shoulder and put on his four-way flashers. Less than a minute later, a second sheriff's vehicle, also with lights flashing, joined the first one behind his truck. Two sheriff's vehicles for one stopped truck wasn't a good sign.

His pulse quickened and his hands were clammy as he watched the deputies exit their vehicles, speak to one another, and then approach his truck from both sides. He grabbed his wallet, took out his license, and reached for the truck's registration in the glove box. He also pulled out the bill of lading for the load of children's clothing he was transporting.

"Are you Chet Carpenter?" one of the deputies said.

He was shocked they knew his name.

"Yes. How do you know that? Why did you pull me over? I wasn't speeding."

"Mr. Carpenter, would you mind stepping out of the vehicle and walking back to my cruiser. There's someone who would like to speak with you on the phone."

Chet didn't know what to make of the situation.

"What's this all about? Who wants to talk to me?"

"Please come with me, Sir."

Chet hesitated for a moment but ultimately did as he was told. He exited the truck and followed the command to walk to the passenger side of the first cruiser behind his truck. The other deputy was standing there with the door open holding a cell phone. He handed it to Chet.

"Chet, this is Tom. Can you hear me?"

Cars and trucks sped by just a few feet away from him, making it difficult for him to hear. He put his free hand over his other ear to muffle the noise and pressed the phone closer to his head.

"Do I need a lawyer already? I wasn't speeding or anything. What's this all about?"

"Chet, listen to me very carefully," Tom said. "I can't get into the details right now, but the deputies will be escorting you to a warehouse near Castle Ridge where they'll take possession of the truck. You're not in any trouble and you haven't done anything wrong. In fact, you're a hero for what you did today. Just follow their directions, hand over the keys when you get to the warehouse, and they'll drive you back to the art gallery, okay?"

Chet had a million questions and wanted to ask them all but recognized this wasn't the time or place.

"Whatever you say, Tom."

"Thanks, buddy. I'll explain everything when I see you. Oh, and if you read or hear anything about Aneilia, know that she's safe. We all are. And you're a big reason why."

The production manager at Societe Robolex's facility outside Bern, Switzerland, read the email when he arrived early the following morning. It was the third email from Waddah in just two days, or so he thought.

Further to my email from yesterday morning regarding accelerated implementation of our Grand Plan, I hereby direct immediate shipment of twenty tons of Zincar for delivery via Global Air Charter to John F. Kennedy International Airport, New York, for onward shipment via Manatee Trucking for delivery to a staging area north of New York City. The specific address will follow. Confirm receipt of instructions and provide a copy of bill of lading.

The production manager read the email twice, but it still didn't make any sense. He double checked the date of the email to make sure it was current. He clicked over to the delivery spreadsheet which confirmed that ten tons of Zincar, disguised as children's clothing, had been shipped less than twenty-four hours earlier and had already arrived and was picked up by a ground courier for delivery to Castle Ridge, New York. This email must have been sent in error. He toggled back to the email and clicked on the reply icon.

Waddah – your email above was well received but must have been sent in error as we shipped product last night as directed by your second email received yesterday. Ten tons of Zincar were shipped pursuant to your instructions. Arrival confirmed at JFK this morning and cargo consigned to an over-the-ground courier for onward delivery to Castle Ridge. Kindly confirm receipt of cargo. To the extent your instructions call for an additional shipment of twenty tons of Zincar, request denied. We have an insufficient supply of product to comply with your instructions. The earliest date for the next shipment will be in thirty days.

Waddah picked up the phone as soon as he finished reading the email.

"Anastasia, we've experienced a major unauthorized network incursion. The American lawyer managed to breach our security protocols and gain access to our network. He arranged for a shipment of Zincar to Castle Ridge. It arrived in New York this morning."

43

Tom told Brooke about Project PAWNED and about Darryl's invaluable assistance. Brooke was frightened and recoiled after learning what Tom had done. She worried hacking into Phoenix Holdings' network meant Tom could be prosecuted and disbarred. But Tom explained his rationale for doing what he did. It was the only option that made sense to him, he said. He needed to get proof of Phoenix Holdings' involvement in the conspiracy and what it was planning to do with the New York City water supply. He told her he needed that evidence before he could guarantee authorities would act and agree to protect him and his family. If he sounded the alarm too soon and went to the authorities before he had enough evidence to allow them to take down Phoenix Holdings, he risked something terrible happening to Brooke and Aneilia. That what the note-cards warned...

Remain silent or Brooke and Aneilia will perish.

He told Brooke he didn't care what happened to him or his career as long as he protected his family and prevented a mass tragedy involving millions of people.

Brooke sat up straight and stared into his eyes. With a steely resolve she often displayed when matters of her family were at stake, she spoke in a firm voice: "There are so many things about you I adore and respect you for. But I have never been prouder of you than I am at this moment. I love you."

With Aneilia resting comfortably, and armed state troopers posted outside her hospital room, Tom and Brooke retired to their room in the McReynolds Residences, the hotel-style wing of Mercy Hospital available at no cost to families of patients in the hospital. It was built with the generosity of Faith McReynolds and her family who paid for its construction and endowed a fund for its future operations.

When they arrived, the troopers who escorted Tom and Brooke told them a visitor was waiting for them in the lobby. As they turned to walk through the lobby doors, Tom saw Darryl standing there in her black leather jacket. He introduced her to Brooke.

"I'm glad Aneilia's okay," Darryl said.

Brooke reached for her hand. "You're an incredible person. Tom told me what you did. Thank you for protecting my family and the resort."

Darryl glanced at Tom.

"She knows everything. I told her what we did."

Darryl softly smiled and exhaled.

"I spoke with my contacts at DHS and arranged for a meeting tomorrow morning with DHS and the FBI to hand over the hard drive. We still need to prevent the mass terrorist attack," Darryl said.

Tom leaned in. "Did you look at the hard drive? Do we have enough evidence?"

"I skimmed the contents of the drive. It looks to be more than enough. A motherload."

Tom pumped his fist and squeezed Brooke's hand.

"Tom, I want to thank you for including me in your plan and allowing me to help you," Darryl said. "When you kicked me out of Faith's office this week, I thought it was because you didn't trust me."

"Just the opposite," Tom responded with an earnest smile. "I wanted to protect you for as long as I could. I'll see you in the morning."

Brooke and Tom were lying in bed in the McReynolds Residences having a tough time falling asleep when Brooke spoke up.

"I've been thinking about everything that's happened and everything you told me, especially the notecards you received. Is it possible that Bradley Mitchelson sent them to you?"

Tom didn't respond. He closed his eyes and silently prayed that it was so, that his former boss was on his team, and hadn't gone rogue to the dark side working against him.

The next morning, Brooke and Tom prepared for what appeared to anyone watching to be a normal day—after a kidnapping. Fresh, clean clothes, winter coats and brand-new sneakers that pretty much fit had been delivered to their room.

Details had been worked out overnight by several agencies coordinating with each other including the New York State Police, Castle Ridge Constable Office, the Monroe County Sheriff Department, and the FBI. DHS and the Department of Defense were informed of preliminary data and the working hypothesis, and immediately issued a code orange alert which meant logistical preparations were underway for potential mobilization within the next twenty-four to forty-eight hours.

When the discharge papers were finally signed at 10:30 a.m., Brooke and Aneilia hopped into the back of a white SUV with blacked out windows and black lettering on the driver and passenger doors reading *Castle Ridge Resort* for the drive back to their cabin. But instead of a resort employee at the wheel, an FBI agent from the Albany Field Office wearing a bulletproof vest, with an earpiece stuck in his ear, sat in the driver's seat. Although the SUV was the only vehicle exiting the hospital's parking lot, within a block of leaving the hospital campus, it was joined by a motorcade consisting of an aged white panel van with a brand new 6.6. liter turbodiesel V-8 engine with Allison transmission—and an armed tactical unit inside; a souped-up Honda Accord with an Uber-Eats placard in the front windshield; and a red GMC 3500 HD pick-up truck with the name of a roofing company stenciled on its sides and back. No government-issued Chevy Impalas were going to be used in this caravan. Each vehicle was driven by a veteran FBI agent specially selected from a group expertly trained in evasive driving maneuvers.

The motorcade missed the Castle Ridge exit on the thruway and continued driving in a loop, first south, then west, and then northeast for several hours until it reached Pratsville AFB in a remote part of northern New York State. For the second time in five years, Brooke, this time with Aneilia in tow, would wait out the approaching storm from a fortified military installation where they would receive round-the-clock protection.

Tom was hustled into the front passenger seat of a black Yukon XL. To his surprise, Aronson, still nursing a headache and on pain meds for his broken ribs, was seated in the back seat. They would keep each other company for the drive to the FBI Albany Field Office escorted by state troopers and armed FBI agents.

"I heard what you did yesterday to help find my daughter. Brooke and I can't begin to thank you."

"Don't mention it," Aronson said. "I figured I owed you one. Maybe it can make up for what happened in D.C. five years ago." Although Tom appreciated the words, he thought there was an edge to Aronson's voice. He wondered if Aronson was the one holding a grudge now, perhaps for the way he was treated when he first visited Tom in the hospital a little over a month ago, or maybe because Tom ignored the advice about not paying ransom to Revolutionary Avengers. They were quiet for most of the ride, and Aronson said they'd discuss specific details of what was planned for the day when they arrived at the SCIF in Albany.

The Yukon XL, followed by the state trooper vehicle and an SUV with armed FBI agents inside, entered the secure underground parking garage of the federal office building in downtown Albany. A perimeter had been set up around the building with federal and state officers carrying assault rifles stationed every hundred meters. Tom and Aronson were whisked to the sixth floor by armed agents. When they entered the SCIF's anteroom, Aronson grabbed Tom's arm and motioned him over to a corner.

"I wanted to wait until we were in a SCIF before raising this with you."

Tom thought Aronson was going to relay details about yesterday's accident with the school bus and finding Aneilia, but he quickly realized Aronson had other things on his mind.

"Based on information that's been conveyed to me, my understanding is that you and Darryl engaged in some pretty risky stuff last night." Aronson sounded frustrated, and Tom assumed this was why he seemed annoyed in the SUV.

"Look, when the stakes are my wife and daughter, and potentially something unimaginable, I'll do whatever I need to do."

Aronson raised his eyebrows and shook his head. Tom wasn't sure Aronson was aware of what they might find on the hard drive.

"Still, I can think of at least seven federal codes you likely violated, as well as multiple ethical rules governing lawyers' conduct. Did you consider the repercussions of what you did for you and your family?"

"I did. And I'd do it the same way again if I had to. I'll do anything to protect my family and innocent lives, and you'd understand if you knew what I know. I'm at peace with the choices I made and have no regrets."

"Tom, think about it. You're the attorney for the Town of Castle Ridge and its mayor, and you're involved in a pending litigation against Phoenix Holdings. You can't go hacking into your adversary's computer systems to obtain evidence." Aronson whispered the last sentence.

Tom held his ground.

"If I lose my law license, so be it. Phoenix Holdings is fucking with my life and my family's life."

"May I remind you that you were also the second highest law enforcement official in the U.S. Government until just a few years ago. President Ferguson still has two years left in her second term. The administration doesn't need a scandal on its hands. Some folks on the other side of the aisle would have a field day with this if they knew what you did. Can you imagine the headlines? 'Former Ferguson Administration DOJ Official Engaged in Hacking to Benefit Private Client.'"

"I'll take the heat. I'll make it clear to everyone that I was acting on my own, as a private citizen, and what I did has nothing to do with the Administration. I'll handle whatever comes my way."

"I admire your principles, Tom, but they don't get you very far in D.C. or in politics these days. Look, I'm on your side, and I'm going to try to protect you," Aronson said, his tone less hostile now. "Here's what we're going to do. When we go into that room, follow my lead and play along. You're here both as a victim and as legal counsel to Castle Ridge Ski Resort and to the Mayor of Castle Ridge, but that's the extent of your involvement in what you did. I've spoken with Darryl and she's eager to help."

Tom was about to explain that he was prepared to deal with this situation on his own when Aronson cut him off.

"Counselor. The decision's been made. You and your family have suffered enough in service to our nation. I told you when I visited you in the hospital that our country is indebted to you, and I meant it. Everyone has much to lose if the truth were to come out, including you. You're a smart guy and this is a good deal. Take it. If not for you, then for your wife and that beautiful little girl of yours. I've got your back. Now let's go in there." Aronson walked away before Tom could say anything.

Darryl was already in the room with agents and intelligence analysts from DHS and the FBI when Tom followed Aronson in. The external hard drive was on the table. She stood ramrod tall and stared right at Tom. For a second, he thought she might salute him again, but then she nodded her head and smiled. Tom smiled back.

As Aronson took his seat, he pressed the red record button on the control panel in front of him and began speaking.

"My name is Douglas Aronson, and I am the Deputy Director of the Federal Bureau of Investigations." After stating the date and time, their location, and reciting the names of the people seated around the table, Aronson read the script prepared for him by FBI lawyers.

"Private citizen Darryl Stratford informed the FBI last night that she is in possession of information she believes constitutes evidence of the commission of certain crimes as well as evidence of a conspiracy to commit future crimes."

As Aronson was reading from the script, Tom was readying his own speech. He had cleared what he was going to say with Faith, and she was on board. If Aronson and Darryl were going to protect his hide, the least he could do was give them cover. Aronson cleared his throat and continued.

"Ms. Stratford advised me that she obtained this information on her own, without assistance from any government or law enforcement agency, or any other person." Aronson looked directly at Tom. "Nor is Ms. Stratford operating at the direction of, or as an agent or instrumentality of, any government or law enforcement agency. This office was unaware of Ms. Stratford's conduct until she informed me of her activities. The FBI has not previously seen the information Ms. Stratford claims to possess, and did not provide any assistance to her to obtain this information. She did this completely on her own." Tom heard the emphasis Aronson placed on the last sentence before continuing with his statement. "The purpose of this video is to record the transfer of this information, for the first time, from Ms. Stratford to the FBI in order to establish chain of custody of the information."

Tom sighed heavily.

"Mr. Thomas Berte is here in a dual capacity. He is a victim of certain alleged crimes uncovered by Ms. Stratford. As such, his presence may be useful to corroborate and confirm information to establish its evidentiary significance. He is also counsel to Faith McReynolds, the Mayor of Castle Ridge, who also happens to be the owner of Castle Ridge Ski Resort, which is also a victim of alleged crimes uncovered by Ms. Stratford. The time now is 12:55 p.m. and the FBI will take possession of the hard drive from Ms. Stratford."

"Before you do, I'd like to make a statement for the record," Tom said in a booming voice.

Aronson jumped out of his chair and was reaching for the control panel, but Tom started speaking before Aronson could turn off the video recorder. Tom spoke quickly.

"Mr. Deputy Director, I wouldn't insist on making a statement unless it was important. As both a victim and counsel to the ski resort, I respectfully request that I have a right to be heard."

Before Aronson could object, Tom glared at him and held his stare. He raised his eyebrows and slowly nodded his head up and down. He hoped Aronson understood his message: trust me.

After a few seconds Aronson relented and sat back down.

"About a week ago, a cyber breach incident incapacitated the Castle Ridge Ski Resort computer network," Tom began. "The resort's management learned of the breach within a day of the horrific incident involving the malfunction of a chairlift and resulting fire that caused the death of hundreds, with hundreds more injured." Tom took a breath. "The resort's management received a message indicating a connection between the cyberattack and the fire. Then perpetrators of the cyberattack threatened to release sensitive and confidential financial information of everyone who's ever visited the resort unless a large ransom was paid to unlock the resort's computer network."

Tom considered saying more, that his vicious attack was also perpetrated by the same evil cast of characters, but there'd be time for that later.

"All of this coincided with an offer to purchase the resort made by an entity called Phoenix Holdings. Ms. Stratford is employed by my client as head of security. I consulted with Ms. Stratford and based on certain information in our possession, suspicion turned to Phoenix Holdings as the possible perpetrator of the cyberattack. Ms. Stratford undertook an investigation into Phoenix Holdings, and I assisted her. As the attorney for the resort. The results of that investigation are contained on the external hard drive on the table in front of us. Discussions between Ms. Stratford and myself, and details of the information in our possession that led to the investigation, are protected from disclosure by the attorney client privilege and the attorney work product privilege. Neither Ms. Stratford nor I will reveal them."

Tom sat back in his seat and looked first at Darryl and then at Aaronson. For the first time in days, he felt at ease. He closed his eyes and images of Aneilia screaming and crying alone in the school bus flashed before him. The memory of Brooke collapsing in the community center came rushing back. He'd promised to do everything he could to protect his family from harm. He almost failed once. He wasn't about to fail again. Hacking into Phoenix Holdings computer network and turning over the download of that information to the government, was his way of keeping that promise. Some evils require a higher justice.

"Mr. Deputy Director, we are pleased to turn over the hard drive to the custody of the United States Government."

The video continued recording as the team leader of intelligence analysts from the DHS connected it to a computer on the table. After a couple clicks of the mouse, she landed on the directory of files. The legend at the bottom of the screen indicated the drive contained two terabytes of data.

Within minutes the lead analyst found a document entitled "Manifesto: Death to the Infidels Resulting from Poisoning the New York City Drinking Water Supply on the Fourth of July."

44

He began hearing increased activity within the compound in the early dawn hours. Looking out the window of his prison cell, in between the bars, he noticed small groups of men scurrying to the security command center. A column of trucks with SCUD missiles stacked in the payload lined the compound's perimeter. In the distance, he saw a battery of anti-aircraft defense systems, likely a combination of patriot missiles left behind by U.S. forces, and Russian-made BUK missiles, being staged around His Eminence's residence. Throughout his captivity at the compound, he'd never seen this type of heightened activity. His messages must have reached Tom.

He was wracked with guilt. He heard rumors of plans for a massive attack, one that would make 9/11 look insignificant by comparison. In the beginning, when he was instrumental in Phoenix Holdings Group's award of a massive contract for the reconstruction of a critical water tunnel bringing fresh drinking water to the residents of New York City, he assumed it was part of the company's strategic growth initiative. When he was consulted on Phoenix's acquisition of a large construction outfit, he figured it was just another step in the expansion of its holdings. He was compensated handsomely, and his reputation enhanced immensely, even beyond the stature he enjoyed as a senator, and then later as Attorney General of the United States. He welcomed the attention and craved the publicity, and took great pleasure in flaunting his newly found status and the wealth that came with it.

When he learned of the purchase of a small swath of land in upstate New York, he considered it insignificant. When the lawsuit was filed and he was informed that attorney Tom Berte represented the plaintiffs, he freely gave his opinion that attorney Berte was one of the finest attorneys he'd ever met. He possessed a brilliant legal mind with excellent judgment, was a savvy negotiator, and would do whatever was necessary to protect his client's interests. He told Anastasia Maine that attorney Berte would be a formidable opponent. He offered to intervene and speak with Tom in an attempt to find a resolution mutually agreeable to all parties. But his offer was rebuffed.

When he later received an invitation from Anastasia to discuss the lawsuit Tom had filed, he assumed his client had reconsidered his offer. But he was wrong. Disillusionment came quickly. Anastasia and Waddah instructed him to demand that Tom withdraw the lawsuit and to take whatever action was necessary to ensure Tom's compliance. When the former Attorney General resisted, he was threatened. Waddah said he was in possession of information connecting him with the illegal activities that brought down the law firm he once worked for before entering politics. The former attorney general called their bluff and refused to cater to their demands. He was soon marginalized and cut off from the financial benefits he long enjoyed.

It was around this time that he began to hear the rumors. When he was shown excerpts of the manifesto and heard audio recordings of His Eminence's rantings and calls for war against the infidels and promises of eternal salvation for the martyrs, he could stay silent no more. He never imagined his client would undertake such a diabolical scheme to seek retribution against the United States. But by the time he decided to alert the authorities, it was too late. While spending a restless night in a hotel room in Dusseldorf, Germany months earlier, he heard the door to his room open. Two men wearing hoods rushed in and threw him against the wall. Before he could react, a handkerchief was placed over his mouth and nose. The sedative worked. He awoke hours later in a room with bars on the window, similar to the one he was now occupying. His wife, Beverly, who had been in the hotel room with him, was also taken prisoner. He had not seen her since.

After several months of confinement, he slowly began to cultivate a relationship with a young guard who would eventually be his emissary to Tom. The guard, too, had become disillusioned with His Eminence's preachings of revenge and martyrdom and agreed to facilitate communications between his prisoner and the American lawyer. The first notecard came too late to prevent the tragedy at the ski resort, but he disclosed all he knew. The guard's understanding of English was rudimentary at best, and the notecard contained only a brief summary of the message he intended to deliver. But, still, he was confident Tom would grasp the gravity of the situation and do whatever was necessary to prevent execution of the Grand Plan.

When he learned about the production of a viral agent in Societe Robolex's facility in Bern, Switzerland, and that a test shipment of an innocuous decoy was being sent to Castle Ridge, he convinced the young guard to contact the courier just before the shipment left Bern and change the consignee's name to Tom's. He hoped that if the shipment was intercepted by the authorities, Tom would be notified and it would provide him with another clue to help him uncover the plot.

And when he learned that Waddah had discovered Tom's investigation into Phoenix's holdings, he and the guard rushed to send Tom the second notecard.

But two questions continued to haunt him: Did Tom have enough information, and did he have enough time to stop the tragedy that would soon unfold?

It was all there. Reports, memos, charts, graphs, maps, pamphlets, correspondence and more. Multiple documents set forth a web of companies and organizations making up Phoenix Holdings Group. Among Phoenix's coterie of businesses were banks, shipping and transportation interests, software development and engineering companies, manufacturing plants and chemical laboratories, oil drillers and refineries, construction entities, real estate developments including hotels, office towers, and residential complexes, and financial services providers, including purveyors of insurance, consulting, accounting services, and securities and commodity brokerages. All appeared to be legitimate businesses on paper. The entities were vast and diverse and spanned the globe, from the Americas to Europe, from Asia to the Middle East. Charts with intersecting lines looked like a spaghetti bowl of interconnected businesses with names like Societe Robolex, Eagle Industries, Manatee Trucking, Global Air Charters, Diversified Financial Services, and Pendulum Holdings. The annual revenue was calculated to be in the tens of trillions and the annual profit was estimated to be in the hundreds of billions. At the top of the organization sat Phoenix Holdings. Its leader was known simply as His Eminence.

The hard drive also contained maps of the desert compound that served as Phoenix's headquarters. Detailed colored drawings showed steel-reinforced fortified bunkers and a web of high-tech gadgetry including security cameras, radar installations, audio transmitters, and thermal imaging sensors built into the compound's perimeter walls. Coordinates showed precise locations for weapon depots and sentry posts. The compound was guarded by an army of soldiers and a network of limited but high-powered precision-guided weaponry.

Due to the volume of data streams on the hard drive, the DHS analysts divided the files among them, each taking a grouping for an initial review. A detailed forensic examination would come later, when the hard drive was sent to Washington. For now, Deputy Director Aronson requested a preliminary assessment, just to understand what he was dealing with.

One of the DHS analysts clicked on a file named *The Promised Prophecy*. After reading a few lines, she asked Aronson to look at the document. Tom and Darryl were invited to look over her shoulder.

It is our divine right to seek retribution against the United States. The infidels have brought forth evils of mind and spirit and seek to eradicate our society and our beliefs. They have occupied our land, corrupted our thoughts, and poisoned our culture. A decade ago the imperialists annihilated our village, our people, and our way of life using weapons of destruction. Innocent lives were taken and the dreams of a people were destroyed. Halima, Zara, and Hamza were but three of the hundreds murdered by the imperialists, their bodies ravaged and pulverized by the arsenal of evil weaponry. While the imperialists and infidels ply their trade of occupation, death, and destruction under the banner of freedom and democracy, the truth is their endeavors are contrary to the will of the Almighty, and undertaken in order to dominate our people and destroy the will of the Messiah. It is just and right to avenge the death of our brothers and sisters. With the remnants of destruction of our village still wafting in the air and lingering in our hearts, I vow revenge and death to those that brought us eternal grief. The loss we endured shall not be in vain, but shall stir within us the strength bestowed upon us by divine mercy to restore our faith and our dignity. We shall rise from the ashes to take our rightful place among the peoples of the world and conquer those who seek to eradicate our cause and do us harm. To accomplish our goal, we must strike at the heart of the infidels. The suffering they have wrought on others will be cast upon them. A decade ago we embarked on formulating the Grand Plan. The time has come to execute the Plan and to reward the sacrifices our people have long endured. Their most critical resource that brings them nourishment and sustains their daily lives shall become their venom.

Aronson, Tom, and Darryl stood in stunned silence as they read the document. Before any of them could speak, the analyst asked them to look at another set of files she'd located. They contained detailed maps showing Bensonville Reservoir and gravity-fed viaducts connecting to aquifers eventually leading to a massive water tunnel connected to transmission trunk mains, distribution pipes, and service lines feeding every home, apartment and business throughout the five boroughs of New York City. Graphs showed the rate of water flowing south and measured time and distance from immersion to reaction.

"They're going to unleash a poison into the drinking water system of New York City," Aronson said, sounding as though he was trying to make sense of what he was saying. "They're planning a mass poisoning to destroy an entire city."

"Sir, there's another file you should see," the analyst urged. With a few clicks of the mouse, she toggled over to a video and pressed play. It was grainy and black and white, but slowly tiny creatures in the video came into view. Dozens of white mice confined in a cage scurried to bottles attached to the side walls. They began ingesting the liquid content of the bottles.

Almost immediately some began to shake violently and foam at the mouth before collapsing. Others stiffened and fell, motionless. The swollen bodies of a few of the tiny creatures turned from a bright white to a sickly yellow before stumbling and curling into a round ball. In each case, death came quickly. Within less than a minute, all of the tiny creatures stopped moving.

When the video finished playing, the analyst brought up a chart containing formulas calculating the volume of a viral agent called Zincar. Small script at the bottom of the graph identified the manufacturer of Zincar as Societe Robolex, Bern, Switzerland. Tom had guessed right.

"We need to get our hands on a sample of Zincar to test its composition and its chemistry," Aronson said to no one in particular.

"I think I can help with that," Tom said, looking at Darryl. "Call Constable Ozzie. He'll know where you can find a sample."

Before Aronson could ask another question, the analyst spoke up again. "Sir, we've found another file you should look at."

The analyst pulled up a calendar on the screen. July 1 was circled in red and the words "Deadline for immersion of Zincar in Bensonville Reservoir" were typed next to the date. Aronson let out a deep breath. July 4 was also circled in red. He slowly read the typed text within the circle. "The effects of Zincar in its victims will be evident beginning July 4." He paused and looked at Tom. "This is fucking unbelievable. That's less than five months from now."

"Actually, Sir, those dates may no longer be accurate," the analyst said.

Tom looked at her in confusion. "What do you mean, we just saw the calendar. It says July 4 and that's consistent with other information I have."

"That may have been true, Sir, at one time, but it appears the timeline of the events we're talking about have been altered. Listen to this." The technician clicked on an audio file, and then clicked the 'play' icon. The voices were clear.

Proceed as you intend with the American lawyer, but I am concerned about what he knows and what he may do with the information he's learned. Our people have labored too hard and sacrificed too much for our efforts to be jeopardized. The lawyer has done much to thwart our use of the reservoir. Let him continue to focus his efforts there. But I want us to move expeditiously to implement the Grand Plan now, without further interruptions.

But how will that help us? The lawyer will continue to delay the sale of the land we covet, a male voice asked.

The first voice was heard again:

We must modify the point of access. Instead of immersing Zincar in Bensonville Reservoir, we must utilize the back-up site to the north of our target area. We already have Zincar pre-positioned there in mobile tank vessels. The effects will not be as widespread, and fewer victims will be sacrificed, but our goal will still be achieved. I will not allow the American lawyer or his client or any official instrumentality of the infidels to derail our plans. Death must come swiftly and our prayers must be answered. I command that Zincar be immersed at the alternate site as soon as possible. Keep me apprised of all developments immediately as and when they occur.

"Sir, that audio was recorded two days ago," the analyst said.

45

"Continue to search the hard drive. Let me know immediately if you find anything related to the location of the alternate site. We don't know how much time we have to stop it!"

Aronson shouted commands to the analysts while he hurriedly called his deputy and asked him to arrange a call with the FBI Director and the National Security Advisor to the President. The stakes had just increased exponentially. Instead of having almost five months to prevent the deadliest mass killing in history, the deadline had narrowed. It might have even passed.

"Tom, Darryl, as you can see, things are moving quickly and I need to pivot my attention to the next twenty-four hours. The analysts will continue to drill down on the contents of the hard drive. You'll both be taken to a secure location to wait out whatever the hell is going to happen. Tom, that's likely the same location where Brooke and Aneilia are, but you'll be provided with detailed instructions." Aronson turned his back and began walking out of the room while continuing to speak to the two of them, but they weren't following him.

"Why are you two standing there, we need to move."

"I'm not leaving. I think I can be more helpful here," Tom said forcefully.

Darryl glanced at Tom and nodded in agreement. "I'm with Tom. If he's staying, I'm staying."

Aronson was about to protest when Tom interrupted him.

"Look, were it not for Darryl and me, you wouldn't have that recording. We got you this far and we want to see it through. These bastards nearly took my life and destroyed my family."

He saw Aronson scowl and knew he hadn't persuaded him, so he pressed on.

"Besides, I think I may know the location of the alternate site Phoenix Holdings will use to poison New York City's drinking water supply."

Waddah gathered his men in an underground bunker deep within the compound. A hushed silence fell over the group, numbering well into the thirties, as they sat cross-legged on the dirt floor and trained their eyes on their warrior leader. Holding a tablet and standing in front of a large screen, Waddah pulled up a satellite image of a park twenty-seven miles north of Times Square. Trees were barren and the landscape was a patchwork of brown bare spots. As he zoomed in closer, it was clear the park was a construction site, with piles of dirt, pallets of material, and heavy machinery and equipment strewn about. Arrayed around a large excavation pit were six tanker-size trucks with large diameter hoses connected to a drilling derrick sitting atop a makeshift bridge over the center of the pit.

"Through the wisdom and courage of His Eminence, and by the grace of the Almighty, we will soon implement the Grand Plan. Our work is nearing completion. The timeline for execution of the Grand Plan, and our salvation and redemption from evil, has been accelerated. This image on the screen is an intake valve chamber that is part of the New York water tunnel construction project intended to connect water supply sources from the northern parts of New York state to the maze of distribution lines in New York City. It extends to a depth of four hundred and twenty feet, from the surface of the land to the immense water tunnel below. In approximately fifteen hours, the sacrifices our people have made over the last ten years will begin to bear fruit, and our long-suffering brothers and sisters will finally receive the justice they deserve."

The men exalted His Eminence with psalms of gratitude.

Waddah focused the image on the tanker trucks arrayed around the derrick and continued with his presentation.

"In fifteen hours, the liquid contents of those vessels, the liquid that is our salvation and was created by servants of His Eminence, will be injected directly into the intake valve chamber. Within three to five hours, the water that flows out of seventy-five percent of the faucets in New York City will be laced with Zincar, the chemical mixture that will bring instant death to the infidels. Long live His Eminence, and may the Almighty grant our people the peace and everlasting salvation they justly deserve."

The men whispered words of thanksgiving and joy for His Eminence as Waddah spoke up again.

"We must prepare for the war of revenge the infidels will no doubt unleash upon us. I suspect the response will be swift and may begin in as soon as several days from now. Pursuant to His Eminence's instructions, we have fortified the compound with the infidels' own weapons that we have captured. Our soldiers must be prepared to wage a long and enduring battle. As leaders of our cause, you must empower your men to do all that is within their power to protect our people. The glory of life everlasting is ours if we choose wisely and defeat the imperialist army that will soon seek to destroy us. Bow your heads in preparation to receive a blessing from His Eminence."

The men did as they were told. They lowered their heads, closed their eyes, and draped prayer shawls over their shoulders. Waddah pressed a button on the tablet and within seconds the sound of His Eminence's voice filled the bunker.

When the prayer was finished, two of the men in the huddle broke away and opened a canvas bag. They retrieved a dirty and stained item and unfurled it between them as others formed the traditional ring of death around the two men. As they chanted the Almighty's prayer, a third man reached for a lit candle and edged closer to a tattered corner of the rectangular fabric stretched taut. Placing the flame against the fabric, the men's chants grew louder as the American flag burned brightly within the circle of death.

From her penthouse apartment on Millionaire's Row near the southern end of Central Park, thousands of miles away from the desert headquarters of the regimen of warriors and their leader to whom she pledged her allegiance, Anastasia listened intently to the sermon and prayers echoing through her phone. In the bright morning sunlight streaming in through the floor to ceiling windows, she caught a glimpse of her reflection as she stared to the north and imagined preparations taking place at that very moment to carryout out the final stages of the Grand Plan. She took a drag from her vape pen and surveyed the city landscape spread before her. She could almost hear the last gasps of life and suffocating pleas uttered by the millions of residents of this beautiful city she had called home for a decade. In just a matter of hours, the prayers of her people would be answered. All that she had worked hard to achieve under the guiding hand of His Eminence and his trusted lieutenant Waddah would be realized amid a deluge of death and agony.

She envisioned the chaos and devastation that would ensue once the water started flowing, but she felt no remorse. Her cause was just and the consequence necessary to avenge the death of her unborn child in the attack on the village of Al-Kharabi that caused her to lose the most important people in her life. The concussive blast struck without warning, killing her husband and throwing her across the room. She awoke in a field, covered in blood, unable to move, bones in her legs and pelvis shattered. Doctors worked valiantly to save her life but were unable to save the life of her unborn child that she'd been carrying for eight months. He was buried next to his father in a mass grave along with hundreds of others killed in the nighttime raid by the infidels. Standing over the gravesite of the only family she had ever known, Anastasia pledged fealty to His Eminence and dedicated her life to the destruction of the government that had wrought so much misery in her life and to her people.

The Grand Plan was devised shortly after the sabotage of her homeland. His Eminence gathered the surviving elders and vowed to exact the type of revenge the world would not soon forget. Surrounded by the brightest minds and a dedicated army of soldiers, His Eminence set out to rebuild his empire. Anastasia's path was ordained. Although she had lost much in the massacre at the village of Al-Kharabi, she was among the survivors who vowed to devote her life to seeking retribution for the atrocities committed against her people. She attended Yale Law School and became legal advisor to His Eminence. She spearheaded negotiations eventually leading to the award of a contract to companies controlled by Phoenix Holdings to reconstruct the massive water tunnel, and she coordinated the acquisition of assets needed to fulfill the mission. She also was instrumental in acquiring land in Castle Ridge, adjacent to the Bensonville Reservoir, to gain access to the water source needed to execute the Grand Plan.

She assumed, incorrectly it turned out, that attorney Tom Berte would not be a formidable opponent. But he was tenacious in his representation of the town of Castle Ridge and the resort, and shrewd in his legal maneuverings. He succeeded in obtaining an injunction preventing Phoenix Holdings from accessing its land, and won many skirmishes along the way. She soon understood the trial scheduled for the spring would be a one-sided affair, with Phoenix Holdings the loser. That's when she altered course and began seeking victories outside the courtroom. First with the attack on Tom, and then with the hacking of the resort's computer network and sabotage of the ski lift after Faith rejected the offer to purchase the resort. The deaths that resulted from the out-of-control lift and ensuing inferno were an unavoidable consequence of the war they had long planned to wage.

The round-the-clock surveillance of Tom's activities proved useful and allowed her colleagues to learn of his investigation into the affairs of Phoenix Holdings. He was getting closer to discovering the truth. It's as if he knew what to look for. Anastasia wondered if he had received information from someone within her organization, a mole or spy perhaps, but she quickly discounted the possibility. His Eminence controlled his people with an iron fist and no one dared betray him.

When his Eminence decided to advance the timetable for executing the Grand Plan, she became less certain of her future with the organization. She suspected His Eminence was losing confidence in her abilities. There had been too many missteps and careless errors for which she would be blamed.

Anastasia glanced at her watch. Her bags were packed and her driver would soon arrive to take her to the private aviation terminal at Teterboro Airport. She did not intend to bear first-hand witness to the atrocity that would befall her adopted city. She would monitor events from a secret location—a location she kept hidden from everyone, even His Eminence.

She clutched the image of her fallen husband tightly in her hand and whispered her unborn child's name as she closed her eyes and imagined the redemption to come.

46

"How could you know where the alternate site is?" Aronson asked.

"Tom, I didn't see anything about a different immersion site in the files I downloaded," Darryl said. "It may be buried somewhere on the hard drive, but where would we even begin to look?"

"It's not in the hard drive. It's in the Holister files."

Tom reached for the phone and started dialing, but suddenly stopped. Even if the phone lines in the FBI's Field Office were secure, the lines on the other end weren't. Phoenix Holdings knew about his investigation into the company, which meant there was a good chance they knew about Claire. He couldn't risk speaking to her on the phone. No matter where he was calling from.

"Douglas, how quickly can your agents in Boston get to the Harvard Law Library to establish a secure connection into this room?"

Less than an hour later, Tom was staring at Claire on a video feed from the SCIF.

"Hi, Tom. This is certainly turning out to be a much more exciting day than I could have imagined when I awoke this morning. How can I help you?"

"Among the files you gave Janet was a photograph. It showed fireworks bursting at night with the New York City skyline in the background. It was some kind of announcement of a construction project awarded to a subsidiary of Phoenix Holdings Group. Do you remember the picture?"

"I do. I thought it odd at the time because a future date was printed on it —July 4 of this year. Yet I found it in a cache file that was inaccessible at first. The caption said something about 'independence is coming' and a water tunnel project."

"Exactly. Can you find that photograph?"

"I think I kept a copy. Let me look through my file."

Tom saw Claire rummaging through a red accordion folder, like the ones Janet brought back from her trip visiting Claire. He didn't realize how impatient he could be. Seconds seemed like hours as Claire searched for the photo. The silence was deafening. All he heard was his heart pounding in his chest.

"Here it is. I found it!" Claire announced, holding up the photo to the video monitor.

"Claire, can you find out the location of that photograph?"

"Well, I don't know. Let me retrace my search to see what I can find."

More time ticked away. Tom felt himself aging by the second. His stomach twisted and his brow was sweaty. He began rocking in his chair staring intently at Claire as she punched the keyboard on her computer.

"I found it!" she exclaimed after a few excruciating minutes.

"Beekman Central Gardens. Oh, it's a beautiful park. I've visited it many times. It's just north of the city. It offers great views of Manhattan and the skyline, and has a lovely children's carousel that my granddaughter adores..."

While Claire kept talking, one of the DHS analysts pulled up a photo of the park. But this was no ordinary photo. It was a real-time image captured just seconds earlier by a military satellite. The image would continue to be updated every ten seconds for as long as the photo remained on the screen.

"Zoom in, down at the fields, at the dirt patch," Tom directed.

The analyst did as she was told and magnified the view until the blurry tan and brown patch came into clearer view. The image was of a construction site with tens of dozens of workers in hard hats scrambling about doing various jobs, with several pieces of heavy machinery parked and in motion around large dirt piles and a large derrick. The site appeared to be walled off with a tall fence covered in black sheathing to prevent anyone from looking in. But it didn't block the view from above.

"Can you zoom in closer? What are those long cylinders around the derrick?" Aronson asked.

The analyst zoomed in tighter. The image came clearly into view.

"They're tankers. Six of them lined up around what looks like a giant hole in the ground covered with a makeshift bridge with the derrick sitting on top of it."

A second analyst pulled up an image on another screen of a similar looking derrick from a heavy equipment website.

"Sir, it says here the derrick we're looking at is a drilling derrick, capable of drilling down a vertical shaft up to six hundred feet."

"Pan over back to the fence," Tom directed the analyst controlling the satellite image. "There, zoom in on that sign, what does it say?"

Almost in unison, everyone in the room read the same words.

WORK IN PROGRESS: The New York City Department of Environmental Protection together with the New York City Infrastructure Cooperative is Proud to Undertake the Construction of an Intake Valve Chamber as part of the Reconstruction of a Water Tunnel to Bring Fresh, Clean Drinking Water to Residents of New York City.

Contractor: Eagle Industries, JV

Anticipated Completion Date: July 1.

Tom narrowed his eyes. "Eagle Industries is owned by Phoenix Industries. This has to be the alternate site. And I bet anything those tankers contain Zincar."

47

DHS analysts in the SCIF in Albany sent documents they found on the hard drive to senior military leaders in the Pentagon and liaisons at the National Security Agency, along with coordinates of the compound's location and details of its security infrastructure. After analyzing the data and confirming its authenticity, they convened a meeting in the Situation Room in the White House with the President, Vice President, Secretary of Defense, National Security Advisor, the Joint Chiefs of Staff, the Secretary of Homeland Security, and the Secretary of State, together with the CIA and FBI Directors.

When he was summoned to the White House, the FBI Director instructed Aronson to immediately get back to Washington, D.C., but Aronson had another idea. He suggested he travel instead to Pratsville Air Force Base, only a thirty-minute ride by chopper, instead of a ninety-minute flight by jet to D.C. Once at Pratsville, Aronson could log into a secure communications portal to monitor developments coming out of the Situation Room. The FBI Director agreed, and plans were made for a military helicopter to land on the helipad on the roof of the federal office building in downtown Albany. Aronson decided not to tell his boss that two guests would accompany him for the ride to Pratsville AFB. Better to beg for forgiveness than ask for permission.

Tom hesitated for a moment when he was invited to take a second helicopter ride in two days. But when he was told he'd be going to the same military installation where Brooke and Aneilia were biding their time, he was all in. Fifteen minutes later, Tom wiped his clammy palms and boarded the helicopter with Aronson and Darryl.

Five minutes before landing at Pratsville, Aronson received an encrypted message on his phone. He read it quickly and silently pumped his fist before speaking in his headset to Tom and Darryl.

"President Ferguson has approved a raid on Phoenix Holdings' desert headquarters. She's also activated a unit of the New York National Guard and soldiers from Fort Drum in New York, along with local, state and federal law enforcement officials, to take control of Beekman Central Gardens to the north of New York City. Satellite images show hurried activity near the tankers lined up next to the intake valve chamber."

Aronson's words hung in the air. Tom stared out a window at the swath of darkened wilderness below as the helicopter sliced through the frozen air toward the northern fringes of New York state. He crossed his fingers the men and women enroute to Beekman Central Gardens would arrive before the contents of the tankers were released into the New York City water supply system.

"When we land, I'm heading into a secure room to monitor events at the compound and in New York City. You're both welcome to join me."

"Seriously?" Tom said.

"I've maintained my stage three classified clearance status. I would like to join you," Darryl said. Aronson nodded his approval and turned to Tom. "What about you?"

Tom shook his head.

"Come on, Doug, you know I don't have that kind of security clearance anymore."

"Who said anything about security clearance? I've been thinking about what you said earlier. Without you we don't get to this point. Now, do you want to watch this thing unfold alongside me and Darryl?"

"Hell, yeah!"

The first drone floated in from the west at half past midnight. The watchmen manning the sentry command station didn't notice the blip on the radar screen and, as a result, didn't raise any alarms. Within minutes several more drones approached from the west forming a large cluster visible on the monitor, this time catching the watchman's attention. The cluster slowly made its way to the compound's perimeter.

Turning on the nighttime visibility sensor, the watchmen saw what he thought were dozens of small fixed-wing airborne devices approximately five hundred meters to the west of the main entrance and hovering approximately two thousand feet above the compound. He immediately switched on the high-intensity flood lights, bathing the compound's perimeter in bright light turning night into day. He pressed the alarm panel emitting a series of shrill, pulsating blasts, broken by intermittent wails of sirens and blaring horns. The pattern repeated every five seconds.

The alarms jolted Waddah awake. He was stunned the infidels were attacking so quickly. He expected it days from now, after the world witnessed the aftermath of the Grand Plan. He prayed the warriors in New York would release the Zincar without further delay. He reached for his prayer shawl and placed it around his head and neck. Grabbing a rifle from the armory cabinet he sprinted for His Eminence's chambers. When he arrived in the darkened chamber illuminated only by candlelight, he saw His Eminence on his knees, in quiet reflection in front of a photograph of his deceased wife and children.

"The time has come Your Eminence. The infidels are at the gate. Our people are prepared to defend our home and defeat the enemy."

His Eminence turned slowly and while still kneeling raised his right hand and placed it over his heart. Closing his eyes he said: "May the power and glory of the Almighty bless our people and the just cause we are about to undertake, and may the souls of our brothers and sisters in paradise illuminate our path to goodness and eternal salvation as we engage in battle to conquer the enemy."

Accepting the blessing, Waddah brought a fringe of the prayer shawl to his lips and kissed it. He then approached His Eminence and helped him to his feet.

"Let us move quickly to the security bunker. I will assist you. We don't have time to spare."

"My son, the only protection I require is that provided by the Almighty. I am at peace with our decision to execute the Grand Plan and to battle the infidels. The spirit of my children and their mother is with me. I am content. May the peace and blessings of our merciful Almighty be with you as you lead our brothers into battle. Go forth and deliver us from evil and free us from the bondage of the infidels. May eternal salvation be granted onto you."

Waddah paused and held his gaze. The look on His Eminence's face told him it was futile to protest his decision. He slowly lifted his arms, embraced His Eminence, and kissed him softly three times on his cheeks.

"You are the light and the path to everlasting salvation," Waddah said. "It is right and just that we heed your teachings. May the Almighty bless you and keep you safe."

With blessings exchanged, Waddah quickly turned and headed for the command center as His Eminence bowed his head and returned to kneel in front of the photograph of his wife and children.

Arriving at the command center, Waddah saw the radar abuzz with activity. A squadron of approximately two hundred drones were heading toward the compound from the west.

"Are the incoming drones armed?" Waddah barked.

"Unknown at this time, commander," said the operator sitting at the control panel. "Our reconnaissance teams confirmed additional inquiries made within the last hour by the American lawyer's operative in Cambridge. This time the operative was zeroing in on the alternate site."

Waddah understood the significance of the information. He needed to repel the incoming attack and hope the technicians at the alternate site would release the Zincar before the infidels made their way to it. With no time to spare, Waddah ordered the launch of ground-to-air defense missiles. One by one, missiles lifted off from ground launchers deep within the compound. They pierced the nighttime sky knocking out the drones, in clusters, and in single strikes. The whistling sound of missiles firing into the sky were soon drowned out by blasts of successful interceptions of the drones. After several minutes, the operator's voice reverberated within the walls of the command center.

"Commander, fifty missiles launched. All known drones, believed to number two hundred, successfully destroyed."

Before Waddah could react, the operator spoke up again.

"Commander, additional drones attacking from the north. Unknown number, but it is a large cluster. At least twice as large as those already destroyed. Request permission to deploy all remaining missiles to neutralize drones."

Without hesitating, Waddah responded. "Permission granted." He was emboldened after his weapons successfully defended against the first wave of the infidels' incursion.

Dozens of missiles ascended into the night sky, turning darkness into light as they thundered toward the heavens. Within seconds they homed in on the cluster of drones, striking them with precision, creating fireballs of roaring explosions echoing throughout the desert valley. On the monitors Waddah saw the trail of smoke of hundreds of destroyed drones streak across the sky as chunks of disintegrated and charred metal fell harmlessly to the barren plains below.

Waddah smiled and relaxed. His Eminence's prayers were being answered. The infidels' weapons were being banished, and the glory of the Almighty was on full display for all the world to see.

After several seconds, the operator spoke with urgency.

"Commander, thirty missiles confirmed launched from seaborne vessels to the west. Time to impact four minutes. Time to intercept two minutes. No other drones or missiles in the vicinity. Request direction."

Waddah rose from his chair. It was a limited strike. Despite the infidel's vast resources and weapon superiority, they had failed to launch a full-blown attack. Through the grace of the Almighty, his people would be able to withstand the attack and defeat the enemy. All that was left to destroy were the last few incoming evil weapons deployed from the sea and victory would be theirs. The Grand Plan would soon be in motion, and eternal salvation would be granted unto them.

Waddah stood tall, thrust out his chest and set his jaw. He took in a deep breath and held it. After a moment, he exhaled slowly and spoke the order to his men: "Launch all remaining SCUD missiles to intercept and destroy inbound projectiles. Glory to His Eminence and victory to our people."

48

Even before the chopper blades stopped rotating, Aronson, Darryl and Tom hopped out of the helicopter at the end of a dark runway. They were driven in silence to a nondescript, one-story cinderblock gatehouse where they were met by a guard who opened a steel door and let them in. The room was dark, damp and cold. As soon as the guard closed the door behind them, he pressed a button on a panel and Tom sensed the floor begin to shake and the room vibrate. He felt his body suspending in midair and his feet almost lifting off the ground. For a second he thought he was free falling. It took him a moment to realize they were in an elevator descending quickly. When it finally stopped, the guard announced they had reached the secure command bunker one hundred and ten feet below ground. A burst of cold air hit Tom's face as soon as the elevator doors opened. They were rushed down a long corridor and into a large rectangular room with floor to ceiling crystal clear color monitors hanging from walls and banks of computer consoles sitting on top of rows of tables.

One of the control operators, a young woman who looked younger than she probably was, announced that the screen on the left wall was a real time display of the air space above the compound. Tom thought it looked like a video game monitor with a series of dots, circles, and dashes representing trajectory lines. He was about to ask what they were seeing when the control operator began to narrate.

"Unarmed good guy drones deployed from the west approaching target area."

Darryl leaned in and whispered to Tom. "We're the 'good guys.'"

Seconds later the command operator spoke up again.

"Unarmed good guy drones intercepted by triple A's and destroyed."

Darryl leaned in again. "Triple A's are the bad guy's anti-aircraft artillery."

Tom was confused and wanted to ask a million questions but he kept quiet, mesmerized by the video war game playing out in front of him.

"Second battery of unarmed good guy drones deployed. Approaching target area from the north." The command operator announced.

The room was still, and Tom could hear himself breathe. He stared intently at the large monitors. Tiny dots crossed in synchronized slow motion, arcing from left to right toward an area marked with a red bullseye. Within minutes the dots closed in on the target. Tom realized he was clenching his fists. As the dots approached the bullseye, the monitor lit up with dozens of broken yellow dash lines moving in the opposite direction, from the target toward the synchronized dots. Quickly, the monitor screen lit up again with bursts of tiny lights. The command operator's sharp voice gave Tom much needed context to what he was seeing. "Second battery of unarmed good guy drones intercepted and neutralized by Triple A's."

What the hell was going on? Tom thought to himself. Why are we sending unarmed drones to the compound and why the hell are they being shot out of the sky? Tom was about to ask those questions when the command operator's monotone voice broke in.

"Three zero good guy tomahawks deployed from tin cans. Time to target four minutes."

Tom's adrenalin was pumping, and he wiped sweat from his upper lip even though the room was cold. He grabbed Darryl's arm and mouthed *what's happening?*

"The US just launched thirty cruise missiles from destroyers at sea headed for the compound. Four minutes until they hit their target."

Tom surveyed the room. It's as if he was hovering from above and looking down at the people in the bunker. It was all so surreal. How the hell did he get here? Lawyers aren't supposed to watch war games play out in real time. His daughter had been kidnapped just hours earlier and he thought his life would end if the unthinkable happened to her. He'd uncovered a mass poisoning plot, and the President of the United States had authorized a military strike against an enemy he'd sued over a spec of dirt in a ski town in New York. None of it made sense. This isn't how his life was supposed to turn out. He left Washington and New York and moved to the mountains to protect his family and to get away from crooks and killers. But they followed him. Different crooks with different motives to be sure, but crooks and killers nonetheless. And they were the worst kind because they targeted innocent civilians, ordinary folks who had nothing to do with whatever psychotic grievances these madmen were seeking to avenge. He almost wished he was back in Washington chasing the Syndicate. At least then he knew who the enemy was, although its leader turned out to be closer to him than he could have ever imagined. This was different. This was a movement of radical extremists intent on destroying an entire nation. Tom's body shook. He wanted to be with Brooke and Aneilia and hug them tightly and never let them go. Finally, he heard the monotone voice of the command operator again.

"Good guy tomahawks intercepted by SCUD surface to air missiles launched from sand dunes. Three zero up and three zero neutralized. Good guys standing down pending further instructions."

Tom leaned over to Aronson and Darryl and this time he wasn't whispering. "What the fuck is going on? Everything we're shooting at them is being intercepted. They're destroying us."

49

President Tayla Ferguson watched Operation Phoenix Spear unfold on monitors in the Situation Room. She shifted uncomfortably as drone after drone was intercepted and destroyed. When thirty tomahawk cruise missiles were shot down over the desert before reaching their targets, she imagined having to answer shouted questions from the press corps and explain to her detractors why the U.S. military had ostensibly failed to defeat a ragtag army of radical terrorists using hand-me-down weapons. But the strategy was explained to her, and she was beseeched to trust her military planners.

The Situation Room was rife with activity. Phones rang, documents were printing, and small groups of advisors were carrying on conversations in corners of the room. Maps and paper littered the large table, and cups of coffee and bottles of water were strewn about. The Situation Room looked like a war room. Operation Phoenix Spear was almost two hours old when an aid to the National Security Advisor rushed in and handed her boss a piece of paper. After a few seconds the National Security Advisor stood up and asked for quiet. She cleared her throat as the din in the room began to settle down.

"Madam President, our intelligence sources on the ground as well as military satellite images confirm that our adversaries' defensive weapons capabilities in the compound have been depleted and their offensive weapons inventory have been located and targeted. US Central Command is standing by to commence phase two of Operation Phoenix Spear on your orders."

Dozens of eyes focused on President Ferguson as they awaited her decision. At that moment, she was bathed in a glowing silhouette of strength and tenacity as the most powerful person in the world. The President sat back in her chair at the head of the long table and took in a deep breath. She wasn't aware the person she once showered with praise, the lawyer she offered to nominate to be her Attorney General during her first term, was responsible for surreptitiously finding evidence that led her to this moment. Nor was she aware that her old friend, the man who once served as her Attorney General, was at that very moment being held prisoner in a darkened dungeon in the same compound that would be obliterated if she ordered the raid. He was no more responsible for the terrorists' vile plan to kill millions in one of the largest population centers in the United States than those who gave the orders that led to the death of His Eminence's family a decade earlier. Nor did she know that it was his silent courage and sharp-witted shrewdness that led him to coopt the young guard into sending Tom the notecards and putting his name on the cargo manifest that ultimately led Tom to uncover the plot.

At that moment, all that mattered was that the administration's military lawyers had concluded she had the legal authority to authorize the unilateral use of lethal force on a foreign country's soil to destroy an imminent threat even without that country's consent due to the exigent circumstances and the very real possibility the foreign sovereign would be unwilling or unable to suppress the threat. Whatever criticism would come her way claiming the military incursion violated international law and rules of engagement would likely be soon forgotten if she succeeded in saving the lives of countless people.

Civilian casualties would presumably be substantial because the compound was home to hundreds of families. But it was the enemy's decision to place its headquarters amidst a community of non-combatants, sprinkling terrorists among children, and bomb-carrying weapons among cribs and strollers. The U.S. didn't ask for this fight, but the President was determined to do what was necessary to end it.

President Ferguson stood and surveyed the room, looking directly at each of her advisors. She squared her shoulders, took in a deep breath, and in a resolute and calm voice gave the order to proceed. Almost immediately, the Secretary of Defense transmitted the orders to military leaders at US Central Command. Thousands of miles away, just as the sun was rising over the compound, seamen on navy ships launched a barrage of tactical guided cruise missiles and glide bombs at the same time a bomber wing of B-52 Stratofortress aircraft circled the skies high above the desert. From a remote desert air base, a C-130 Hercules cargo plane set a path for its target. A squadron of fighter jets were also scrambled from decks of the USS Abraham Lincoln and USS Theodore Roosevelt for a rendezvous above the compound. And long-range tactical assault missiles were fired from military installations in neighboring allied territory.

The cruise missiles struck first, targeting the compound's radar installations, anti-aircraft artillery capabilities, and destroying the weapons depot. Several missiles targeted video surveillance systems and security camera systems that had been located using high resolution satellite imagery. Fighter jets launched dozens of AGM-130 air to surface missiles targeting soldier barracks and a fleet of trucks suspected of carrying IEDS and parts used to assemble crude dirty bombs. Infrared imaging from drones circling above relayed a visual display of targets, and their obliteration, back to the Situation Room.

The C-130 Hercules cargo plane patiently flew a zig-zag pattern over the compound as round after round of missiles destroyed the enemy's offensive weapons capabilities and the warriors who vowed death to America who manned them. But the compound's command and control facility remained intact. The enemy's military headquarters, a warren of underground caves, tunnels and bunkers housing the enemy's leaders, its brain trust, and the presumed location where the Grand Plan was conceived and planned, and where the fateful orders for its execution were given, had thus far been untouched. It was to be the final piece of the U.S.'s raid of the compound and its most consequential.

The C-130 Hercules approached from the east at an altitude of ten thousand feet. When it was two miles out, the pilots pushed forward hard on the yoke, directing the nose of the massive plane toward the ground. As it came in at a steep angle, the pilot adjusted the plane's speed. The electronic warfare officer steadied himself and lifted the metal cover over the toggle switch used to open the payload doors. "Ready to fire on your command, Sir," he said into the microphone connected to his helmet.

Seconds later he heard the words he'd been trained to receive. "Three, two, one. Fox 2!"

The most powerful munition was reserved for the grand finale.

As the payload doors opened, the GBU-43/B Massive Ordinance Air Blast, the largest non-nuclear weapon in the U.S. arsenal, nicknamed the "mother of all bombs," fell from the sky on a direct route to its prey below.

Waddah stood in the compound's darkened command-and-control facility deep underground. His orders to launch additional missiles to intercept the incoming barrage of ordinances went unheeded. The stockpile was depleted. The video monitors went dark when the first missiles struck, also destroying the compound's communications systems. He had no way of commanding his warriors. But it would have been useless anyway. Hundreds of them had been killed when bombs demolished their barracks and pulverized the muster stations. He thought of making his way to His Eminence's chambers but he knew he'd never make it – even if it was still standing and even if His Eminence was still alive.

He fell to the floor and tugged on his prayer shawl, attempting to wrap himself in it. He lifted the prayer shawl to his lips and gently kissed it. As he raised his right fist into the air and proclaimed "death to the infidels," the mother of all bombs struck deep into the command-and-control center obliterating everything in its path.

The operator in the underground bunker at Pratsville AFB had been providing a play-by-play narrative of the strike on the compound. Her final words caused Aronson, Tom, and Darryl to finally breathe. “The compound is destroyed.”

50

Four helicopters, two each from the New York City Police Department and the New York State Police hovered over Beekman Central Gardens shining their Night Sun spotlights. Hundreds of workers in hard hats and reflective safety vests scurried about, appearing unsure what to do. The police pilots of the helicopters shouted commands through loudspeakers directing the workers to move away from the tankers. The helicopters were soon joined by two massive CH-47 Chinook tandem-rotor helicopters ferrying soldiers and equipment from Fort Drum.

A column of police cars, national guard trucks, tactical armored vehicles and fire trucks raced over bridges heading toward the park. Near the front of the motorcade was a blue police van filled with scientists from the New York City and State Departments of Environmental Protection as well as two chemists from Columbia University. Air traffic controllers cleared the airspace over New York City, grounding flights at every airport in the region and directing all airborne traffic to land immediately at the nearest air strip. Fighter jets scrambled from Otis Air National Guard Base in Massachusetts and Langley Air Force Base in Virginia, travelling at speeds over Mach 2.0, arrived in the skies over New York City in minutes.

President Ferguson briefed the Mayor of New York City who was monitoring events from the City's Emergency Operations Center. He was told the fighter jets were authorized to take offensive actions to prevent threats emanating from the park, the first time in history the U.S. military would take such action on American soil.

At Pratsville AFB, the command operator switched to a live feed of the scene over the park provided by drones launched by the New York City Police and Fire Departments. It was the same live feed streaming into the Situation Room at the White House. The strike on the compound was critical to decapitate the enemy's command structure, but it would be window dressing if Zincar was already released into the City's drinking water supply. No one knew for sure if the tankers in the park contained the lethal concoction or if it was already flowing into the homes of millions of New York City residents. Messages intercepted by government satellites and monitoring of chatter on the deep web were inconclusive.

The President and Mayor debated whether to announce a health emergency and warn the public. There was no way to shut down the water system from a central location. If Zincar had already been released into the intake valve chamber, it would be too late to stop its flow. Announcing the threat would create immediate panic and cause mass hysteria throughout the City—and soon the world. Those who received word after drinking a cup of tea or glass of water, or after brushing their teeth, would likely clog the city's streets and highways on their way to the nearest hospital. Emergency wards and medical centers would be filled with thousands of people, perhaps hundreds of thousands. And the 911 emergency call center would be inundated with calls, which threatened to bring down the entire system.

If an announcement was made that later turned out to be wrong, the economic and psychological impact could be devastating, so much so that the City and region might never recover. After weighing all considerations, the decision was made to await confirmation from personnel on the ground before issuing any alerts. If Zincar had been released, it was already too late to save millions of lives. Sure, sounding the alarm now instead of five minutes later might save countless others, but the risk of being wrong based on a lack of information proved too daunting. In the end, economic considerations won out and the President and Mayor and their advisors decided to stand down until they knew for sure whether poison had been released into the water system.

Tom studied the scene at the park as events unfolded. The swirling lights from the helicopters above arced over the construction site, illuminating sections of it for seconds at a time before plunging it into darkness. The drones' audio feeds were clear enough that he could faintly hear sirens off in the distance. Workers in hard hats appeared to be heeding commands from the hovering helicopter pilots and quickly receded to a corner of the site, although Tom noticed several workers running into the darkness after shedding their reflective vests. He knew it would likely take just a few adherents lurking amid the tankers to pull the right controls to release their contents through the hoses connected to the derrick stationed above the intake valve chamber. Worse yet, on-site workers might not even be necessary if releasing the agent could be accomplished by someone pushing the right buttons on a computer or a hand-held device.

Tom shuddered at the thought. A cold sensation ran through him. He looked at Aronson and Darryl and noticed they also looked pale and anguished. He reminded himself to breathe. He was safe and so, too, were Brooke and Aneilia. So far, as horrible as events in the past twenty-four hours had been, he'd been able to keep his promise to keep them safe. But what about millions of people in New York and their families who were right now enjoying a Saturday night oblivious to the catastrophe that could be moments away from changing their lives forever?

He saw the flashing lights of dozens of vehicles and trucks descending on the park. The overhead shot from the drones provided a wide-angle bird's-eye view of the scene. The thudding sound from hovering helicopters grew louder as their beams of light shined intensely. Dirt kicked up, and anything that wasn't battened down began to swirl in the dust storm. The helicopters were now close to the ground, and it looked like they were coming in for a landing.

The command operator continued her narration and told those assembled in the room that four F-15E Eagle jets were patrolling the skies above New York City and accounted for the roaring sounds picked up by the drones' audio receivers. Tom saw dozens of agents leap from their vehicles as they arrived at the park. A contingent of armed officers, weapons drawn and wearing bulletproof vests and helmets, ran to the workers ordering them to kneel with their hands clasped behind their hard hats.

A second group of armed law enforcement officers escorted a group covered head to toe in white hazmat suits, with breathing tanks strapped to their backs, toward the tankers.

"Scene secured. Inspection of tankers underway," the command operator said in clipped sentences.

Tom watched intently as a dozen or so people clad in hazmat suits inspected the tankers and hoses connected to the derrick. Scene lights from firetrucks and emergency vehicles shined directly onto the tankers, helping to light up the park like Yankee Stadium just a few miles away, giving Tom a crisp, clear view of events as they were unfolding. Minutes passed as personnel on the ground pulled out what looked like probes and inserted them into the tankers' hatches and into the intake valve chamber and checked controls on handheld monitors. Tom sat motionless watching and waiting for what was to come. The only sounds came from shrill sirens and shouted commands, and the roar of jets flying overhead.

"Contents of six tankers confirmed to contain a viral agent." The words from the command operator landed hard.

Tom's heart sank. He sucked in a gulp of air but felt his airway constrict. He hoped he misheard and wanted to ask the command operator to repeat herself, but watching Aronson shake his head while mouthing an expletive and seeing Darryl close her eyes and bring her hands to her face told him he'd heard her correctly. How could this be happening, he asked himself. Was he too late? Should he have done something different? If he had been smarter about his investigation the terrorists might not have accelerated their plans and maybe he would have had more time to uncover the plot. He began questioning whether he should have gone to the authorities sooner, when he received the first notecard. He could have found a way to protect Brooke and Aneilia and still foil the attack. Doing so could have prevented the tragedy at the ski resort. His mind raced with alternative decisions he could have made. He thought of Faith. She was devastated when so many people were killed on her mountain. He felt responsible for that catastrophe. It was his lawsuit that set in motion the chain of events that led to sabotage of the resort and the deaths of so many. He was beating himself up when he noticed hurried activity around the tankers. People were running and pulling out their phones. Something was happening.

"They've found something. They must know whether the chemical was released," Aronson said, speaking quickly. Tom held his breath as he and the others looked to the command operator. She was listening to her headset, staring straight ahead. Tom noticed her flinch. She appeared to lower her shoulders and he noticed her chin drop. He was sure he saw it. She closed her eyes before appearing to regain control. She turned to face everyone in the room and began speaking.

"Tankers remain at full capacity." She took a deep breath before continuing. "No release of viral agent and no trace of any chemical detected in the water system. The New York City water supply is safe."

51

Almost a week had passed since the strike on the compound and the raid in the park, but neither event garnered much news.

The bombing of the compound made it to the third page, below the fold, of the international section of the *New York Times* a few days after the incident, and it got even less coverage in other newspapers. It was buried in the middle of national news broadcasts on the three major networks. While cable news channels devoted a bit more time to the story, it was only because it had occurred during a particularly slow news cycle. March madness was still weeks away, and there hadn't been any government shutdowns, wildfires, overdoses by celebrities or, thankfully, mass shootings to monopolize the airwaves.

The stories that were reported were mostly the same. The United States' military engaged in a limited strike on a suspected terrorist hideout and munitions storage facility. A handful of militants were killed, a stockpile of dangerous weapons was destroyed, and there were no American or civilian casualties or injuries. The mission was a success, and the world was a safer place because of the United States' military leadership and might, blah, blah, blah.

The raid at Beekman Central Gardens got even less attention. Only local TV stations in New York City covered it and reported that a police investigation resulted in the arrest of dozens of suspected drug dealers. In breathless clips, reporters earnestly ran with a story of drug pushers overrunning the park, and the construction site within it, using it as a hub for distributing fentanyl and other illegal narcotics to a web of street peddlers and addicts. Luckily, no videos of the raid were played on TV, which would have shown an armada of vehicles and a swarm of officers, much more than would have been necessary to take down even a drug kingpin. Instead, they showed the Governor of New York at a sparsely attended press conference with representatives from the DEA and FBI, and everyone spraining their arms to pat themselves on the back for a job well done. Just another typical day in New York City, and another victory for the good guys.

Tom read the articles and watched the news reports in the early morning before he left for his office. He wondered how many other newsworthy events went unreported or ignored completely by the news media on a daily basis. But maybe it was better to keep the truth from the American people, he thought, because if they knew what really happened and how close the world had come to another major terrorist attack, one that was so unfathomable in magnitude and utterly devastating in consequences, Americans might never feel safe again.

Just as he was preparing to leave the cabin for his office, his cell phone rang. It was Aaronson. He said he wanted to fill Tom in on certain details about the strike at the compound the news stories didn't cover. He swore Tom to secrecy before he did.

His Eminence's body had not yet been recovered, DNA testing was underway on body fragments and limbs located in sleeping quarters near the command center. Pathologists believe the results of those tests will confirm His Eminence perished in the strike along with hundreds of others including, regrettably, multiple women and children who called the compound home.

"As for Phoenix Holdings' General Counsel and part owner, Anastasia Maine, she was intimately involved in devising and executing the Grand Plan according to documents downloaded onto the hard drive, and her whereabouts are still unknown. She was last seen hours before the raid on the compound getting into a dark SUV outside her luxury high-rise building in Manhattan."

Tom wondered if it was a Range Rover.

"Traffic video cameras along several routes lost track of her SUV as it headed north out of Manhattan," Aronson explained. "Her photograph has been dispatched to law enforcement authorities across the United States, and customs officials and border crossing agents are on high alert for a woman matching her description. So far, authorities have no leads and all potential sightings have turned up nada. It's as if she's disappeared into thin air."

Aronson wasn't done sharing bad news.

"Among the casualties from the strike on the compound was the former Attorney General."

The news struck Tom hard.

"As shocking as it sounds, it's true. A search of the information you and Darryl obtained revealed a trove of documents relating to Mitchelson. He was hired by Phoenix Holdings Group as a strategic consultant a few years ago. At first, his advice was sought because of his stature and geopolitical relationships around the world and his insight into the functioning of the United States government, including his close ties to the Administration of President Ferguson."

Tom nodded along.

"Based on an in-depth review of information on the hard drive, backed up by U.S. intelligence reports and statements obtained from undercover confidential informants in the days since the strike, we're certain Mitchelson had no prior knowledge of the Grand Plan and no involvement in devising it in any way. In fact, we believe after Mitchelson learned the truth about Phoenix Holdings' intentions and the plot it was planning to carry out, he tried to sound the alarm, but it was too late."

Tom was trying to make sense of what he was hearing.

"A number of months ago he was picked up in Dusseldorf, Germany, where he was speaking at a conference, and imprisoned in the compound while Phoenix Holdings was putting the finishing touches on the Grand Plan. He was killed in the strike, and U.S. Marines recovered his body from a bombed-out prison cell. His wife, Beverly, was also being held captive in the compound and she, too, is presumed to have perished in the strike."

Tom bowed his head and closed his eyes. "I can't believe it. That's why he didn't return any of my calls or messages. He was being held hostage."

Tom suddenly remembered what Brooke said to him last night, right before she fell asleep.

"Doug, I received two cryptic notecards within the last month alerting me to Phoenix Holdings' involvement in my attack, the massacre at the resort, and that it was planning a devastating attack on the Fourth of July. You should investigate whether Mitchelson had anything to do with the notecards."

"He did."

Tom grabbed for a chair and fell onto it.

"Mitchelson was able to sway a young guard in the prison barracks in the compound. The guard had become disenchanted with His Eminence's increasingly dark rhetoric about death to innocent Americans. It appears that as soon as the guard learned that Phoenix was behind your attack as a means to punish you for the lawsuit you filed, and uncovered evidence that Phoenix was planning a more devastating attack at the ski resort, he decided to put an end to the madness. He and Mitchelson worked together as quickly as they could, in secret, to warn you and send you the first notecard. Later, when Mitchelson and the guard learned that Phoenix Holdings knew of your investigation, and were planning the plot against your family, they sent you the second notecard. There's no indication Mitchelson knew the specifics. He didn't know Aneilia was going to be kidnapped. But he knew enough, including that you would do whatever it took to stop Phoenix Holdings."

"How do you know all this?"

"The guard who was Mitcheson's emissary survived the raid and surrendered. He gave up everything he and Mitchelson had been working on, including copies of the notecards. His English is limited, and the means he had available to get the messages out of the compound and over to you were rudimentary, which is why the notecards were so brief and vague."

"Mitchelson kept his oath to defend and protect America and was a patriot till the end. Were it not for Mitchelson sending me those notecards, I would have never learned that Phoenix Holdings was behind all of this. He died a hero. We need to let President Ferguson know."

"She already does. She's been briefed on all of this. There's talk that when this all becomes public, probably in a few months' time, she'll award the Presidential Medal of Freedom posthumously to Mitchelson."

"That will be an appropriate honor," Tom whispered.

"The President is also aware of your role in uncovering the plot and gaining access to Phoenix Holdings' network."

"Oh. Is this where you read me my rights?".

"Hardly. The President was as amazed as anyone about your involvement, but said she wasn't surprised that you did what was necessary to protect your family and serve your country. You'll soon be receiving an invitation to meet privately with her at the White House. I hear she has a special announcement planned for you."

"I can't wait to hear it."

"Tom, the information you obtained has tremendous value to our intelligence community. Not only about Phoenix Holdings and attacks it was planning, but also about other terrorist organizations. We'll be able to foil a number of plots and save countless lives because of you. I know I've said it before, but I'll say it again. You're a hero in my book. Our nation is once again indebted to you. If there is ever anything I can help you with, just let me know."

Tom thanked Aaronson for the call and told him he looked forward to seeing him in a few weeks' time at a gathering Faith McReynolds was planning at her home to thank folks in town for standing by her throughout the ordeal at the resort.

"Oh, there's one more thing," Aronson said. "Be on the lookout for a judgment from the judge presiding over your case against Phoenix Holdings. I think you won."

Tom sat alone in his kitchen replaying the events of the last few days. Despite the senseless loss of so many lives in the inferno at the resort, and the trauma he, Brooke and Aneilia endured, he was grateful so many more lives were spared. For the moment, anyway, he was also grateful he'd been able to keep his promise to keep his family safe from harm.

Brooke came into the kitchen and sat next to him. She was happy when he told her that she was right about Bradley Mitchelson being behind the notecards. But her happiness soon turned to sadness, and she welled up, when Tom shared the news that Mitchelson and his wife had died a few days earlier when the U.S. military attacked Phoenix Holdings' headquarters halfway around the world. He said they were unintended casualties of the strike. He was certain Brooke suspected there was more to the story, but he also knew she was smart enough not to ask questions now. There would be time later for the details and he would eventually come around to telling her everything.

Late that afternoon, Tom received an email from Phoenix Holdings' *new* lawyers who had been appointed by the court to replace Anastasia Maine to wind up the company's affairs. It said Phoenix was throwing in the towel and dropping its opposition to the lawsuit Tom had filed. It also said Phoenix was withdrawing its offer to purchase the resort, and giving up control of the land it owned adjacent to the reservoir which it would surrender to a conservancy run by the state. The email noted the judge would soon issue an order granting the permanent injunction barring any development on the seven-acre parcel abutting the reservoir.

When Tom delivered the news to Faith, she was ecstatic, even as she continued to mourn the tragic loss of life that occurred on her mountain.

52

It had been a long week and Tom was enjoying a peaceful Friday afternoon in his office. He had just grabbed a cold *Yoohoo* out of the fridge, leaned back in his chair and admired the view up Main Street. Traffic was light and the town was quiet. There was still a lot of uncertainty among the locals about what the future held and whether Castle Ridge Ski Resort would ever reopen. Even if it did, many wondered if it would ever reclaim its former glory as a premier ski and snowboard destination. In any other year, Main Street on a Friday afternoon in late February would have been bubbling with activity as skiers and riders counted down the days to the end of the season and savored their last weeks on the slopes. But this year was different, and it was bittersweet. While Tom bemoaned the loss of a pastime he loved on a mountain he cherished, he still rejoiced at the way things turned out. The bad guys had been caught, Faith got to keep her resort, and the world was spared another devastating terrorist attack.

Tom's cell phone rang, and when he looked down at the screen, he saw Aronson's name. After speaking with Aronson a day earlier, he wondered how long it would take to hear from him again. He just got his answer.

"Tom, where are you? Can you talk?"

"Hi Doug. I'm in my office enjoying a quiet Friday afternoon. And, yes, I can chat for a few minutes. What's up?"

Tom heard Aaronson sighing on the other end.

"Tom, we've been through a lot in the past few weeks, and despite the way you felt about me in the beginning and what I thought of you, I've grown to like and trust you. I told you I think you're a hero. But..." His voice trailed off.

Aronson sounded serious and Tom tried to match his tone. "If there's something you want to say to me, Mr. Deputy Director, you should just come out and say it. There's no need to beat around the bush."

"FBI technicians have gone through the hard drive with a fine-toothed comb." Aronson paused.

"Great. So why do you sound so gloomy?"

"Is there something you want to tell me about the information you and Darryl duplicated and downloaded?"

"No, nothing comes to mind," Tom said, wondering if Aronson finally discovered the "extra" wire transfer only he and Darryl knew about.

"Tom, I'm trying to be a friend here. I can help you. But I need you to level with me."

"What do you mean? Like a get out of jail free card? Thanks for the offer."

"Come on, Tom. Get serious. If you come clean, I'll see what I can do for you."

Tom leaned back and took a sip of *Yoohoo*.

"I'm sorry, Mr. FBI Deputy Director, but I don't know what you're driving at."

"Goddammit, Tom." Aronson was angry now. "We found evidence of the previously unknown wire transfer the night you hacked into Phoenix Holdings' servers. The one transferring funds into your attorney escrow account. Did you really think you were going to get away with it? You've put me in a very difficult position. I was about to nominate you for a fucking Nobel peace prize. Now I need to consider what to put in an indictment."

Tom was enjoying listening to Aronson getting worked up when he finally decided to put him out of his misery.

"Doug, let me ask you: When your people went through the information on the hard drive, did they find evidence of any cash other than this wire transfer, anywhere? Did they find money in any bank accounts that could be tapped into?

"No."

"And if they had, what would happen to that money?"

"I don't know. The government would have sequestered it and eventually, hopefully, taken possession of it? What does that have to do with anything? We're talking about money that wound up in your account, Tom. We're talking about larceny and a dozen other crimes."

"I've been accused of worse, remember?"

"Tom, I don't know what games you're playing. You're in deep shit."

"Answer one more question for me. If the government takes possession of the money in my attorney escrow account, which is a big if, what then? Where does the money wind up?"

"I don't know, but again so what? What does it have to do with what you did?"

"Because you know as well as I do that even if the government got its hands on the money, it would go into some general fund to be spent on some bullshit pork spending program. Besides, it's a drop in the bucket when you consider the trillions our government wastes every year. I can do something better with the money."

"Tom, I think you should retain a lawyer. A good one."

"I'm that lawyer, Doug. A few days ago, you told me if there was anything I needed, I should let you know. Well, I'm letting you know. I'm asking, okay? I need you to do something for me. Only it's not for me. It's for a lot of other people who are hurting right now and need that money more than our government needs it."

"What the hell are you taking about?"

"I didn't steal that money, Doug. You should know better than anyone that money doesn't motivate me. I don't do things for money. I do what's right. That's what motivates me. Doing the right thing. Every time. I know the right thing to do with this money and I've already set the plan in motion. The question is: can I count on you to back me up?"

53

At about ten to six, Tom, Brooke, and Aneilia arrived at Faith's mansion. Tom drove past the open gated entrance and up the winding drive to the covered portico. Faith insisted that Aneilia come to the party, and Tom and Brooke jumped at the chance to take her along. Ever since the kidnapping, they were uncomfortable letting her out of their sight and had become hypervigilant, making sure they always knew where she was. Aneilia, too, was looking forward to the party after Brooke told her about the other children who would be there, including Darryl's daughter who was just a few years older than Aneilia, and Chet's son who was also three. The invitation said face painters, clowns, and magicians would entertain the kids while the adults enjoyed dinner.

The celebration was slated to kick off at 6:30 p.m., but Tom called Faith earlier that afternoon and asked if he could arrive a bit early and speak with her privately. As soon as he parked his truck, he saw two other vehicles pull up behind him, right on time. Darryl, her husband, and her daughter greeted Tom, Brooke and Aneilia, and they were soon joined by Doug Aronson and his wife, both of whom flew up from Washington, D.C. for the occasion. It was a balmy night for early March, and they spent a few minutes chatting under the portico, with Brooke greeting Aronson's wife and introducing Aneilia to Darryl's daughter.

Faith's butler met the group and ushered them into the large foyer. A few seconds later, Faith made her way down the sweeping staircase and welcomed her guests. Tom could see she was surprised to see the large group arrive so early so he pulled her aside.

"I hope you don't mind but I asked Darryl and FBI Deputy Director Aronson to join me a few minutes early. The three of us would like to speak with you. Can we meet in your study?"

"Of course, come this way."

The butler showed Brooke, Aneilia and the others to the two-story great room while Tom, Darryl, and Aronson followed Faith down the long, winding hallway to her study. She offered her guests a drink, but each declined, saying there'd be time for drinks later.

"So, what is so important that it takes three of you, including the Deputy Director of the FBI, to tell me?" Faith said with a nervous laugh.

"We come bearing good news," Tom said, "and we all wanted to share it with you." Faith visibly relaxed and took a seat on the sofa across from the fireplace.

"Well, that's always nice to hear. Do tell. Please."

Darryl and Aronson took seats on chairs flanking the fireplace, leaving Tom as the only person standing.

"Earlier today, I opened a bank account at First Hudson Bank with you and me as the named custodians," Tom began. "I used the power of attorney you gave me in connection with the proposed sale of the resort, and the bank manager was only too eager to accommodate me."

Faith tilted her head and Tom could tell she didn't have a clue what he was talking about.

"A bank account? What for?"

"It's a charity trust account. I named it the McReynolds Family Castle Ridge Resort Relief Fund."

"Well that's thoughtful. But I don't need charity. I've kept all my employees on the payroll, and I intend to pay their salary through next year when I expect to reopen the resort. I've decided to try to make a go of the business and to donate all profits from the first year of operations to the victims of the fire and to local businesses. I also spoke with my insurance carriers, and they will try to expedite payments to the victims as soon as possible."

"I know you don't need money Faith and, frankly, the charity fund isn't for you. It's for all the people who were injured as a result of the fire and for the families of those who perished. You get to decide how to distribute the money, and I'll assist you."

Faith looked at Darryl and Aronson and each smiled and nodded.

"That's a wonderful idea, Tom. I'll call the bank manager tomorrow and donate to the fund. I'll donate a million dollars."

"You won't need to do that Faith. Use your money to continue to pay your employees and for the work needed to reopen the resort. There's enough money in the charity fund to help the victims and their families."

"How can that be? Where did the money come from? How much could you have possibly raised?"

Tom turned to Aronson. "Doug, would you like to do the honors?"

"Faith, the U.S. Government is blessed to work with some highly capable, good people, who put the wellbeing of others before themselves. Modern day Robinhoods, if you will." He turned to Tom and smiled. "As a result of the efforts of these talented folks, a large sum of money was located belonging to the group that committed the heinous atrocity on the mountain that killed and injured so many. I brought this matter to the attention of the highest levels of our government, and everyone agreed the money should be used solely for the benefit of the victims of the tragedy. Tom, Darryl, and I spoke with the President of the United States this morning and she signed an Executive Order this afternoon authorizing use of the funds for such purpose."

Faith looked stunned but managed to collect herself. "That's simply amazing. Thank you, Mr. Deputy Director." She then turned to Tom and Darryl. "Tom, that's absolutely wonderful. Darryl, thank you for all you've done. How were you two involved with all of this?"

Tom and Darryl looked at each other and smiled. "There'll be time to discuss all of that later," Tom said. "Your guests should be arriving soon and we don't want to be late for the festivities."

"I can't wait to hear all the details," Faith said, a huge smile crossing her face. They all stood and shook hands and congratulated one another when Faith turned to Tom as they were heading out of the study.

"Tom, you didn't mention how much money is in the account?"

He glanced at Aronson and Darryl, biting his lower lip.

"Darryl, would you like to tell Faith?"

"Ah, no, I think you deserve the honor."

He took a deep breath and stood tall. He was proud of what he'd done and prouder still that so many people were going to benefit from it. He knew it wouldn't bring back their loved ones, or heal their wounds, or cure their trauma, but it was a start and, hopefully, in some small measure, it would help in their recovery and allow them to turn the page on the darkest day of their lives.

"Five hundred million dollars. The same amount you were offered for your resort."

More and more guests kept arriving. Janet and her husband, Hank, arrived first with his oxygen tank in tow at the same time as Claire Holister and her husband Phillip arrived. Brooke spotted Claire and Phillip and ran over to give them a hug, and began introducing them to the other guests. Faith included Claire and her husband on the guest list after Tom shared with her how instrumental Claire was in uncovering evidence of Phoenix Holdings' plot.

Constable Stuart Ozzie and his wife, followed by a number of his deputies—those who rotated through the daily watch duty at Tom's office and home, and who loved Aneilia's cookies—arrived a short time later. Brooke and Aneilia had spent the better part of the day baking cookies to bring to Faith's house for all the police *mens*.

Chet was also there with his wife and son, and he was soon regaling guests with stories about the ski lines, including his technique for keeping them moving. He might never know the important role he played in taking down Phoenix Holdings, but Tom did. It was a risky job, and Tom had debated whether to involve him, but he knew Chet would be up to the task and he didn't disappoint. The cargo of Zincar was a crucial piece of evidence, and shutting down Societe Robolex's operations in Switzerland likely prevented more poisoning of scores of people around the globe.

Millard Jensen and his wife Phyllis also arrived for the dinner. Millard looked like he was having difficulty getting around. He quickly spotted Tom and made a slow beeline straight for him. "I hear congratulations are in order, Counselor, regarding the land case and the permanent injunction you obtained. You're gaining quite a reputation in these parts as a first-rate, get-it-done attorney."

"Thank you, Millard. It's always nice when the good guys win."

Millard looked around to make sure no one was within earshot, then he leaned into Tom and whispered. "I received the handwritten letter you sent me. I needed to use a magnifying glass to read the instructions. They said I was to unseal the folder that came with the letter only if something happened to you because it would reveal the duress you were under and explain your actions. I trust since you're alive and well, I should keep the folder sealed and its contents confidential."

Tom smiled. With all that had happened in the last few weeks, he'd forgotten about the letter and sealed folder containing the notecards he sent Millard the day Aneilia was kidnapped.

"Yes, please continue to keep it in a safe place, and follow those instructions if they ever become necessary. But for now, a higher justice has prevailed. You're a smart man, Millard, and I'm grateful for your advice." Millard smiled and the two men walked into the great room, where Millard headed for the bar.

After a bit, Tom saw Terrie and walked over to her. He thanked her again for everything she did for him, and repeated that he wouldn't be where he was today without her help. She was a godsend.

The owners of the art gallery, Peak's Perk Coffee Chalet, and several other business owners in town also attended the celebration, as did Sheila, Constable Ozzie's secretary, Ms. Plessy, Aneilia's teacher from the Regal Preschool, and Detective Samantha Kaplan from the Monroe County's Sherriff's Department. When Brooke saw Sam, she ran over and embraced her, thanking her for all she did for her during her darkest hours.

In a large playroom on the other side of the mansion, a dozen or so children between the ages of three and ten were being entertained and, based on the howls of laughter and shouts of joy, it sounded like they were all having a wonderful time.

As the guests gathered in the cavernous dining room, Faith used a spoon to tap her water glass and ask for everyone's attention. After a few repeated taps, the chatter quieted down. Fifty-eight guests were seated around a horseshoe table under two enormous crystal chandeliers. A fire crackled in the hearth as servers filled everyone's flutes with champagne. Faith rose from her chair and gazed at her guests.

"I'd like to take a moment to thank all of you for gracing us with your presence tonight. These have been an incredibly difficult few months for all of us." Faith paused and looked at Tom. "Starting, of course, with Tom's vicious attack." Brooke reached over and grabbed Tom's hand. "I'm told the authorities are working diligently to find the possible culprit." All Faith was told was that Phoenix Holdings was behind Tom's attack and The Turret fire, and that both incidents were related to the lawsuit Faith retained Tom to bring on behalf of the resort and the town. She, wisely, decided not to get into the details.

"I will, of course, fulfill my pledge of paying the one hundred-thousand-dollar reward to anyone who comes forward with information that leads to an arrest." Tom sheepishly bowed his head and wondered if he could lay claim to that money. He glanced over at Darryl and Aronson and wondered if they, too, were thinking the same thing. Faith went on to say she was happy he had made a full recovery, and all the guests clapped.

"Tom's nightmare, unfortunately, wasn't the end of our town's nightmare. The malfunction of the chairlift and the dreaded fire that resulted from it will live in my memory forever. The senseless death of so many people, coupled with the injuries sustained by all those innocent victims, will haunt me for as long as I live. The investigation into the tragedy revealed that Castle Ridge Ski Resort was targeted by foreign cyber terrorists whose motives are still unclear." Faith looked at Tom, Aronson, and Darryl. Aronson suggested she keep her comments vague and intentionally omit the part about paying the ransom. News might leak out eventually, but since the government's investigation into Phoenix was continuing, the less she said publicly, the better. Tom agreed and Faith complied.

"I could not have handled the fallout from the tragic fire without the dedicated work of Darryl, the head of security for the resort, and Tom, my trusted legal advisor." Another round of applause filled the room.

"Initially, I considered shutting down the resort. The memories of that horrific day are too painful and the hurt still too raw. I feared the many families who visited the mountain over the years would be afraid to return to a place of such grief and sorrow. But in the last several weeks, I've heard from so many friends and families who consider Castle Ridge their second home. They shared with me how important this mountain and this town are to them. They offered their cherished memories of growing up on this mountain, and how they look forward to bringing their children and grandchildren to enjoy all that we have to offer. And without exception, they pleaded with me to reopen the resort so they and countless others can continue to experience the same joy and happiness Castle Ridge brought to their own lives. I considered their sentiments, and I prayed deeply over what to do. In the end, I decided the best way to honor the lives of all those who were touched by the tragedy is to not give in to the evil that brought about so much pain and suffering, but to rise up from that terrible event and rebuild this resort into the beautiful resort it once was and still can be. I want to help fuel the economic recovery of this town and this region and the people who work and live here. With God's help, we will turn tears of pain and suffering into cheers of triumph and joy. I'm proud to announce that Castle Ridge Ski Resort will reopen next winter. Everyone who was here on that fateful day when fire destroyed so much of what we've built, will forever be able to ski and ride here at no cost to them or their families, and I pledge to donate all profits from our first year of operations to victims of the tragedy and to local businesses."

Audible gasps were heard throughout the room followed by loud applause.

"And," Faith continued, "through God's grace and the extraordinary work of a number of people around this table, a charitable fund has been set up to compensate the victims and their families who lost so much as a result of the tragic events on the mountain."

Tom, Aronson, and Faith had also discussed how much Faith should say about the fund. She wanted to let everyone know that it contained five hundred million dollars, but in the end they all agreed it was best that she not disclose the amount and instead let her actions speak for themselves.

"Each of you in some way, large and small, contributed to Castle Ridge surviving this long winter nightmare and have made this day possible. And for that my dear friends, I am eternally grateful. So please raise your glass with me as we toast ourselves for the strength, courage and resolve we've shown in the face of misery and evil, and for our shared commitment to the town of Castle Ridge and its people. As my grandfather Earl used to say, 'may the saddest days of our future be no worse than the happiest days of our past.'"

Shouts of 'here, here' were soon replaced by the clinking of crystal as guests stretched and reached to tap their champagne flutes and raise them in the air.

As laughter and chatter continued to fill the vast room, it was suddenly plunged into darkness. Nervous laughter quickly gave way to an uneasy stillness. Brooke reached for Tom and grabbed his arm. Seconds passed. No one moved.

The explosion was immediate. Concussive blasts reverberated throughout the room. Smashing glass, tumbling china, churning and twisting metal, and the roar of a hundred freight trains drowned out all other sounds. The floor buckled upward and the enormous chandeliers came raining down crushing everyone and everything in between. Smoke and dust filled the air and choked the guests. Loud shrieks of panic gave way to sorrowful whimpers, and howls of agony were silenced by the final gasps of life.

Pushing away rubble from his face, Tom looked up and saw stars twinkling in the nighttime sky through a massive hole in the ceiling. Plumes of black smoke and ash quickly obscured his sight and he began to choke. The last thing he heard before losing consciousness was Brooke's gut-wrenching scream:

"Aneilia!"

54

Tom saw the snowdrop flowers when he looked out the kitchen window. Baby shoots were sprouting from in between a pile of dead and decaying logs in his front yard, their white petals drooping downward as if in mourning. Next to them were tiny purple crocuses just beginning to bloom in the thawing ground, a sure sign of the advancing spring, even in this tiny upstate hamlet where winters often lingered until the start of summer. He slowly cranked the handle on the windowsill with his left hand to let in the fresh early morning breeze. Almost all the snow that had piled high on the road in front of his cabin had melted, and whatever blackened frozen pellets remained would surely disappear over the next few days as temperatures were expected to climb well into the sixties. But while the retreating season brought with it promises of new beginnings, Tom knew there would be no renewal for him. Not this year. Not with scars from pain that might never heal, and memories that may never fade.

The cabin was quiet. He was still recovering from his injuries and hoped his doctor would tell him on his next visit the cast on his right arm could come off. He had been breathing easier the last few days and the scarring in his throat from inhaling boiling hot smoke was beginning to heal. Bandages still covered his legs and feet to protect skin grafts on burn wounds suffered in the explosion three weeks earlier.

Tom moved slowly and limped into the den, using the cane to steady himself. He approached the chair next to the fireplace, turned and fell into it. He stared at a framed photograph of Brooke and Aneilia on the small table next to him. He'd snapped that picture just a few months earlier, in the fall, when Aneilia and Brooke were playing in a pile of leaves on the front lawn. It was the same one they used for the back cover of their Christmas card. Brooke loved that photograph because she said it captured Aneilia's sweet smile and her big brown eyes sparkling in the sunlight. Tom helped Brooke and Aneilia design the card and even pitched in to write the "year in review" summary of their family's adventures, including Aneilia's first day at summer camp, and her first day of preschool. He choked up as those memories came rushing back.

They were happier times, when he and Brooke would spend hours talking about their future, including the dream of growing their family. It was a time of innocence and kindness, when Castle Ridge was a refuge from violence and crime and danger that lurked elsewhere in the world. But that was all in the past.

As much as things had changed, much had remained the same. Evil had once again intruded on his life. The names and faces were different to be sure, but the twin goals of death and manipulation were the same. He found it odd, but when he was in the hospital recovering from his injuries, he felt no solace at having struck at the heart of Phoenix Holdings and preventing the mass poisoning it had planned. Yes, he was thankful that a devastating and unthinkable terrorist plot had been foiled, and even more grateful that countless lives had been spared, but he was tormented by the loss of innocence and peace he longed for when he moved to Castle Ridge. Maybe he was naïve, but he had dreamed of a future without senseless violence and evil. He realized now he was no more capable of protecting his family from bearing witness to such atrocities than he'd been in preventing them from occurring in the first place. A few weeks ago he thought he'd succeeded when his government toppled the enemy, but the carnage that resulted from the explosion changed all that. Defeat had erased victory, with the final verdict leaving him reeling and empty. His fifteen minutes of gloom had returned with more hardships to endure before he'd bask in glory again.

He glanced out the window and stared vacantly at the Castle's peaks. Where white, chiseled trails once stood, the landscape now looked forlorn and weathered. Living amid tall, majestic mountains has a way of making you feel small he thought to himself. He wondered whether he'd be able to continue to call this bucolic place home.

There was a time when loud noises scared Tom. Now it was silence that frightened him the most. Silence that comes from unspeakable loss and tragedy. Ever since that fateful evening at Faith's house, he'd been alternating between pangs of profound sadness and periods of quiet reflection. He fought back tears when he saw his baby girl's toys in the corner of the room and heard the sound of her laughter replaying in his mind.

The last few weeks had been a reminder of how fragile life can be. Perhaps because of that dawning reality, he decided now was the right time to reach out to his mother. She had suffered enough and had been punished too long. Holding grudges became difficult to condone. She had her reasons for doing what she did, and he was beginning to understand them better now. He kept asking himself whether, in light of what he'd been through these past few months, his choices would have been different than the ones she made. When he didn't answer as quickly as he once did, or with as much certainty, he knew it was time to forgive and reunite. He would do that soon, after the solemn vigil of the next few days.

As he sat alone in the den, he closed his eyes and replayed in his mind the memorial services he had attended thus far for the souls of those who perished in the explosion. The first were for Millard and Phyllis, followed a few days later by a service for Janet's husband, Hank. Each one tugged at his heart, and he shed tears of sorrow and grief.

The largest funeral, and the one that had attracted the most attention and the most mourners, was for Constable Stuart Ozzie. His family and friends came from faraway places to pay their respects and say goodbye to a man of deep faith and unwavering courage and strength in the face of both triumph and tragedy. Thousands of law enforcement officers from around the state and around the country lined Main Street, five deep in some places. Three New York State Police helicopters flew in formation low over the mourners as part of the services for the fallen decorated veteran lawman. He was remembered as a stalwart of the community and a committed and fierce protector of the town of Castle Ridge. Mayor Faith McReynolds, still nursing her own injuries from the explosion, and the Castle Ridge Town Council honored Ozzie with a posthumous promotion to Inspector First Grade, and his family was presented with a plaque commemorating his tenure as the longest-serving Constable of Castle Ridge. The plaque would hang in the rotunda of town hall.

Douglas Aronson's remains were flown back to Washington, D.C. several days after the explosion and he was interred at Arlington National Cemetery in a private ceremony. Tom was unable to pay his respects because he was in the hospital recovering from his injuries, but he promised Doug's wife he'd return to Washington as soon as he was strong enough and he'd lay a flower on Doug's headstone. It was a promise he intended to keep.

The cause of the explosion was determined to be several bombs planted in Faith's home, two of them hidden in the dining room, detonated by remote operation. No arrests had been made, but associates of Phoenix Holdings were suspected of being responsible for the blast. An international manhunt was underway for them, and an INTERPOL arrest warrant had been issued for Anastasia Maine. Tom was especially interested in her capture, not because it would bring back those whose lives were taken, or erase the pain their deaths caused, but so justice could be done.

It was almost 8:00 a.m. when Tom climbed the stairs one step at a time to his bedroom to prepare for the difficult day ahead. The floors creaked under him as he shuffled and leaned on his cane. He stopped in the doorway and looked into the empty, quiet space.

He turned and took a long look at the closed door to Aneilia's bedroom. His mind took him back to the morning of the explosion, when he tiptoed in to kiss his baby girl's forehead before she awoke. Tom welled up with emotion again at the memory of Aneilia sleeping peacefully, unaware of the hatred that surrounded her in the world. He was drawn to her bedroom now and felt himself being carried effortlessly toward her. Arriving at the closed door, he raised his left hand and gently brushed the nameplate. They had purchased it last summer on a trip to the Jersey shore. She was so excited when she saw her name stenciled in colorful script, and was eager to help Tom hang it.

He took a deep breath, and with his hand shaking, reached for the handle. He nudged the door open, careful not to make a sound, and just enough to peer in. Through faint light filtering through the blinds, he saw Aneilia's treasured teddy bear neatly arranged with her other stuffed animals on the window seat next to her favorite bedtime storybook. Her baby scent filled the air.

As he gazed around the room, his eyes settled on Aneilia's little bed. For the first time since the devastating explosion, he smiled watching his sleeping baby girl, her small body rising and falling with each peaceful breath. Curled up next to her was Brooke, and lying at their feet was Bentley, his tail wagging as he looked up at Tom.

System of Justice
Book 3 in The Tom Berte Legal Thrillers

A Supreme Court justice murdered—and Tom Berte is the only lifeline for the accused.

Comfortably settled into a civil law practice in Albany, Tom Berte has finally left behind the conspiracies and threats of his past. But when a shocking murder strikes the Supreme Court, Madison Redding reaches out with a desperate plea for help, and Tom can't ignore her call. A young Supreme Court clerk accused of killing Tom's former mentor, Madison swears she's innocent; the victim of a ruthless set-up carefully engineered to frame her as the perfect culprit.

Reluctantly stepping into criminal defense for the first time, Tom swiftly finds himself maneuvering through Washington's hidden corridors of political power and personal betrayal. Influential lobbyists, jealous spouses, and ruthless operatives close ranks, determined to protect their dark secrets at any cost.

With each revelation pushing Tom deeper into unfamiliar moral territory, he becomes trapped between defending Madison and safeguarding the peaceful life he's carefully rebuilt.

ACKNOWLEDGMENTS

I never set out to write a second book after *The Manipulator*, let alone write a multi-book series. But the incredible team at Severn River Publishing, including Amber Hudock, Cate Streissguth, Julia Barron, Julia Hastings, Megan Copenhaver, and the rest of the wonderful folks behind the scenes who make it all happen, saw something in my writing and convinced me this was a journey worth taking. I am eternally grateful to the entire team for this opportunity and for their amazing support. A special thanks goes to my rock-star copy editor Amie Swope whose advice, insight and thoroughness were spot-on. And orchestrating it all and encouraging me to persevere when my cursor simply blinked on a blank page is the best cheerleader literary agent anyone could ask for, Terrie Wolf of AKA Literary Management.

I am grateful to my social media whisperer and all-around marketing guru, Elliana Olivo.

Thank you to my wife and three kids for allowing me the time to create the story of Tom Berte, and for creating a loving and supportive home when writing time was over. Their ideas, critiques, and suggested edits made this book immeasurably better. Everything I do, I do because of all of you.

Last, to you, the readers of my books, thank you again for taking the time to read what I've written. I never take it for granted that, with all the books you could choose to read, you chose mine. I hope you enjoyed it.

ABOUT THE AUTHOR

Dan is a litigation partner in a national law firm with over 1,100 attorneys, and a mafia aficionado. His series is inspired, in part, by a fascination with all things mafia and an actual case where he worked closely with the Department of Justice and FBI. After several years, Dan's team succeeded in recovering over $240 million on behalf of thousands of innocent investors swindled by foreign nationals. He is a graduate of Tufts University and Fordham Law School. In his spare time, he enjoys traveling and skiing with his wife and three children. He is also a volunteer firefighter in his hometown of Colts Neck, NJ.

Join the reader list at
severnriverbooks.com